PRAISE FOR THE
KEY WEST FOOD CRITIC MYSTERIES

Death with All the Trimmings

"Like a spiked glass of eggnog or s'mores over a cold night's cozy fire, *Death with All the Trimmings* is a holiday treat that any book lover should be pleased to find stuffed in their stocking or neatly wrapped beneath the tree." —The Florida Book Review

"A contemporary comedy of manners sprinkled with gastronomical glitter, delectable danger, and goodwill . . . delightful." —*Florida Weekly*

"Juicy, entertaining, and twisty . . . this is a perfect seasonal treat for readers who love both a turkey dinner and a good mystery." —Shelf Awareness

"Sheer fun. The twists and turns keep the reader guessing until the very end, as Lucy Burdette serves up a spectacular mystery." —Fresh Fiction

Murder with Ganache

"Gourmets who enjoy a little mayhem with their munchies will welcome Burdette's fourth Key West mystery." —*Publishers Weekly*

"Sprightly and suspenseful . . . like a gourmet meal, it will leave you wanting more." —*Fort Myers Florida Weekly*

continued . . .

"One crazy adventure ride. This page-turner kept me up half the night."   —MyShelf.com

"[Lucy Burdette] once again crafts a complicated mystery that incorporates delectable descriptions of Key West cuisine."   —Kings River Life Magazine

Topped Chef

"Burdette fills *Topped Chef* with a fine plot, a delightful heroine, a wealth of food—and all the charm and craziness of Key West. You'll wish you could read it while sipping a mojito on the porch of a Conch cottage in mainland America's southernmost community."
                                         —*Richmond Times-Dispatch*

"In addition to a compelling murder mystery, readers are treated to a dose of spirited competition, a pinch of romantic intrigue, and a hearty portion of local flavor. It's enough to satisfy both casual readers and cozy fans alike, though be forewarned: You'll be left craving more."   —Examiner.com

"The characters remain as fresh as the breeze off the ocean, as does the plot."   —The Mystery Reader

"The descriptions of the coastal cuisine, snappish and temperamental cheftestants, and drag queens all combine to make this a very well-written and tasty mystery, sure to please fans of food, reality shows, and mysteries."   —Kings River Life Magazine

Death in Four Courses

"Anyone who's ever overpaid for a pretentious restaurant meal will relish this witty cozy."
                                         —*Publishers Weekly*

"Breezy as a warm Florida Keys day, *Death in Four Courses* is a fast-paced mystery that easily combines food and writing with an intricate plot to create an engaging mystery."   —The Mystery Reader

An Appetite for Murder

"What fun! Lucy Burdette writes evocatively about Key West and food—a winning combination. I can't wait for the next entry in this charming series."
                              —*New York Times* bestselling author
                                     Diane Mott Davidson

"Food, fun, and felonies. What more could a reader ask for?"—*New York Times* bestselling author Lorna Barrett

"For a true taste of paradise, don't miss *An Appetite for Murder.* . . . The victim may not be coming back for seconds, but readers certainly will!"
                              —Julie Hyzy, *New York Times* bestselling author
                                     of the White House Chef Mysteries and
                                             Manor House Mysteries

"You'll eat it up."   —*Richmond Times-Dispatch*

"Not only does Burdette capture the physical and pastoral essence of Key West—she celebrates the food."
                                     —The Florida Book Review

"Hayley herself is delightful. . . . Readers will be happy to make her acquaintance and follow her through future adventures."   —*Florida Weekly*

Other Key West Food Critic Mysteries
by Lucy Burdette

FATAL
RESERVATIONS

A Key West Food Critic Mystery

Lucy Burdette

AN OBSIDIAN MYSTERY

OBSIDIAN
Published by the Penguin Group
Penguin Group (USA) LLC, 375 Hudson Street,
New York, New York 10014

USA | Canada | UK | Ireland | Australia | New Zealand | India | South Africa | China
penguin.com
A Penguin Random House Company

First published by Obsidian, an imprint of New American Library,
a division of Penguin Group (USA) LLC

First Printing, July 2015

ISBN 978-0-451-47482-7

Printed in the United States of America
10 9 8 7 6 5 4 3 2 1

For Barbara Thomason, Donna Johnson, and Sheila Dolan, for their gifts of my furs, Yoda and Tonka

ACKNOWLEDGMENTS

Like so many writers before me, I love my adopted hometown, Key West; it's a pleasure to show you around. Most of the places and restaurants (and some of the people) mentioned really exist, though this story of course is fiction. And if Hayley is forced to give a bad review, I've made that restaurant up. Occasionally, I tweak geography or facts to suit my story.

I would like to express great appreciation to Matthew Carroll from the Make Do and Mend band for permission to quote a wonderful line from their song "No Words." I saw this line tattooed on a young man's arm while waiting for a plane in the Miami airport and knew it would become important in this book.

Thank you to reader Sue Peterson, who strongly suggested that Hayley needed a challenge in her love life. Thanks to Jane Newhagen for the cemetery tour and for helpful information about digging up graves. She also fixed some factual errors—thank you, Jane! Any remaining mistakes are mine.

I'm grateful to Jonathan Shapiro for legal advice on Lorenzo's dilemma and to Dr. Doug Lyle and Michelle Clark for helpful information on body decomposition. Thank you to Barbara Ross for the clever name of the floating restaurant, For Goodness' Sake, and to Hallie Ephron for help with back cover copy. Thanks to Ben

Harrison for describing the spear gun, and to the Key West Ambassador program for introducing me to layers of the city I never knew existed.

Thank you to Ron Augustine for sharing insights on tarot, though any mistakes Lorenzo makes are mine. Same goes for Steve Torrence, who helps out with police-procedure questions—boneheaded moves by characters in this book are not his responsibility.

Thank you to my writer friends, who are always willing to lend a shoulder or an ear. Angelo Pompano and Chris Falcone ask all the right questions and are so steady in their willingness to read drafts and make comments and suggestions. Thank you! The women at Jungle Red Writers and Mystery Lovers' Kitchen have become true and dear friends. Thank you! My sister, Susan Cerulean, was there at the beginning and is with me each step of the way. Thanks to every reader (I love you guys!) and to the libraries and bookstores that help them find my books.

Thanks to Paige Wheeler and her folks at Creative Media Agency for helping me navigate this crazy publishing business. And thanks to the team of professionals at New American Library, who bring the books to life, especially Sandy Harding, whose editing is truly a gift.

As always, thanks to my John. His loving support and good humor make all this possible!

Lucy Burdette
Key West, Florida
February 22, 2015

"What's inside it?" asked the Mole, wriggling with curiosity.

"There's cold chicken inside it," replied the Rat briefly; *"coldtonguecoldhamcoldbeefpickledgherkinsaladfrenchrollscressandwichespottedmeatgingerbeerlemonadesodawater—"*

"O stop, stop," cried the Mole in ecstasies: *"This is too much!"*

—Kenneth Grahame, *The Wind in the Willows*

1

Sometimes spaghetti likes to be alone.
—Joseph Tropiano and Stanley Tucci,
Big Night

The first time Miss Gloria almost died, she came out of the hospital rigid with fear.

The second time, just before Christmas, she came out fighting. In spite of having been jammed into a small space for hours, with hands and feet bound and mouth taped shut, she was determined to embrace life with all the risks that entailed. For weeks, she'd brushed off my concerns about conserving her energy, going out at night alone, and piloting her enormous Buick around the island instead of calling a cab. Good gravy, wasn't she almost eighty-one years old? And besides that, she could barely see over the steering wheel.

I took a deep breath and lowered my voice so the entire marina wouldn't hear us squabbling on the deck of her houseboat. "Your sons will have conniptions if they hear you're driving again," I said. "Lots of things can go wrong—the traffic is terrible this time of year—"

She gripped my wrist with her tiny fingers. "When you look at it without your blinders on, Hayley Snow," she said, "isn't life just one big series of close calls? We all have to go sometime," she added with an impish tilt to her head. "And I've realized that I don't want to go feeling any regrets. And I'd definitely regret spending the rest of my life acting like a scared old lady." She grinned and patted my hand. "My training shift at the cemetery starts at three. You're coming for a tour at four so I can practice, right? How about we compromise and you'll drive me home? That way you can walk over to the cemetery, burn off a few calories, and earn points with your gym trainer," she finished with a sly wink.

I sighed and nodded my agreement. I'd been had and we both knew it.

She hurried down the dock to her metallic green car and I buried myself in my work in order to avoid watching the big sedan back and fill. When she'd extracted the vehicle from its tight parking space, she careened across the Palm Avenue traffic, tires squealing and horn blaring.

I plugged my ears and tried not to look. I had my own problem to attend to: roughing out a plan for my latest restaurant review roundup, tentatively called "Paradise Lunched." My new boss, Palamina Wells, was turning out to be a lot more hands-on than any of us working at *Key Zest* had expected when she assumed half ownership of the magazine in January. Instead of the cheerleader I'd anticipated, she was watching me like a pastry chef eyes salted caramel. Like I might turn on her at any moment.

"I know I'm giving a lot of suggestions right now. I'll back off once I get a handle on things," she'd told us in a staff meeting yesterday. "In the meantime, let's work on making our lead paragraphs truly memorable. Think tweetable, think Buzzfeedable, think Instagram envy. Let's make them irresistibly viral, okay?"

Irresistibly viral felt like a lot to ask from an article on lunch.

At three thirty I put my overworked, underperforming first paragraph aside and told the cats I'd be back in an hour, lord willing that Miss Gloria allowed me to drive home. If the lord didn't will that, I couldn't promise anything.

By the time I fast-walked from Houseboat Row to the Frances Street entrance of the cemetery, I was sweaty and hot, which meant my face had to be its most unattractive tomato red. I took a selfie on my phone and texted it to my trainer, Leigh, as proof of my aerobic exertion. She had been on the money last week when she pointed out that my fitness program had lots of room for improvement. "Increasing your walking from zero miles per week to any positive number would be good," she'd said, snapping her iPad shut with a flourish.

The Key West Cemetery sits in the center of the island on its highest point, where it was moved after the hurricane of 1846 washed the graves and bodies into the Atlantic Ocean. Because of the tight space on this island, many of the burials are now handled in aboveground crypts—which makes for an interesting and spooky landscape. That—along with some interesting inhabitants—makes the cemetery one of the biggest tourist attractions on the island.

I'd put off agreeing to this tour for as long as I could. It's not that cemeteries scare me exactly. It's that the idea of people dying makes me sad, especially people like Miss Gloria, who's probably closer to that transition than most of the people I know. I love her like a grandmother, only more so, because she's a friend, so our relationship is free from the baggage that family relationships can hold. And now here she was, training to be a volunteer guide at the cemetery, where the radio station would play all dead people, all the time.

She was waiting for me at the gate, positively vibrating with excitement. "How much time do we have?" she asked. "I've learned so much, I'd like to tell you all of it."

I laughed. "I have to be at the city commission meeting by six o'clock sharp. And I definitely need something to eat before—the commissioners have a reputation for running hot and late. So let's say half an hour?"

She straightened her shoulders, the serious expression on her lined face at odds with her cheerful yellow sweatshirt, which featured sweet bunnies nibbling on flowers. "In that case, maybe we'll start in the Catholic part of the cemetery, since it's closest." She pushed her glasses up the bridge of her nose. The hinge at the left temple, still held together with silver duct tape, caught on a clump of white hair. She had gotten the lens replaced after it was crushed in the scuffle last December, but she refused to spring for new frames. "I like old things," she'd said, laughing. "They go with me."

She waved me forward. "So we'll start on the right. Then we can work our way around the edges and I won't forget where we left off."

"How long are the tours you'll be giving once you're finished with your training?" I mopped my face with my sleeve and paused in the scanty shade of a coconut palm.

"It depends if it's a special event. In that case, I could be here two hours. But most tourists don't have that kind of attention span. They want to see the gravestone that says, 'I told you I was sick.' And maybe the double-murder-suicide grave."

"The double-murder-suicide?"

"Yes." She nodded enthusiastically. "He shot her and then killed himself. And the poor woman is stuck in the same grave site with him for eternity. What's up with that?"

"Somebody with a sick sense of humor made that decision," I said. "Though Eric always says you never know what's going on in a marriage unless you're living in that space. I guess it's possible that she drove him to it?" My childhood friend Eric is a psychologist and, besides that, the most sensible man I know.

She cleared her throat and started to speak in a serious public-radio kind of voice. "Okay, in this right-hand corner that runs along Frances and Angela streets you will find the Catholic cemetery." Miss Gloria wove through the mossy stones, pointing out the plot for the Gato family, prominent in cigar-manufacturing days; the English family plot, honoring school principal James English and his father, Nelson, Key West's first and only African American postmaster; and a gravestone reading DEVOTED FAN OF SINGER JULIO IGLESIAS.

She adjusted her damaged glasses again. "I hope you'll find something more personal to say than that when my time comes."

"Definitely," I said. "Miss Gloria, spark plug, wonderful roommate, and mother of fabulous sons. But that's too wordy. How about—'She was up for anything'?"

I glanced at my watch, hoping to change the subject. "It looks like we have time for one more."

"Oh, I have to show you this one, then," she said, and led me to the grave of Mario Sanchez, an artist who had recorded scenes of early Key West in his folk-art woodcut painting. "His artwork's shot up in value. Can you imagine, I had the chance to buy one of his pieces, twenty years ago," she said. "But my husband thought two hundred dollars was out of our price range." She looked up at the sky and shook her fist. "Honey, you weren't right about everything. Those paintings are selling for close to a hundred grand now."

Then she hustled up ahead of me. "Here's one more—isn't it amazing? Their monument looks like a collapsed wedding cake."

Tiers of cement pocked by dark patches of mildew crumbled from their redbrick base. "It was beautiful," I said. "Too bad it's falling into disrepair."

She waved at two plots side by side, separated by a spiky metal fence. "Apparently these two families were feuding. Maybe they bought the plot before they started to fight? But anyway, now they're stuck next to each other for eternity with only this fence to separate them."

As we headed out of the graveyard to her car, Miss Gloria darted ahead of me so she could slide into the driver's seat. She waved me to the passenger's side. "Since I'm thinking of driving more often, maybe it's a good idea if you check out my technique."

Crossing my fingers behind my back, I got into the car and fastened my seat belt. Then I gripped the handle above the door with my right hand and the seat with my left. She looked over at me and laughed.

"I swear it won't be that bad." She put the key in the

ignition, turned the car on, and revved up the big engine. We jolted away from the curb on Olivia Street and headed up toward White. At the intersection, cars, bicycles, and scooters roared by in both directions. The town definitely felt busier than usual, but with Miss Gloria at the wheel, all my senses were heightened. She turned on the radio and scooched up the volume so I could barely hear myself worry.

"I'm going to take a right here," she yelled over the Beach Boys singing "Fun, Fun, Fun," "because I'm afraid turning left will make you too anxious."

"You could be correct," I said with a pained smile.

She drove the few blocks from White to Truman without incident and pulled into the left-turn lane. "See now," she said, craning her neck around to look at me. "I'm putting on my directional signal. And my hearing is perfectly good, so I'm not going to leave it on after I turn like the other old people do." She cackled out loud, but I kept looking straight ahead through the windshield, praying she'd get the message and do the same.

"Green arrow!" Miss Gloria sang out, more to herself than to me. She piloted the Buick like a boxy Carnival Cruise ship from the left-turn lane onto Truman Avenue and lurched across the intersection to the right lane. "What are you working on today?" she asked.

I tried to ungrit my teeth and relax my jaw. "It's an article on lunch," I said. "I'm planning to include Firefly, and maybe Azur and The Café."

"What about Edel's bistro?" she asked. "Aren't they serving lunch?"

"Everyone knows Edel and I are well acquainted after all that publicity," I said. "I'm going to give her place a rest for a couple months." Edel Waugh had opened a bistro on the Old Town harbor last December. A fire and a murder had almost tanked the restaurant— I'd been a little too involved in that situation to be considered a disinterested party when it came to restaurant reviews. "Besides, she's gotten so popular lately, it's hard to get a table."

"Jesus Lord!" Miss Gloria yelped and leaned on the horn as a Key West police car cut in front of us. She slammed on the brakes and rolled down her window. "Where did you get your license, Kmart?"

"That's a cop car," I muttered. "Roll up the darn window and keep driving."

"I don't care who it is. He's driving like a horny high school student late for his date."

I goggled at her in amazement. As we reached the intersection of Truman and Palm avenues, where another left turn led to our marina, I noticed the flashing of blue lights from the water.

"The cops," said Miss Gloria. "Let's pull over and see what's happening."

Before I could protest, she had hurtled up onto the sidewalk, thrown the car into park, and scrambled out. A tangle of orange construction webbing floated in the brackish water closest to the new roadway, dotted with assorted trash and a lump of something bigger. Three or four policemen stood on the sidewalk looking down, seeming to discuss how to drag the whole mess ashore. One of them glanced up and then hurried toward us, scowling.

"Get back in the car and keep moving, ladies. This isn't a sideshow. And you're blocking traffic, ma'am." He looked pointedly at my roommate.

"Let's go," I said, herding Miss Gloria to her sedan. "You can watch them from the back deck with the binoculars."

"I swear, Hayley," she said, twisting around to look again. "I think they've snagged a body."

2

Our former back-door neighbors on the next finger
over had finally had their old tub dragged away when
the renters trashed it beyond repair, which left our
view open to the garden spot (not) that is Roosevelt
Boulevard leading into Key West. While I dressed for
the city commission meeting and warmed up some of
last night's chicken enchiladas, Miss Gloria hollered in
with the play-by-play from the deck.

In addition to the two sets of flashing blue lights
we'd seen as we drove by, two more police cars and
then a rescue vehicle arrived at the corner. Traffic had
backed up in both directions, all the way out to our
marina's entrance off Palm Avenue. Miss Gloria spent

ten minutes trying to adjust our elderly binoculars, then finally begged me to buzz her over on my scooter so we could rubberneck along with the rest of the locals and tourists and homeless. All the flotsam and jetsam that added up to the population of Key West seemed to be out looking. I was curious, too, but the possibility of seeing another waterlogged body made me utterly queasy.

"We'll read about it in the paper in the morning," I said as I carried plates of food out from the galley. "Dinner's ready."

We moved a couple of tomato plants off the bench facing the water and sat down to eat. I'd made the green sauce yesterday using a rare cache of tomatillos that I'd snagged at the Restaurant Store's monthly Artisan Market last Sunday. After rolling flour tortillas around shredded chicken, onions, peppers, cheese, and sour cream, I dredged them in the sauce and baked them until they bubbled. We'd liked them so well, we considered consuming the entire 13 by 9 inch pan between the two of us. In one sitting. Reason had finally prevailed when I remembered my feeble attempt to diet—or at least eat smart—and, a few beats later, the fact that I wouldn't have time to cook tonight.

"This is just as good as it was last night, maybe even better," said Miss Gloria after a few bites.

"I love cooking for an appreciative audience," I said, squeezing her shoulder.

Miss Gloria picked up the binoculars and took another look at the scene down the road. Then she gasped and sprang up to point. "It *is* a body!"

I balanced my plate on my knees and grabbed the binoculars to focus on the melee. Several cops had dropped over the railing into the brackish water and were now wet up to their waists. Working together, they snagged a tangle of the orange plastic left over from the Roosevelt Boulevard construction and pulled it toward the road. They heaved the whole mess onto the concrete, including what appeared to be a body, bloated and sodden. A lady detective in a black pantsuit with a turquoise shirt moved forward to snap photos.

I put the fork down on the plate and handed the binoculars back to Miss Gloria. "I've lost my appetite. I'm going to wrap my supper up for after the meeting." I gestured at the knot of cops and gawkers. "Don't go down there, promise?" She sighed and nodded.

Fifteen minutes later, I climbed the very steep steps to the Old City Hall building, an imposing redbrick structure with ornate black railings and a bell tower. For a hundred years, the city commission has been meeting here on Greene Street, a half block from Hemingway's favorite watering hole, Sloppy Joe's, and the chaos of Duval Street. I doubted that visitors had any idea how much city business was conducted while they swilled beer and shouted out choruses of Buffet's "Margaritaville" and Kenny Chesney's Key West theme song, "No Shoes, No Shirt, No Problems."

The hall was cavernous, handsome, and clearly designed to differentiate the commissioners and city staff from any interested onlookers. A text from Wally, my boss and sort-of boyfriend, buzzed in, which reminded me to turn off the ringer on my cell phone.

Let me know outcome tomorrow? Mom's chemo today brutal. I'm going to watch a marathon of Breaking Bad and then crash. See you a.m. @ staff meeting.

As my relationship with Wally took a turn for the better over the last couple of months, his mother's health had taken a turn for the worse. In that sense, our new half owner, Palamina Wells, had been a godsend. She was smart enough to step right in and run the day-to-day nitty-gritty details of *Key Zest* while Wally took care of his mom. She was also smart enough to recognize the attraction between me and Wally and to remove me from reporting directly to him, so we could see where this love train might take us.

I pulled my lizard brain away from that happy thought, deflecting a few niggling concerns in my executive-function lobe that things with him hadn't moved along as quickly as I'd expected—or hoped. I grabbed an aisle seat on the left side of the hall. If by lucky chance the floating-restaurant discussion came up early, I'd be able to slip out. The truth is, I'd rather stick needles in my eyes than attend a Key West city commission meeting. But since food was my beat and since the new floating restaurant on the historic harbor was an item of interest, both Palamina and Wally agreed that I needed to be there to report on the controversy.

For a tiny place, Key West has had a remarkable string of entrepreneurs descend on the island, looking to make their fortunes on *the next best thing*. In the 1800s, it was wreckers scavenging the reefs to make their livelihoods on someone else's misfortune. Following them came the spongers and the turtle harvesters, who moved on after the populations in question were decimated. And then the drug trade. And after that, the gay pride people. In the almost year and a half since I'd moved here from New Jersey, it had been all about the tourists. And high-end real estate. There are big bucks to be made on this island. Which means some entrepreneurs spend a lot of time figuring out how to game the system—how to avoid running their plans through the gimlet-eyed gauntlet of the Historical Architectural Review Commission, for example. Or how to duck city taxes and regulations while raking in the most money.

In the foodie world, the latest brouhaha over the past six months had been about food trucks. Should these mobile food vendors be allowed to operate in the city? Should our commissioners and planners get busy crafting an ordinance that would control where they parked, their hours, their size, their signage, their proximity to other restaurants? Or do nothing? The administration seesawed back and forth on these issues, its fluid stances all duly reflected with varying amounts of hysteria in the newspapers. So it didn't surprise me at all that a floating restaurant would attract the same scrutiny.

Up on the dais behind a wooden railing, the six city commissioners plus the mayor and a smattering of Key West city staff filed into position. The commissioners took seats in large brown leather chairs behind a wooden desk, with carved wooden signs identifying each of them. The mayor called the meeting to order, the clerk called the roll, and a Navy chaplain offered a short prayer, followed by the Pledge of Allegiance.

Onlookers continued to stream into the room as the mayor ran through the items on tonight's docket. Anything that invited comments from the public was removed from the regular agenda so it could be brought up for discussion later. I followed along on my written copy—the floating restaurant, a dispute among the Mallory Square street performers, and a police report on the burglaries in the vicinity of the cemetery were all removed for comments and discussions. Then the mayor gave out commendations to the Boys and Girls Club for their prizewinning float in the Hometown Holiday Parade, and the latest class of Key West Ambassadors was congratulated and installed.

Edel Waugh, the chef/owner at the Bistro on the Bight, entered through the main door, blinked to get her bearings, then clopped up to the podium to pick up an agenda and sign her name as a speaker. Then she hurried down the side aisle and took a seat in the row ahead of me. Had she seen me and chosen to sit by herself anyway? We'd worked out some, but not all, of our prickly feelings after the death and fire at her restaurant last December.

I assumed she was here to comment on the floating restaurant, which had been docked only a hundred yards down harbor from her bistro. I tapped on her shoulder and whispered, "Are you planning to speak?"

She gave a curt nod. The clerk read the description of the agenda item. "Ordinance of the City of Key West Florida . . . granting grandfather status to Edwin and Olivia Mastin's request for zoning variance to operate their floating restaurant, For Goodness' Sake, until further notice." Then the clerk added, "A petition in support of the variance is attached, signed by one hundred residents. A petition protesting the variance has also been attached, with seventeen signatures. Ms. Edel Waugh will be the first to comment."

Edel scrambled out of her seat and hurried to the podium at the front left of the room. She barely reached the microphone, and I had to strain to hear her introduction. The city clerk lumbered over to lower the mic so she could be heard. Edel nodded her thanks, placed her notes down, and looked at the commissioners.

"You've probably read my name in the newspaper in connection with the fire this past December. Bistro on the Bight is my new restaurant and I'm extremely grateful for the local support which allowed me to open the bistro and proceed with renewed vigor after the tragedy." The smile on Edel's face faded away and her cheeks flooded pink. "The proposed floating restaurant lies approximately a hundred yards west of my place, even closer to the restaurants Schooner Wharf and Turtle Kraals. My hope is that city officials will consider matters of fairness when they approach this zoning request." Edel breathed deeply and patted her dark curls.

"We all live together in this small space—newcomers, old guard, visitors—all of us. I don't need to tell you that our island occupies less than ten square miles." She fixed her gaze on each of the commissioners in turn. "As you folks know better than most anyone else on this coral rock, the rules and regulations that the city establishes make life here not only bearable, but beautiful." She flashed her most charming and grateful smile.

"When I applied for the lease last year for my restaurant on the old harbor and then plans for the renovations, I had to show my design to the Historical Architectural Review Commission. There were many *discussions*."

She made air quotes with her fingers and then barked a tight laugh. A smattering of the audience and two commissioners laughed along with her.

"I had to demonstrate that my building would meet the standards of the committee, that it would fit in with other historic structures in Key West. As many business owners and homeowners in the town have done, I spent a lot more time and money than I'd planned to during renovation in order to comply with these regulations." She sighed. "This is the cost of doing business in Key West, and I determined that it was worth it."

A light began to flash, indicating that Edel's time limit for commenting was approaching. Her voice grew louder.

"The question of the floating restaurant raises a question of fairness."

Two ladies down the row from me had begun to rustle. "She already said that," said a woman in blue jeans. "She seems to think she's the only business in Key West."

"A hundred yards from some of the busiest streets in the city, should one restaurant be allowed to bypass the city's regulations?" Edel went on, her voice taut with outrage. "Dismiss regulations about appearance and noise levels and the environment? I, for one, don't think so. People warned me that I'd run into a Bubba system in Key West, but I chose not to believe them."

I was surprised to hear her mention Bubbas, the so-called old-boys network that some folks believe dominate city politics behind the scenes. This was a little like complaining about communists in Cuba. You had to be careful because you never really knew to whom you were speaking.

"Excuse me, Miss Waugh," the clerk began, but Edel barreled over her.

"I don't mind competition; in fact, I welcome it. Competition helps every chef cook better. In the restaurant business, it helps us stay on our game to have someone else nipping at our heels." She banged a fist on the podium, causing several of the commissioners to startle. "But what's not fair is restaurants that don't have to pay the same taxes or jump through the city ordinance hoops with the Historic Architectural Review Commission or the Planning and Zoning Department. Restaurants that have been allowed to open without all the permits in place—"

The city clerk cut her off again and a police officer escorted her away from the podium.

Next, Edwin Mastin, the owner of the floating restaurant, was announced. A solid man with a sunburned face, wearing a green Hawaiian shirt over a small potbelly, approached the dais. I was surprised to recognize him as the proprietor of another restaurant in town—one of the busiest and most lucrative on the island, if not the highest level of gastronomy. He swung around and fixed an angry gaze on Edel.

"Thank you, Miss Waugh. I'm a little surprised to hear you say you welcome competition, because in our view, you appear to be doing as much as you can to destroy it." He turned back to the commissioners, raised his shoulders and then lowered them with a loud exhalation, and finally smiled. "As you know, I've lived in Key West my entire life. I am not a newcomer intent on walking on the backs of other businesses in order to succeed. I own two other restaurants and am in full compliance with all city regulations. In this case, For Goodness' Sake is not a building; it's a boat. It's not covered by the regulations of the Historic Architectural Review Commission, as much as Miss Waugh might wish that it were." He cleared his throat, ran his fingers through his bushy hair. "Should the commission determine that regulations should be written for floating restaurants, we will certainly comply with them. Thank you for the opportunity to speak." He stepped away from the podium well before the warning light flashed,

which honestly left him looking organized and competent, and Edel, long-winded and a little hysterical.

"Thank you," said the mayor. "Are there any other
remarks?" He took a few questions about the size of the
boat (one hundred feet) and the number of customers it
could seat (forty) and allowed several other attendees to
comment in support of Mastin's new project. "Thank
you for all that. The commissioners will take this input
into account and revisit the matter at our next meeting."

"Damn it," Edel muttered. "I should have known
they wouldn't do anything about this." She collected
her papers, grabbed her sweater from the seat back,
and swept out of the room.

As she went out, a man with a very tan face wearing
a pith helmet woven from palm fronds staggered in. He
stumbled across the area in front of the commissioners,
mumbling loudly, and then scribbled his name on the
docket and collapsed into a front-row seat. I'd seen him
regularly on Duval Street accosting visitors and bad-
gering them into buying his hats. But right now the
hairs on the back of my neck stood at attention.

Too many times this past year, we'd heard in the
news that citizens and professionals had not paid
enough attention to the warning signs of people who
seemed a little off—who later turned out to be violent.
And people died as a result. I'd seen no metal detector
at the entrance to the door. Other than the officer who
had escorted Edel away from the microphone, I hadn't
noticed a police presence in the room. I glanced around
and felt relieved to spot my friend Lieutenant Torrence
standing against the back wall, his eyes narrowed and
focused on the man in the palm-frond hat.

The mayor piped up. "The next item on the agenda

will be a discussion of the lease renewal on Mallory Square for the Artistic Performance Preservation Society. The first speaker will be Commissioner Greenleigh. To be followed by Lorenzo."

The only female commissioner on the dais pulled her microphone closer to her lips. "I've been attempting to work with the steering committee of the APPS for the past few months." She wiped her hand over her eyes and looked at the clock. It felt as if we'd spent hours here already and there was plenty more to come. "'Steering committee' in this case is a term that should be used loosely. In all my years in government and business, it's hard to say where I might have witnessed a more dysfunctional group. You will already know that for many years the APPS has received the lease for the performance space at Mallory Square, and then they've taken care of assigning performers to individual places in the square. But it's my impression that the city may have to rescind the lease and begin running the Sunset Celebration events itself."

A noisy rustling burst out in the audience and the man with the palm-frond hat staggered up toward the podium, shouting. "You people have been looking for any excuse to take over. Damn it, this is none of your business! The trouble with the Artistic Damn Preservation Society is right here in this room." He spun around to point a shaky finger at a tall man several rows behind me: my friend, the tarot card reader. Lorenzo.

The mayor rose to his feet. "You need to return to your seat or you'll be removed from the premises."

But instead of sitting, the palm-hat man darted down the center aisle, heading for Lorenzo. He flung himself across two startled women and circled his hands around my friend's neck. Lieutenant Torrence and a uniformed cop roared up the aisle from the back of the room, yanked him off Lorenzo, whipped his hands behind his back, and cuffed them. He fought and cursed as they ushered him out of the room and down the stairs. Outside, I heard the whoop of several sirens.

The mayor's face was now beaded with sweat, his wire-rimmed glasses askew, and his wide forehead lined with concern. He removed his glasses and wiped them on his white shirt. "Are you all right, sir?" he asked Lorenzo.

"I think so." Pulling a crisp handkerchief from his pants pocket, Lorenzo patted his face and neck, now mottled red, and smoothed his hair.

"If you're able to speak, sir, it's your turn at the microphone," said the mayor, and sank back into his leather chair.

Lorenzo nodded, adjusted his collar, and came forward. By dress alone, he stood out from most everyone in attendance: long-sleeved white dress shirt, high-waisted black pants, black tie, tortoiseshell glasses—even his wavy hair had been smoothed into a neat ponytail. All very proper and distinguished. But his face shone in the spotlight and large damp circles spread from his underarms to the body of his shirt. He looked very hot. And rattled.

"I should make clear that I am speaking for myself tonight, as a concerned artist at the Sunset Celebration, not in an official context." He ran his finger around his collar and straightened his tie. "Next to the ocean itself, the Sunset Celebration is the biggest tourist attraction on our island. Everybody in the world has heard of it, and that's a major reason why they come to Key West." Lorenzo touched his forehead again with the hankie. "I hate to say it, but I must agree with Commissioner

Greenleigh. Our present steering board seems unable to solve—"

"The city government cannot be allowed to take control—they will ruin this just the way they've ruined everything else," a man called out from the audience.

Lorenzo waited with a pained expression on his face while one of the cops went to quiet the disgruntled spectator. "As I was saying, I'm not convinced that our internal organization can handle itself well enough to make certain that the Sunset Celebration remains the city's crown jewel. That's all. Thank you." He nodded at each of the leaders and returned to his seat.

After some discussion among the commissioners, they decided that several of them should attend the Artistic Performance Preservation Society's meeting in two days to see if some informal assistance could be rendered. If this proved impossible, more drastic actions would be considered.

The mayor, who appeared tired and haggard, glanced at the big clock on the wall. "It's late. I'd like to have a quick discussion on this final item, which concerns the ongoing robberies in homes around the cemetery. We pride ourselves on the safety record of our island," he said, "and now we've had what—six? seven? ten? burglaries in what is touted as one of the safest residential areas in the city."

"More like twenty!" called a woman from the audience.

The mayor ignored her. "The so-called cemetery burglar is making a laughingstock of our police department." I was more than a little surprised that he'd be publicly critical of the KWPD. He must have been feeling a lot of pressure. He looked around the hall. "I don't see our police chief in attendance. Lieutenant Torrence, perhaps you could come to the podium and speak to these issues?"

The crowd rustled and muttered as Torrence muscled his way to the front of the room, managing to look official and friendly at the same time. For fifteen minutes, he answered questions from the city officials and the audience, assuring everyone in the calmest of voices that the police were very vigilant and close to arresting the burglar. "In fact, due to our vigilance, there have been no new burglary episodes in the past week. In spite of the millions of visitors we welcome each year, our city remains one of the safest places to live in the United States."

A white-haired woman in the front row waved her hand frantically and the mayor allowed her question. "What about the body pulled from the water today near Palm Avenue? That does not make us feel the least bit safe."

Another man yelled out, "Is it true that the victim was Bart Frontgate?" The crowd buzzed.

Torrence's face reddened and he ran a finger around his collar, replicating the motion Lorenzo had made while on the hot seat. "I can assure you, ma'am," he repeated, "that the police are very close to an arrest. I'm not able to say anything further due to the sensitive nature of the investigation."

Miss Gloria, who tended to be an early bird rather than a night owl, was still up when I got home to our boat.

"I found a couple of your double-chocolate brownies in the freezer," she explained. "I'm so jazzed up from the caffeine, I may not sleep until Friday. Tell me about the meeting."

I had just begun to describe the antics of the various

town folk when my phone rang. Lorenzo. I accepted the call.

"Hayley, I need your help," he whispered before even his customary polite greeting. "The police think I murdered Bart Frontgate."

3

*Julia Child, goddess of fat, is beaming some-
where. Butter is back.*
　　　—Mark Bittman, "Butter Is Back,"
　　　　　　The New York Times

The next morning I forced myself to postpone reading
the paper until after I'd walked the two miles prescribed by my daily exercise program. Then I skimmed
my e-mail and scanned the newspaper headlines online while I waited for the second pot of coffee to per-
colate.

Both the *Key West Citizen* and the *Konk Life* e-blasts
were buzzing with reports of the city commission
meeting the evening before. I was not the only one who
had found the tension uncomfortable. The police chief
had refused to comment on his own absence or on the
attack on Lorenzo to the *Citizen*'s most dogged ace reporter, but he assured her that he had full confidence in
the lieutenants reporting to him, including Torrence.
They were in the process of organizing a community
meeting to discuss the state of the cemetery burglar in-

vestigation. And they were vigorously pursuing leads on the latest tragic death on the island. I got the feeling that under the headlines there lay a serious crisis of confidence in our law enforcement.

A photo of the crime scene—the deceased covered in a blue tarp—took up most of the space below the fold in Miss Gloria's paper copy of the *Citizen*. A quote from the mayor expressed sorrow at the loss of a member of the Key West family. At the bottom of the article a passage read:

> *The murdered man, Bartholomew Frontgate, was recently involved in the controversy over the lease renewal at Mallory Square for the Artistic Performance Preservation Society. He has been a staple at the nightly Sunset Celebration for almost fifteen years, performing his trademark juggling act with oversized kitchen utensils studded with flaming chunks of meat. Mr. Frontgate had recently drawn the ire of the SPCA when he announced his plan to add kittens to his act, which he planned to juggle along with the forks. Responding to pressure from the local police and a tirade of comments in the Citizens' Voice, he backed away from the animal component, while assuring the public that he had no intention of setting the animals on fire.*

Miss Gloria came out of the bathroom, toweling her white curls dry. "You were up and at 'em early today. Are you off somewhere important?" she asked.

"I'm having brunch with Eric and Lorenzo in a little bit," I said, "for the lunch roundup. I invited Lorenzo to join us because he's a total basket case." I tapped the paper spread out on the counter.

Miss Gloria had heard my end of the conversation

last night, so I wouldn't be breaking any confidences by telling her what was happening—that Lorenzo believed he was a lead suspect in Frontgate's murder. "I think Eric will be able to calm him down and help him sort out his options. And even maybe figure out why he's been fingered. I can't imagine Lorenzo would hurt a fly, never mind kill someone. He's a Buddhist and truly the most gentle soul I've ever met."

"He's a darling man," she said, her eyes narrowing. She draped the towel over the back of a kitchen chair and picked up Sparky, her purring cat. "Probably someone else set him up to take the fall for this, right? You should call that nice Steve Torrence and tell him the cops are on the wrong track."

I nodded reluctantly. I doubted that Lieutenant Torrence or any other member of the Key West Police Department would welcome my theories. Or, despite her recent status as local hero, Miss Gloria's.

"Would you mind dropping me off at the cemetery on your way downtown? My boss, Jane, is holding a special class for us guides on symbolism in the monuments."

"With all the time you're spending there, I hope she's paying you well," I said with a laugh. And then I wondered why Miss Gloria wasn't taking her car, although it seemed better not to even ask. Why take the risk of planting the idea back in her head?

Once we were both dressed and groomed, I zipped Miss G over to the graveyard and then continued to the restaurant, located in the Bahama Village section of town, which formerly housed mainly people of Bahamian descent. Firefly Restaurant, serving home-style Southern food, is just a block down Petronia Street from two other Key West tourist eatery favorites, Blue

Heaven and La Creperie. New places like Firefly, part of the creeping gentrification of the island, are good for foodies, but not so good for average working people looking for affordable meals and livable rents.

I arrived before Lorenzo and Eric and managed to snag a seat upstairs on the porch overlooking Petronia Street. Sitting with one eye on the street and the other on the door so I could watch for my friends, I perused the appetizers on the menu. My eye caught on pimento cheese with spiced saltine crackers and a plate of fried green tomatoes—was it too early in the day for pimento cheese? My mouth watered at the prospect, which I interpreted as a definitive no. The waitress filled a mason jar with unsweetened iced tea, and I sat back to watch the slow parade of people and chickens below me and jot a few notes about the setting.

A few minutes later, a tall man with tousled blond hair, plummy cheeks, and wire-rimmed glasses appeared in the doorway. Eric. I waved and he came over to join me. We exchanged hugs and he sat across from me.

"How are the doggies? How's Bill?" Bill is Eric's husband, and also co-parent to their two beloved Yorkies.

"All good. How was the city commission meeting?"

"Awful," I said. "Long and tense. And then this thing with Lorenzo." I'd told him the bare bones of the story when I'd called to set this meeting up.

Lorenzo fluttered in, still wearing the same black pants, white shirt, and black clogs he'd had on the night before—minus the tie. He looked as though he'd slept in his clothes or, more likely, hadn't slept at all. His wavy hair was uncombed and he was missing an earring. He was usually so fastidious that this downturn in appearance alarmed me. He took the seat next to me.

"Just ice water. With lemon," he told the waitress when she asked him about a beverage. "If I have one more jot of caffeine, I may blast off," he said to me.

I introduced him to Eric. "I feel like you two should know each other already."

"By reputation, certainly," said Eric. "Hayley speaks very highly of you."

"Thank you," said Lorenzo in a soft, earnest voice. "She's a dear friend. And a good person. And if you're a friend of hers, that's all I need to know."

"Tell us what's happening," I said. "I'm so worried about you."

Lorenzo lowered his voice so we could barely hear him. "You saw the charade at the city commission meeting. And that idiot Louis trying to choke me." One hand fluttered to his neck. "Maybe half an hour after I got home, two cops knocked on my door. They had questions about my whereabouts for the past twenty-four hours and my relationship with the dead man."

The waitress returned with water for Lorenzo, coffee for Eric, and the appetizers I'd ordered for the table. I reeled off a list of dishes that we would also share. "Anything else you're craving?" I asked them.

"I don't have much of an appetite," Lorenzo admitted.

"You've pretty much ordered everything on the menu already," Eric added with a laugh.

"One thing I have to ask," I said to Lorenzo once the waitress had bustled off with our order. I tried to think about how to word the question so he wouldn't take offense. "Did you have any kind of premonition that Louis attacking you last night was going to happen?"

He looked so distressed that I wished I hadn't said anything, hadn't appeared to question his special vision. "I'm not trying to be fresh or rude," I said. "I'm really serious. Did you have any sense something bad might happen with the Artistic Preservation group? Or Louis himself?"

Lorenzo mopped his forehead with a limp white hankie. "Of course things have been terribly stressful at Mallory Square for the last—let's say, even the past year or so. I felt every bit of that anxiety." He patted his chest.

Which didn't really answer my question, but I hated to press him harder. Let him tell the story in his own time. I spread a spoonful of pimento cheese on a saltine cracker for each of us and waited. Eric and I began to eat. The cheese and pimentos were a lovely combination of creamy and tangy, and the crackers crispy and salty. I could eat an entire order of this and nothing else and feel perfectly happy. Lorenzo's fingers trembled as he picked up his cracker. He set the treat back down on the small plate and peered over the railing to the street below.

"How does the organization work down at Mallory Square?" Eric asked as he loaded a second cracker with cheese. "It always looks like barely controlled chaos." He waved his cracker at me. "By the way, I never imagined I liked pimento cheese, but this is amazing."

"It's too complicated and convoluted to tell you everything," Lorenzo said. "Basically, we elect a board of directors to set up the performer guidelines and negotiate the contract with the city. The organization leases the space from the city," he explained. "Across the years, the biggest conflict has been over seniority. If you've visited Mallory Square at Sunset you might have noticed that some of the positions are worth a lot more money than others."

"If you score a square of space near the water," I suggested, "your traffic will tend to be better?"

"Of course," said Lorenzo. "When the sun actually dips into the water, tourists want to be right there on the edge, where they have the best view. Performers who've been around a long time don't want the space to be portioned out according to who gets there early in the day to set up. They want a primo space reserved for them." He sighed and crossed his hands neatly, reminding me of a big tuxedo housecat. "The newer people don't like this."

"I see the potential problems snowballing," Eric said. "I suspect that many of the performers are living on a shoestring, so tips matter a lot?"

"You got it." Lorenzo huffed. "There's more. One of our other hot issues has to do with voting. When an important vote is about to be decided, some people have been salting the membership with new members who will vote the way they want them to. You can only imagine the ways the rules can be twisted." He heaved another big sigh. "These people aren't Harvard-educated, polite politicians. They're street performers. Cagey. And ruthless."

Eric nodded, keeping his gaze on Lorenzo, concentrating with every cell. I could definitely see why his patients found his empathy compelling enough that they were willing to spill their toxic secrets to a complete stranger.

"I'm not on the board or anything, but I try to stay involved, push for changes if they're needed. My hope is that we keep everything transparent. Just like our government." He grimaced. "Not that that's been working out so well in Washington. Or even Tallahassee. But people don't like that—me saying we have to establish meaningful rules and follow them, quit relying on backroom politics. Some of our performers who have been around the longest are starting to feel entitled, and that grates on the newer people. We all pay the same fees—well." He stopped and frowned. "Some of us don't pay at all."

"What do you mean, some don't pay?"

"Right now, you only pay if you're selling something—a physical object like food or T-shirts or souvenirs. But that's got to change. It's all got to change. But if people are going to die over it . . ."

"So you think Frontgate's murder was related to what's going on with this organization?" Eric asked.

Lorenzo's lower lip quivered—he looked exhausted and hopeless.

I reached across the table to take his hand, which was moist and hot. And I suddenly felt like I was intruding on his privacy. I let go and tried to smile. "I wanted you to meet Eric because he was also wrongly accused of a murder. Of course he was innocent. But he learned some important lessons about the process." I turned to Eric. "Could you give him some suggestions?"

"Definitely," said Eric, "if he's interested."

I cut the fried green tomatoes into pie-shaped slices and slid a few bites onto each of our plates. Nobody but me was eating much—Lorenzo was too upset. And Eric was completely focusing on the other man.

Lorenzo finally shrugged. "Advice is welcome. How could it make things worse?"

Eric said, "When I first fell under suspicion, I didn't tell the police everything I knew about the crime because I was trying to protect someone. It had to do with my obligation as a psychologist. The obligation that I felt to keep the secrets of a patient private. But I also thought I was protecting myself. I believed that keeping that secret would keep me out of trouble. Wrong. My judgment, I'm sorry to say, was not that great. In fact, it stunk." He wrinkled his brow. "Maybe you have some of the same feelings about your clients."

"Of course I do," said Lorenzo. "I'm helping people with heavy burdens. They've carried them around for years, some of them. And they've told no one until they come to my table. They are so desperate to unload the weight. To get some guidance. You may laugh, because I sit at a booth on the pier with crowds of tourists and crazy circus performers all around, while you sit in a fancy office with a waiting room full of expensive magazines and classical music. But my work is a big responsibility." He clasped his hands over his heart. "I feel it here every day."

I was afraid to look at Eric, thinking that he might find Lorenzo's parallel between tarot cards and psychotherapy ludicrous. But when I snuck a glance, his face was utterly serious. "Listen," Eric said, "you have to tell the police whatever you know. This business of the artist performance committee or whatever—it sounds very complicated. And there are obviously sides being taken and I'm guessing maybe your side is not popular? And the fellow who attacked you last night—you should tell them your theories about that. Why has he singled you out? These are fringe people with histories of drugs and violence—some of them, anyway. They're not your usual upstanding citizens. You have to be careful."

Lorenzo nodded.

"Why are the cops coming after you?" Eric asked. "What exactly was your connection with the dead man?"

Lorenzo swallowed, his Adam's apple bobbing, and shook his head. "No connection, other than sharing the public space at Sunset."

I met Eric's gaze and he lifted his eyebrows, as though he, too, thought Lorenzo was holding something back. "Who was Bart Frontgate?" Eric asked.

"He was a juggler," Lorenzo said stubbornly. "I only knew him in the context of our business connection."

"Then help us understand why the cops are after you."

Lorenzo's shoulders lifted in a tight shrug.

"Do you have a lawyer?" Eric asked. "You're going to need one."

"I don't mean to be rude, but I think I'm going to be sick." Lorenzo pushed to his feet and clattered away from our table. He crossed the porch and shot down the stairs. Within minutes, we watched him clop down Petronia Street and disappear into an alley.

4

"The only thing that makes a soufflé fall,"
he was talking almost to himself, "is if it
knows that you are afraid of it."
—Ruth Reichl, *Delicious!*

Once it was clear that Lorenzo was not coming back (and how much more clear could he have been?), Eric and I did the best we could with all the food I'd ordered. The fried chicken with a thin crisp waffle and spicy maple syrup was my favorite, although Eric was crazy about the cheese grits and the kale salad.

Finally he pushed away from the table. "Two hundred thousand calories later, I can't eat another bite."

I called the waitress over and asked her to bring samples of her most popular desserts and wrap up the other leftovers so I could take them to *Key Zest*. Palamina didn't strike me as a big eater, but Danielle was always happy to graze. And I could use some auxiliary opinions.

"What do you think's going on with your friend?" Eric asked after our server had whisked the plates away.

"Like I said to Miss Gloria this morning, he's a practicing Buddhist. He's gentle and peaceful. I can't believe he would murder another living being."

"But how well do you really know him?"

All the food I'd eaten, in combination with Eric's tough question, was making me feel a little queasy. "Not that well. But I knew you very well and you still kept secrets about a murder."

"That's my point," Eric replied. "There's obviously something he isn't able or willing to talk about. You don't think he'd murder someone, but you never know what will happen when someone's pushed hard."

I shook my head. "I don't see it. If one of the Sunset performers killed Frontgate, it's more likely it was the crazy man who attacked Lorenzo last night. Now, there's a guy who is capable of violence."

Eric frowned and tipped his head in the direction that Lorenzo had disappeared. "Bear with me here. Just for starters, is Lorenzo a local? If not, where did he come from? What do you know about his background?"

"I don't know too much. His name was Marvin growing up. Once he became an official tarot card reader, he decided that no one would want their cards read by a man named Marvin. Hence, Lorenzo." I snickered but then fell silent. Nothing about this situation was funny. "And I know that he visits friends in Connecticut in the summer when it's the slow season down here. But I've never heard him talk about his family."

Eric's face had grown very solemn. "And that's the thing about this town," he said. "Many folks end up here because they don't fit in anywhere else. And so you have no idea whether they're running from something or whether they just love this island."

"Really? That's your theory? He's running?"

He flashed a lopsided grin. "Lots of times it's something as simple as not wanting to grow up. But lots of folks don't have normal families. Current company excepted, of course. There's always the exception that proves the rule."

"Oh, I was definitely running from something, too," I said. "Maybe you've forgotten, I had no idea where my life was going. I just knew I couldn't spend the rest of it in my mother's back bedroom."

"Speaking of which," said Eric, "how is your mother?"

"Of course you remember that Sam had surgery and Mom went up to see him through it?" My mother had come down to winter in Key West last December, and to everyone's surprise—especially mine—had instantly landed a plum catering position. She flew north only to nurse her new fiancé, Sam, through his hip replacement. "The docs had Sam up and walking the evening they put in the new hip," I said. "It's kind of amazing what they make people do right after surgery. I'm sure in the old days he would've stayed in a hospital bed for a week."

"And suffered for it," said Eric. The waitress brought two brown bags of leftovers, two kinds of dessert in plastic containers, and the bill.

"Anyway," I added, once she'd left with my credit card, "Mom wants to stay up north long enough to make sure Sam can fix himself a cup of soup or cup of coffee, and then she'll be back down to finish her season at Small Chef at Large. Jennifer's got her covered for three weeks, so there's no hurry. Except that it's fifteen degrees and snowing every other day in New Jersey."

Eric groaned. He'd come from my hometown, too, and he knew what winters were like. "I bet she can't wait to get out of there. But for you, maybe it's a smidgen of relief to have her out of town for a bit? She's larger than life."

"No comment." I grinned and took a bite of the key lime cake, which was both light and sharp, and then the fried blueberry pie. I jotted some notes in my phone.

Eric glanced at his watch. "I need to get going. Don't you get involved with this case, okay?"

"Only if Lorenzo needs me."

Eric chewed on his lip. "Not loving that answer."

"Only if he's flat-out desperate, and I'll call the cops first, okay? Thanks for everything. I bet talking to you helped him a lot." I kissed him on the cheek, gathered up my stuff, and followed him out into the perfect Key West day—a little sun, a little wind, a few clouds, and air that was as warm as bathwater. I zipped back to the *Key Zest* office feeling edgy and tired. Last night's commission meeting had worn me out, and my worry about Lorenzo was piling on top of that.

And now that I was closer to the office and unable to push the feeling aside, I realized that I wasn't quite comfortable with Palamina Wells running the staff meetings while Wally was out of town. "Not quite comfortable" didn't really describe what I was feeling. "Worried sick" was more like it.

Oh, this first month with Palamina was definitely miles better than my time working for Ava Faulkner had been, with her nasty digs, impossible demands, and poorly disguised threats. But what if I couldn't live up to Palamina's expectations? I had never written for a New York City magazine, as she had for years. I felt less sophisticated in every way. Plus, *Key Zest* didn't feel quite the same with her installed in Wally's office and him Skyping on the computer screen—at least until his mom was stable. Eric would say I working myself up over nothing. I tried taking a couple deep breaths. *Whoo-ha, whoo-ha.*

Then I remembered that Palamina had promised to make some changes in the decor, too. She insisted on doing this overnight, by herself—like we were hapless contestants in a desperate office makeover. Nothing that would cost a lot of money, she assured us, but a step above the fake palm trees and flowered chintz that we had been satisfied with before she came. How I hated familiar things changing.

Most of all I wished that I'd had time to spit shine my opening paragraph on lunch. The last thing I wanted was to have her suspect that Wally had hired me only because he thought I was cute.

I parked my scooter in the back lot and raced up the stairs, already fifteen minutes late. Paint fumes grew stronger as I approached the second-floor landing. Pushing open the door to the reception area, I was shocked by the bright yellow color of the walls. And then I noticed a series of large framed photographs behind Danielle's desk. A plate of pink shrimp and a glass of wine on a table overlooking the ocean—Louie's Backyard?—polydactyl cats lounging at the Ernest Hemingway Home, a rooster flapping his wings in front of the Little White House, and finally, the quotation "Leap and the net will appear" in elegant calligraphy, superimposed over two bright red butterflies.

"Wow," I said, a little stupefied by the changes. "It looks amazing."

"Hurry," said Danielle, beckoning me to follow her into Wally's office. "We've been waiting for you to start the meeting."

I hustled into the office and took my customary seat

catty-corner to the desk that had been Wally's. His familiar face was on Palamina's oversized screen, and she was sitting in his chair. His back wall, on which he had thumbtacked our best articles from the past year, was now papered with textured burlap, and his prized ceramic flip-flop lamp had been replaced with two Asian-style table lamps made of arcing fish. Gone were the cascades of garish-colored beads from Fantasy Fest and New Year's Eve, which had been looped on a couple of random nails on his walls. The room seemed neater and more elegant. And maybe a little bit sad.

"Sorry I'm late; the brunch went slowly at Firefly. But I did bring leftovers."

I held up two brown bags, now unappealingly stained by grease and smelling to high heaven of cheese and onions.

Palamina's nose wrinkled slightly.

"Let me stick those in the fridge for you," Danielle said, snatching them out of my hands.

"I've just taken Wally on a tour of our new look," Palamina said with a grin, once Danielle was back in place.

"All I can say is wow," I said with an enthusiastic accent on the "wow," knowing that anyone who knew me—as Wally and Danielle did—could see right through it. The changes looked glamorous and upscale and upbeat, too—none of which I was feeling.

"Wow is right," said Wally from the computer screen. "I didn't realize how much we were in need of a makeover."

I squirmed and pasted a sickly smile on my face. I loved the way the look of our old office had evolved, a kitschy style that I thought suited *Key Zest* perfectly.

"And," Danielle added, pointing at me, "hold on to your hat, because we are no longer obligated or even encouraged to wear the yellow polyester *Key Zest* shirts! Palamina is thinking of ordering us these." She tapped the page on a catalog spread open on the desk, which showed a flowing silk blouse with an asymmetrical hem and a low neckline. Still the yellow color that brought out the jaundice in my skin tone, but with the addition of a style guaranteed to keep me twitching to hide glimpses of brassiere and even breast.

"A polyester Hawaiian shirt doesn't do much for anyone," said Palamina. "Do you think?"

"Wow," I said again, because I couldn't think of anything else that wouldn't be rude. Of course our team shirts were homely, but to me, they were like a badge and a blue polyester uniform were to a cop. They meant we belonged. They meant we were on the case, on the hunt for the best food—the best everything—in Key West. The brotherhood of *Key Zest*. "Wally's going to look adorable in that," I finally added when it became clear that Palamina was waiting for my reaction.

Palamina laughed. "Let's get the meeting started. Bring us up to date on the floating restaurant."

"The commission meeting was wild," I said. "Edel Waugh spoke up against the new place and tried to invoke the regulations of the Historic Architectural Review Commission and so on. But she was overruled because it's a boat, not a building, so the present regulations don't apply. They plan to reconsider the situation, but it sounds like they are likely to grandfather in the Mastins' restaurant anyway."

Palamina's forehead wrinkled up a little. "So, hmm, what are you thinking about for the angle of your story?"

I felt my mouth sag open—I hadn't thought for a minute about my angle. I pulled my jaw shut. "Actually, I hadn't noodled that out yet. I had planned to go home and work on the piece last night, but right after that, Lorenzo was attacked right there in the meeting. And then there were contentious discussions about the Sunset Celebration at Mallory Square and the cemetery burglar. It was too tense to leave. And this morning I devoted to Firefly." I had to stop blathering—to Palamina it must have sounded as though I was making excuses for doing a shoddy job.

She nodded, looking thoughtful, and then turned to focus on Wally's image on the computer screen. She tapped the tip of her pencil on the desk. "I don't know what your policy has been in the past, but I'm kind of thinking Hayley should maintain her focus on the food angle, rather than get caught up in the town politics. I like the idea of Hayley's brand being food and restaurants, sort of the Key West Pete Wells or Frank Bruni. And then you or I can cover politics as needed. Once you get back down here, of course."

"Sounds okay to me," said Wally. "Okay with you, Hayley?"

Pretty clear that she didn't think I could handle hard news, because I hadn't produced an "angle." But what was I going to do, pitch a fit about covering fluff? "Sure," I said. "But rest assured that I can write about anything. What I mean is, I'm capable of writing on any subject."

Palamina gave a brisk nod. "If it sounds okay to the rest of you, I took the liberty of making a reservation at For Goodness' Sake for Hayley for dinner tomorrow. While the other news organizations are waiting to see what shakes out with the regulations, we'll get the jump on what the meals are like. Table for four at seven thirty under the name Wells. I have a date with Commissioner Greenleigh for drinks tonight. I bet I can get something quotable from her on the zoning controversy."

We spent another fifteen minutes in the meeting—a record short length for *Key Zest*. I did miss the usual chit-chat and gossip, but each time we veered in that direction, Palamina briskly steered us back to work. Within those fifteen minutes, she'd admired and approved my lunch article's title and slashed the lead to a stylish two sentences that would get necks snapping. Or salivary glands watering or eyeballs popping, whatever. Once Wally had signed off the conference call, I said, "How did he look to you? Don't you think he looked pale?"

"But he sounded strong," Danielle said. "I think work is good for him, something to keep him occupied that isn't sad."

"Agreed," said Palamina. Then she turned to me. "So you've got Firefly in the bag; do you think you can get two more lunches in and have the article to me by Tuesday? Actually Monday would be even better, so I have time to edit."

"Of course." I gathered up my papers and computer and slunk down the hall to my cubicle, which had not yet been decorated in the world-according-to-Palamina style. I phoned Wally as soon as I'd shut the door.

"I didn't get a chance to find out how you're doing," I said.

"We're doing well," he said. "Mom's feeling better and I may even get down to Key West for part of the weekend."

"Fabulous!" I said. "Can't wait to see you. Let me know when you get here." And then I touched my toe in the water: "That Palamina is a whirling dervish, isn't she?"

"A breath of fresh air," Wally said. "Nothing negative about her. It takes a weight off me to know she's quite capable of handling things until I get back full-time."

Which hadn't exactly been my experience—not this morning, anyway. In the past, her fringe of red hair and striped leggings had reminded me of a friendly woodpecker. But this morning? A vulture, a crow, a starling: She'd scared me to death.

After making reservations at two other restaurants, I hunkered down at my computer to pull my notes about Firefly together. I was deep into a digression about the merits of Southern comfort food in a world that seemed to embrace nonfat everything when my phone rang. Torrence's name flashed onto the screen.

We exchanged greetings, and I complimented him on his performance at the city commission meeting. "These days, it must not be easy for cops to sound competent without coming off as arrogant," I said. "But you managed it. And it didn't seem like you were going to strangle any of the crazy questioners, either. Even though the meeting dragged on forever. And what was with the nut case who attacked Lorenzo?"

He laughed. "Plenty of practice. Listen, I have a question about your friend. Would it be convenient if I swung by the office and we chatted for a couple of minutes?"

I let that sit for a second. Would it be convenient? Not at all. I had a new boss who was watching my every move. "How about I grab something for a late lunch and bring it down to the police station?" I wasn't hungry in the slightest, but if he was, I'd gladly sacrifice my waistline to keep him out of the office. "Anything you're craving?"

"You got me," he said.

"You're easy to get." I snickered. "What is it?"

"I drove by the Old Town Bakery this morning and they had a special sandwich on their chalkboard. Italian with ham, soppressata, basil pesto, fontina, spinach, and tomato. On one of their homemade French bread loaves. Doesn't that sound like heaven?"

"Absolutely. Dessert?" I asked.

"I'm on a diet," he said, his voice halting and mournful. "I have to tap everything I eat into this smartphone app that adds the calories up on the spot. I think I'm already over the limit for today."

"So the chocolate OMG brownie?"

He groaned.

5

Their tree is full this year, the fruit thud on the roof all night, but he doesn't like this varietal; they taste like old butter.
　　—Diana Abu-Jaber, *Birds of Paradise*

I drove up to the pink stucco Key West Police Department with yet one more fragrant bag of food, thinking that I'd visited this place over the past year and a half more often than a normal person should. How could it be, I wondered, that I knew so many people accused of murder? And how would I manage to squeeze information from Torrence without ratting out Lorenzo? Not that he'd really told me anything incriminating, but he sure was acting guilty.

The person manning the security camera and the station's locked front door must have recognized me: I was buzzed inside without even picking up the phone. I made my way down the left-hand hall to Torrence's office and tapped on his door.

"I'll be right there. Just chill a minute, okay?" he answered, his words muffled.

It was more like five minutes, but then the door banged open and instead of Lieutenant Torrence, I faced a bristling wall of testosterone: Detective Bransford. In white dress shirt with sleeves rolled up, a burr of whiskers on his face and tie askew, he looked like an escapee from *GQ*—ready to be photographed for an article on messy looks that ooze sex appeal. I tried to play chicken, seeing who would speak first, but I caved within fifteen seconds.

"Hello," I said in a reedy voice that barely sounded like me. "It's a beautiful day in the neighborhood."

He looked puzzled.

"You know, the song?" I warbled the line this time, still reedy, but now off-key, too.

But Bransford didn't crack a smile. Maybe his mother hadn't tried to relive her childhood by sitting him through dozens of reruns of *Mr. Rogers' Neighborhood*, the way mine had. Or maybe he'd sprung full formed from someone's forehead, like Athena had from Zeus. All head, no heart.

Last year, we'd dabbled with dating. But then his ex-wife materialized and persuaded him to try their marriage again. As my mother liked to say, why would I want a man who didn't want me? But every time I'd seen him since, the air between us had crackled with unexplored tension. Before I could stop myself, my gaze dropped to his left hand, empty except for a fine line of pale skin where his wedding ring had been. His eyes followed mine.

"I brought Torrence for lunch," I stammered nonsensically, feeling completely embarrassed. "I mean lunch for Torrence. You know how hungry that man gets. His blood sugar dips down and he turns into a grouch. It's a public service I'm doing—"

"Things didn't work out with my wife," Bransford said, tapping his ringless finger. "She hoped things would be different, but they weren't." He grunted out a mirthless laugh. "People don't change, you know? If all the evidence points to one truth, only a fool ignores that. You might want desperately for something to be a certain way because you're soft on someone. But that doesn't change how life is. Right?"

How could I possibly answer that? In truth, I sort of believed what he was saying, but that didn't mean I liked it. Eric wouldn't agree—he said people could change, if they wanted to work at it hard enough. But why was Bransford telling me this, anyway? I squeezed my hands into fists and kept my silence.

"I'm certain that Lieutenant Torrence will cover this in your discussion," he finally added, lips barely moving but mustache undulating. "We know that Lorenzo is a close acquaintance of yours."

I interrupted him, my voice flat and definite. "A friend."

"A friend of yours," Bransford corrected himself. "But if he gets in touch with you or if you hear anything that might explain his absence, it's absolutely urgent that you let us know."

"His absence?" I asked.

"He's not at his home, and he's not answering our calls."

I nodded, worried to hear this but not surprised. "I don't know a thing about that," I said, which in the technical, narrow context of his question was true.

He frowned. "People are often not what they seem. And they don't often change for the better. Keep that in mind when you get the overpowering urge to defend your *friend* Lorenzo."

I just stared at him.

"Evidence doesn't lie, Hayley. Understood?"

"I know you believe that. I'm not sure I do." I gave a snappy salute, slipped past him into Torrence's office, and shut the door behind me, leaving him out in the hall.

"Oh, we'll both pay for that," said Torrence, barely suppressing a grin.

I rubbed a hand over my eyes, feeling suddenly like I might cry. "What's up with that crabby bastard?" I asked, a little more fiercely than I felt.

Torrence sighed and waved me to the chair across from him. "There's a lot of pressure on this department right now, Hayley. You saw some of it at the meeting last night. People are not feeling all warm and fuzzy about police departments in general. And they're freaked out by the burglaries of the homes around the cemetery." He shook his head, frowning. "You can imagine the hysterical calls we're getting about this latest death. Which is why I need to talk to you about Lorenzo."

"He wouldn't kill someone," I said.

"Hayley—"

"It's not right for you guys to pin a murder on Lorenzo because the department feels pressured. Without a shred of evidence, as far as I can tell." I crossed my arms over my chest and glared straight at him.

Torrence looked at me, fingering the dimple on his chin. "I'll tell you what I can, if you can agree you'll stay out of it. And share anything that you know or that you hear bearing on the investigation. Deal?"

"Okay." I collapsed into the chair, dropping the lunch on his desk.

"The dead man, Bart Frontgate, was a juggler at the

Sunset Celebration. He was the only performer to use flaming barbecue forks with actual chunks of meat on them." He grimaced. "He even fed some of the spectators after the spectacle. Which would not comply with any public health guidelines, I assure you. You've seen his act, I'm certain. What did you think?"

"I never stayed through the whole thing." I paused for a minute, thinking about why. Because lord knows, I'd spent hours watching other performers, including the Cat Man, who worked his felines through their paces across high wires and through flaming hoops. And I loved Snorkel the Pig's show, too. Not that a Vietnamese potbellied pig has that many tricks up his proverbial sleeve, but the pig bowling act made me laugh every time. So why didn't I care for Frontgate?

"It bothered me how he bullied the crowd for money," I finally said. "I know they all have to make a living, but if you put on a good show or have something to offer, people fight to give tips when it's over. Frontgate made me feel as though I was personally going to cheat him if I didn't drop money in his bucket. I totally get performers giving the audience a little nudge at the end of the show, but harassing us all the way through? Not cool."

"I can see that," said Torrence. "But not everyone agreed. He was one of the biggest draws at Sunset."

"Maybe it wasn't only his personality that I disliked," I added. "Probably anyone juggling on a high wire would make me nervous. Never mind that the utensils he was lobbing around were on fire."

"Aha! That's how I feel when you get involved with police work," said Torrence. "Like you're on a high wire tossing flaming objects with not one nanosecond of training or experience." He reached into the paper bag and took out the sandwiches.

"I got the French dip, too," I said. "I already ate a big brunch but I thought I might get hungry by the time I got here. Not so much." I picked up half a sandwich, nibbled, then put it down again. Two meals within twenty-four hours where I'd lost my appetite—not like me. Not like me at all. At least I'd managed to choke down the brunch—I wasn't in danger of wasting away. "Back to Lorenzo . . ."

"Lorenzo and Frontgate squared off about the problems with the Mallory Square committee, from what we've heard," Torrence said. "People have mentioned a lot of angry exchanges. You know there's a Webcam on Mallory Square, right? We're reviewing the tapes for confirmation right now."

My heart plummeted. Lorenzo had told Eric and me he had no relationship with Frontgate. "Speaking of angry, what was the deal with Louis the palm-hat guy, who attacked Lorenzo? He looked like the sort of character who would kill someone. He tried it last night right in the official business meeting, with a hundred witnesses."

Torrence huffed a big sigh. "Probably Lorenzo didn't mean to kill Bart. Probably they had an altercation and Frontgate threatened him and maybe Lorenzo was trying to protect himself and he lost control." He wiped his lips on a napkin. "But you know the drill—things will go a lot easier if he turns himself in. Then we have a chance to sort out the facts."

"Sure." I flashed a compliant but fake smile. The longer we talked, the clearer it became that Lorenzo was in their sights. And that Louis was not. "But you wouldn't arrest a guy just because he didn't like the victim. Even if the victim is irritating as hell, most folks' default response would not be murder. A lot of people probably couldn't stand Frontgate. How did he die, anyway?"

Torrence groaned with exasperation. "The autopsy results aren't in yet, but he had puncture wounds in his chest and his neck, consistent with a fine boning knife. Or even the tines of a big fork."

I shuddered, trying to shut out a horrible mental picture of Bart's death. "And this relates to Lorenzo how?"

"You know that Lorenzo brings his table and lamp and all that tarot stuff to the Sunset Celebration? Then he sets up and decorates the table with a special cloth."

I nodded again, not liking the way this was going. Feeling the contents of my stomach grinding.

"We found one of Frontgate's forks wrapped up in the tablecloth that your friend uses to cover his table— the dark blue one with the stars and the moon on it," he added. "It's very distinctive."

"Where? Where did you find it? Did you have a search warrant?"

His eyes widened. "Police Procedure 101: We don't need a warrant to search for a murder weapon with probable cause."

"But where did you find it? Why did you look there?"

Torrence smiled, regret on his face. He wasn't going to tell me anything else.

"Anyone could've planted a fork in his tablecloth," I said, but a pit was opening up in my gut.

Torrence said, "People could have, but why would they?"

"The hat guy—he hates Lorenzo. You saw it. He probably tried to set him up."

"Why, Hayley? What sense does that make?"

"If he's trying to shift the blame to Lorenzo, it makes perfect sense. He figures the cops would be dumb enough to fall for something that obvious—"

My phone buzzed with the arrival of a text message. I took a quick glance. Lorenzo. *Can u take care of Lola a few days? Won't come in and I have 2 go. Food etc inside.*

I could feel the heat rushing from my neck and flooding across my cheeks—the redheads' dead-giveaway scourge.

"Something wrong?" Torrence asked, his eyes all wide again.

"Big-time boy troubles," I stammered as I sprang up, flipping a dismissive wave. "Got to run."

I left Torrence with the lion's share of the lunch, including the Oh My God brownie, with its central lake of rich chocolate pudding. It was his problem if he ate the whole thing and spoiled his diet. Out in the parking lot, I texted Lorenzo. *R U ok?*

I waited a couple of minutes but heard nothing back. Even though I'd sort of promised Torrence that I'd stay out of the case, how could I not support my friend? Lorenzo had absolutely come through for me every time something in my life looked bleak. He'd offered free readings when I needed them and advice on everything from murder to my love life. Which sometimes felt like the same thing.

So I took a left out of the back entrance of the KWPD parking lot and buzzed over to New Town. Lorenzo's cottage is a small concrete-block structure about fifty yards from a man-made canal that feeds eventually into the Gulf. This neighborhood had been hit hard by the double-whammy storm surge of flooding during

Hurricane Wilma. Since then, most all of the damage
had been repaired, though some folks who'd lived
through it retained the high-water markers on their
walls and foundations. Badges of courage, I supposed.

Lorenzo had built a Zen garden around his home,
with a wash of small white rocks taking the place of
grass. The rocks were punctuated by short, spiky pal-
mettos and tropical bushes and trees, including sea
grapes, shortleaf figs, and an autograph tree, the totally
cool plant I'd seen in the botanical garden with actual
autographs inscribed on its smooth green leaves. People scribbled on those leaves as if they were writing on
the wall of a public bathroom stall. I knocked on the
front door, but no one answered. So I walked around
the back of the house to look for signs of activity. In the
backyard, gorgeous avocado, mango, and banana trees
were bursting with life. But no lights were on, no win-
dows cracked, no air conditioner humming, no evidence of Lorenzo. He was really gone.

I tapped on the back door, then called his cell phone.
Nothing. A small white cat with brown patches around
her ears and a brown tail crept out of the bushes and
began to wind around my legs. She purred and uttered
breathy cries like a worried baby. I scooped her up, remembering my friend's recent joy about adopting a
kitten.

"Daddy will come home soon," I said, and rubbed
my nose in her fur.

"Marvin loved that cat," said a gravelly voice from
the next yard over, startling me half out of my mind. A
woman with bleached blond hair and black roots
leaned over the fence separating her front yard from
Lorenzo's—hers green and weedy in comparison to his

orderly pebbles. Why was she talking in the past tense, as if he was dead—or maybe gone for good?

"He left a while ago in a pink taxi," she continued. "With a little suitcase and a train case. Remember those? All the fancy ladies would carry their cosmetics and potions in a train case." She lifted her chin at the white cat. "He called for Miss Kitty but she wouldn't come. He sounded kind of desperate, but then the cab pulled up and he had to leave without her. I'd take her in but my pit bull would eat her for lunch."

Who was this woman? At first blush, she struck me as completely annoying, but if she was Lorenzo's friend . . . "Miss Kitty? That's not her name, though, is it?"

"He called her Lola, but that seems like a big name for that little bit. I think he liked the idea of singing her all the songs with Lola in them." She chortled and began to croon "Copacabana": "'Her name was Lola. . .'"

"Any idea where he went?" I asked. "Or when he'll be back?"

She shrugged. And held up two crossed fingers. "We're not that close." Her eyes narrowed to watchful slits. "But I can tell you that the cops swarmed all over this block last night. He's in some kind of hot water—that much is for sure."

If they weren't close, why was she calling him by his given name? Most people didn't know him as Marvin. And changing the name of *his* cat? This seemed like the kind of neighbor who might have snooped in his mailbox. Or even his trash. The kitty rubbed her jowls against my chin. "Tell him if you see him that Hayley took the cat to her houseboat? Thanks. I'm just going to go in and collect a few supplies."

Wishing I hadn't felt as though I had to explain myself to her, I marched over to the back door and went inside. I closed and locked the door behind me and pulled the shade on the window so the nosy neighbor couldn't spy on me.

Then I scanned the kitchen for signs of cat supplies. If Lola had to move in with strange cats and humans, at least she should be able to eat something familiar. I sorted through the cabinets, looking for her food, and finally opened the door leading into a very neat pantry. Dozens of cans of Fancy Feast were arranged on a shelf to the right. I loaded half a dozen of these and a sack of dry food into a cloth grocery bag, then reached for a couple more cans. Who knew how long he'd be gone? I searched around for a cat carrier, but no luck. But the kitty was sticking close to me, so I didn't think the transport would be a problem.

I texted Miss Gloria. *Furry company coming. Warn Evinrude and Sparky, they should trot out their best manners.* After hoisting the bag of food over my shoulder, I wrapped the quivering kitty in my jacket and tucked her under the other arm. Then I went back outside, clamping down on the thoughts that were whirling in my mind so I could concentrate on getting my cargo home safely.

6

*In the stress-reduction class I learned to go
to the cake inside my mind, but these were
darker days. To escape the level of stress in
my house, I had to go inside a much more
literal cake. I had to surround myself with
cake, build a foxhole out of cake in which I
could hide.*

—Jeanne Ray, *Eat Cake*

While Miss Gloria fussed over the white kitten and kept
our cats from rushing her, I filled her in on the police
findings and Lorenzo's subsequent disappearance.

"His neighbor said he called for the kitten before he
left. And that he looked desperate and took some luggage."

I pulled out my phone and texted Lorenzo again. *I
have Lola. Where r u?*

"The cops found a bloody knife in his stuff?" she
asked.

"Not a knife, a fork," I said, realizing after I'd said it
that "fork" sounded almost worse. Who stabbed some-

one to death with a fork? Someone vicious and angry and possibly crazy—that's who. Torrence hadn't said anything about blood, but it surely had been there.

Then my mother phoned, and I explained the situation to her.

"You can't just let him rot in jail," she said once I'd finished outlining the high—or low, really—points of the conversation.

"Put her on speakerphone," said Miss Gloria. "Hi, Janet!" she called, and my mother greeted her back.

"Lorenzo isn't in jail," I said, working to tamp down the impatience that had crept into my voice. She had to be stir-crazy, shut in by a frigid New Jersey winter, nursing Sam. She wouldn't be able to listen carefully under those circumstances. "I don't know where he is."

"But you know what I mean," my mother said. "Somebody has to be in his corner."

The irritation spiked again and I took a big breath. "We are all in his corner. But I promised Torrence that I'd stay out of trouble. And I know you would agree," I added pointedly. "I felt okay about dropping by Lorenzo's house, and I'm glad I've got the kitty, but that's as far as I'm willing to take it."

Lola the kitten danced around Sparky, and he batted at her and hissed. Evinrude Halloweened up and backed away, taking refuge under the kitchen table. He crouched low, growling like a dog and watching.

"We could just take a swing around the Sunset this evening," said Miss Gloria. "Check out the vibe."

"Check out the vibe?" I asked. I could feel my eyeballs bulging.

"Not a bad idea," said Mom. "You could mostly listen—see what the word on the street is about last night's meeting. And then if you recognize someone who knew Lorenzo, you could chat with them. No trouble there, right?"

"I'm not sure Torrence would see it that way," I said. Since when did my mother encourage me to look for trouble? But the idea was growing on me.

"Any other problems I can help with?" Mom asked.

"This next one isn't really a problem," I said. "More of an opportunity. And that is, Palamina made a reservation for four on the floating restaurant for tomorrow night. I have to fill out the table."

"I wish I could be there," Mom said, her voice full of yearning. "We're expecting another snowstorm tonight and Sam can't go anywhere anyway."

"I've got a special mah jong game," said Miss Gloria, "or I'd be glad to go with you." She winked at me. "I'm the designated driver."

I groaned and thunked my forehead with my palm.

"Do you suppose Palamina wanted you to invite her?" Mom asked.

I thought back to the meeting. Had there been any hint that she was fishing for an invite? I honestly didn't know her well enough to say.

"And what about Wally? Add Danielle and you can make it all *Key Zest* all the time."

"That's an idea," I said. "But by the time Wally gets down here, I'd like to spend some time alone with him."

"Hot dog!" said Miss Gloria, and we all laughed.

"Speaking of romance, how is Sam doing?" I asked.

Mom was silent for a minute—not her usual state. "The doc wants him to walk as much as he can. But the sidewalks and the backyard are sheets of ice. So the poor man circles around and around the kitchen island and then out to the living room and back. With his

walker. In his boxer shorts, because it hurts to dress."
More silence. "Oh lord, how I miss Key West."

Around four o'clock, as we prepared to head down to
Mallory Square to check out the "vibe," we separated
our resident cats from the white guest cat and put the
kitten in my bedroom just to be sure there wouldn't be
any incidents while we were gone. As we left, one tiny
white paw reached through the crack under my door.
Laughing about how cute she was, Miss Gloria and I
piled onto my scooter and headed down the island. I
had managed to persuade her that there wouldn't be
parking for an oversized Buick and thus to sidestep the
issue of riding shotgun with her again.

"I'd like to walk a few blocks on Duval Street and
see if the man who weaves those palm hats is around.
If we wait till later, I'm afraid he'll be fried."

"Drunk again," warbled Ms. Gloria.

"He's an explosive personality," I warned her, "and
he could be very dangerous. So please let me do the
talking."

On Southard Street, I parked in a small space that
had been set aside for bicycles and scooters, and we
started to walk west. The sidewalks were already busy
with tourists wearing flip-flops, sundresses, and T-
shirts, most of the visitors shiny and red from too much
time in the sun. Under the overhang of Willie T's bar,
its ceiling papered with messages written on dollar
bills, a rock band played. The crowd spilled out onto
the street, drinking beer and dancing. We stopped for a
minute to listen and watch the fun.

"Mr. P and I used to come to Duval Street once a
week back in the day," said Miss Gloria, the expression

on her face all nostalgic and sad. "We figured if we didn't act old, we wouldn't get old."

"It worked pretty well for you." I squeezed her hand. "Let's get going, okay?"

The palm-hat weaver was sitting in a low beach chair on the sidewalk, not far from Starbucks the next block over. He had a pile of palm fronds next to him and several completed hats and bowls on display. Behind him was a rusty metal grocery cart full of more supplies and products. He was shouting at a stream of passersby, explaining about his merchandise and his reasonable prices as his fingers worked the palm fronds. When there was a break in the action, I moved closer.

"Hi," I said in a perky voice. "I'm Hayley and this is Miss Gloria."

"We would love one of those hats," said Miss Gloria, "for this young lady's father."

I glared at her—I hadn't intended to buy anything. And my father would not—no way—be caught dead in this ugly green hat.

"Freaking awesome," he said, pushing the hat into Miss Gloria's hands. "I'm Louis. These hats here are woven from only the finest coconut palm trees. I harvest them gently and legally and they cure in approximately three weeks and provide excellent protection from the sun."

"How much?" I asked, pointing first to the green pith helmet and then to a smaller basket, hoping one of them wouldn't break the bank. And feeling a bit like a cop who had to pay his snitch.

"Thirty-five for the hat and twenty-five for the basket. Fifty for the both."

"We'll take one of each," piped up Miss Gloria. "And

while you're wrapping those, we would like to extend our condolences on the loss of Bart Frontgate."

He looked up, surprised, and grunted his thanks. "Though truth is, we weren't more than working acquaintances." He scratched his stomach through a gap between his shirt buttons and then placed the hat and the bowl into a rumpled plastic bag with a CVS logo on it. "Still, he was one of us. And he put a hell of a lot into making things run smooth."

"What's happening with the group managing the Sunset Celebration now?" I asked. "We thought we might have seen you at the commission meeting last night."

He twirled a finger around next to his ear. "Loco," he said. "That crap has all gone further than it should. I tried to take a leadership role, but apparently I wasn't leader material. Or so thought our precious fortune-teller."

He guffawed, releasing a gust of alcohol-laced air. "Apparently he didn't see me in his cards. But that isn't working out so well for him now, is it?" He leered and thrust the sack of hideous woven items at Miss G.

I handed over the last of my cash. Then I took Miss Gloria by the elbow and steered her down the street toward the Westin pier. She perched the green palm hat on her head, though it was large enough that it fell over her forehead and just caught on her ears. She could hardly see from under it.

"So what did we get from that conversation?" asked Miss Gloria. "Besides this attractive hat." She giggled and shifted it to a rakish angle. "Your father's going to go bananas for this."

"And let's don't forget the lovely bowl that set me back another twenty-five bucks. I can't think of a thing

I would serve in it." I put the bowl on my head and we both snickered.

"What I learned," said Miss Gloria, returning our woven purchases to the plastic bag, "was there was no love lost between him and Lorenzo. Everyone knows that Lorenzo drags his stuff to Sunset in that cart hooked up to his bike. So if our weaver had a reason to get rid of Mr. Frontgate but wanted to shift the blame on someone else, it wouldn't have been much of a stretch for him to see Lorenzo's cart, grab the tablecloth, and wrap the murder weapon in it. And then dump it where he could be sure someone would find it."

I stopped on the crosswalk in front of the redbrick Custom House Museum and squinted down at her. "I haven't heard that they're looking for new detectives at the KWPD, but I'll keep my ears open. You'd be a shoo-in." I took her elbow again. "Although planting a bloody implement seems so obvious and cruel. And risky, too. He'd have to have a big grudge against Lorenzo, right?"

"Lorenzo," she said, "is like that perfect nerd from high school. The one who made all A's and also ran the yearbook or the school newspaper. Maybe ran for treasurer of student council too. Someone who didn't have his you-know-what together could easily resent him."

"Point taken," I said. "Though if the man was killed down by Tarpon Pier—and that's a big if—where was Lorenzo's cart? Wouldn't it have been at his house that time of night? Where would the murderer find the cart? There are just too many questions we don't have answers to."

Around us, the crowd thickened as the time approached for people to abandon their Duval Street barstools and stumble, stagger, and weave toward the entertainers on Mallory Square. We fell in with the tide.

The first performer we passed was Dominique, dubbed the Cat Man of Key West, who had probably been performing his act longer than most of the other entertainers. And he was also arguably the most popular. A slender man in capri pants, cat kneesocks, and a white Farrah Fawcett hairdo, Dominique charmed the customers who flocked to Mallory Square with a faux French accent and a stable of trained house cats.

Eight cages of cats had already been unloaded with their backs facing the water and the sunset. He was setting up several padded stools and ladders and a tightrope that his cats would scramble across during the show. A cluster of tourists was pawing through the boxes of Cat Man merchandise for sale—T-shirts, socks, and postcards.

"We'd better chat with him later," I said to Miss Gloria. "He's got his paws full."

Both of us grinning, we continued along the water and crossed the small bridge in front of the aquarium that led to Mallory Square proper. Vendors selling jewelry, artwork, and other Florida-related paraphernalia were laying out their wares on card tables. A trolley car set up as a bar was doing a brisk business in beer and mojitos. Now the humid sea air was thick with the scent of hot grease wafting from stations offering fried conch fritters, hot dogs, and popcorn. I could almost feel the oil settling on my skin.

Further along on the pavement, performing grids had been marked off on the cement with heavy black ropes. The best location in the entire square—front and center, looking across the water to Sunset Key—was empty, except for piles of flowers and cards and stuffed animals. The place where Bart Frontgate would have been juggling his barbecue implements had been turned into an impromptu shrine. We moved a few steps closer to study the memorial.

We love you, Bart! one note read, written in red crayon and tied around the neck of a blue rabbit.

Another letter, nestled among some droopy green carnations, featured a stick-figure drawing of a man on a high wire holding several enormous forks, with a gold halo hovering over his head. *Juggling in Heaven*, the caption read.

This I very much doubted.

I spotted three men chatting underneath a palm tree twenty yards away; one of them I recognized as my homeless friend, Tony. I hadn't seen him around in several weeks and I had begun to wonder whether he'd moved on from Key West. Maybe found a less expensive town where the cops didn't know him well enough to hassle him. Sometimes he was happy to see me, other times not so much. But it seemed worth a try to see what he knew.

"Good evening, everyone," I said in a cheerful voice. I prodded Miss Gloria ahead of me toward Tony. "I'm not sure if you ever met my roommate, Miss Gloria."

She thrust her tiny hand out to him and he shifted his beer bottle from his right hand to his left. He grasped her fingers and then removed his battered cowboy hat and bowed.

"It's a pleasure to meet you, young lady," he said. He gestured to the other two men, who had grizzled faces and looked to be in their early twenties. They were dressed in shabby pirate costumes. "Couple of my pals here," he added. "There's no need to learn their names, because their act sucks, so I doubt they'll be around much longer."

He cackled with laughter. The other men grunted and barely smiled.

"Are you performing tonight?" asked Miss Gloria of the closer pirate.

"That's the plan," he said. "Although the spot we were assigned stinks to high hell. The only traffic we'll get is tourists looking for the damn restroom. I was just asking Tony here whether we might use Mr. Frontgate's square since he sure ain't gonna be performing."

Leave it to Tony to act like he was in charge of the performers' grid, when I doubted he had anything to do with it. But on the other hand, with all the time he spent observing from the sidelines, he knew plenty about what happened on this island. And even if he had a low database of factual information on a topic, he never lacked confidence in his own opinions.

I squeezed Miss Gloria's arm just above the elbow, hoping she'd get the message to allow the man to talk. In my experience, pressing Tony for information didn't work nearly as well as cutting the lead loose and letting him run.

Tony set his beer on the curb and lit up a cigarette. "And as I was explaining to you before these lovely ladies stopped by, spaces are assigned according to how long you've been around. Mr. Frontgate, for example, had been here since the Dark Ages. You, on the other hand, washed in with the latest tide. And your act stinks like that, too."

The pirate puffed out his chest. "But at least we have something unusual to offer. At least we've tried to work on our performance." He scrunched up his face in an expression of disgust and disbelief. "You want to tell me that replacing knives with barbecue forks was considered a juggling innovation?"

"It's all about the schtick, man," said Tony. "It's all about how you sell your story. And Frontgate had a smooth patter." He lifted his cowboy hat and swept his fingers through his oily curls. "And who you know—that matters in this backwater. Don't you imagine that it doesn't."

He sucked in a big drag of smoke, which made the skin around his lips pucker into a sea of wrinkles. Then he blew it out and said, "There was a new guy showed up here last year from California. I don't remember where, exactly—Santa Barbara, maybe? He thought he was the cat's pajamas."

He sucked on the cigarette again and I watched the ash burn red hot, almost singeing his knuckles. "The thing is, this dude went around and watched everybody. He was clever that way. And then he took what was best about each of those acts and copied it right into his own stupid routine." He waggled his finger at the pirates. "People didn't take kindly to that. Not only did he get the lousy space; he got the crap beat out of him one night." Tony shook his head slowly and sadly. "The cops never did figure out what happened to him. Mr. Frontgate wondered if maybe he'd had a few pops too many and then experienced an altercation with his own bicycle." He gurgled with laughter, dropped the butt, and ground it into the cement with his heel.

"There's something you have to know about this place," he added. "And if you don't learn it, you aren't going to last. It looks like every man for himself. But it's an island, man, and there's an underlying fabric, a connection that an outsider can't see until he's been here awhile. But you start messing with that—you start trying to jump ahead of people or steal their thunder—that fabric could end up smothering you or choking you if you're not careful." He leered at the two new-comers. "That's your words of wisdom from Cap'n Tony. Got it, yahoos?"

The larger pirate kicked over Tony's beer and stomped off in the direction of the Waterfront Playhouse.

7

It is hunger that makes you crazy, whether it's one appetite or another.
—Norman Van Aken, *No Experience Necessary*

We left Tony fuming and sputtering and made our way through the crowd toward the open area where Lorenzo usually set up his card table. We walked past tables and booths hawking paintings, Key West photographs, jewelry, and T-shirts of every color, design, and size. Lorenzo, of course, was not there. I realized from my disappointed reaction that I'd been hoping he had returned to Mallory Square as if nothing was wrong. As if the cops had realized they were looking at the wrong man and that someone had let him know he could resurface into life as usual.

A woman with pitch-black hair, circles of sparkly rouge on her cheeks, and deep blue eye shadow that almost reached her brows was sitting at a booth in his place. The sign hanging from her table indicated that she was a palm reader, though at the moment, she had no customers. I edged a little closer.

"Oh my goodness," I said in an innocent voice. "I was looking for that tarot card guy. Last time I talked with him he was so helpful. I was hoping he could tell me what's wrong with my boyfriend. Isn't this where he usually sits?"

The woman's eyes narrowed, and the glitter on her cheeks and in her hair glinted in the light from the streetlamp directly above her. "I don't know what's happened to him," she said. "But I was told I could have his place."

"Who told you that?" I asked. "Isn't there a committee that decides where people perform?"

She fidgeted in her folding chair and looked away from me, then finally waved a dismissive hand. "When you commit a serious infraction, you lose your privileges." She lowered her voice to a whisper. "We heard he might have had something to do with that murder." She pressed both hands to her cheeks and blinked.

Did she know something about what had really happened, or was she spreading vicious rumors? "Oh no, you mean he actually killed someone?" I asked, taking another step closer to her table.

"So I hear. Everyone's talking about the fights he had with the dead guy." She tapped her fingers to her forehead and looked up at the sky. "God rest his soul." She smiled as she turned those blue-rimmed eyes to me. "But I would love to do a reading for you. I use the human palm rather than cards because the hand taps into the heart in a way that a deck of cards could never do. I'm very good with relationship problems." She grabbed my hand with one of hers and stroked it with the other.

Goose bumps spread from my wrist all the way to my neck.

"Already," she said, her eyes fluttering shut, "I feel some unrest. Perhaps there is a troubled engagement? Come sit with me and let's puzzle this out together."

"Lordy, lordy," muttered Miss Gloria under her breath. "We'd better get out of here before she eats us alive."

I extracted my fingers from the palm reader's and assured her I'd return another time. Miss Gloria doused my hands with a little spray bottle of hand sanitizer and I rubbed them together. Then we headed for the alley in between the Cuban restaurant and the Waterfront Playhouse, which would funnel us out of the square, pausing for a minute to admire the antics of Snorkel the Pig.

"Not for nothing," said Miss Gloria, "but if you have an adorable animal in your act, you really need have no talent at all." She laughed and then turned to look at me straight on. "Is it possible that Lorenzo really did kill a man? I admire your loyalty and all, and I love him, too, but if everyone says the same thing . . ."

"All that tells us is the place is thick with mean gossip." I pinched my lips together until they quivered.

She patted my arm. "You're right. Do you mind waiting a minute while I use the restroom?"

"Of course not," I said. I wouldn't be caught dead in the public bathroom, but at eighty, if she had to go, she had to go. I moved to the side of the alley and leaned against the wall to wait. Across from me, a dark-skinned man piped out new age music from what looked like a homemade reed instrument into a microphone. How many CDs could he possibly sell in a night? Enough, I supposed, since he'd been here every time I'd walked by. To my left, two more homeless men were watching a couple of stray cats squabble with loose chickens over kibbles.

"Did the damn cops hassle you again this morning?" asked one man of the other.

"They were all over me like fleas on dog-park dogs," the second man grumbled. "Get used to it—they won't back off until that GD murder is solved."

"I thought it was that fortune-teller. That's what Louis told me."

"Louis told you? You might as well read the local rag as listen to that fool. He makes crap up just to hear himself talk. Wouldn't surprise me one bit to hear he was the one stabbed poor Frontgate."

Out of the corner of my eye, I saw him joust and feint with an imaginary sword. Fork, I supposed, was more accurate.

"Why would he do that?"

"Just for the pure mean fun of it," said the second.

Miss Gloria emerged from the bathroom, wiping her hands dry on her slacks. "Ready to roll."

By the time we'd tromped the blocks back to my scooter on Southard Street, we were exhausted (Miss Gloria) and starving (me). We stopped at the Kojin Noodle Bar takeout window and ordered a Saigon salad and a big bowl of sesame noodles with shrimp.

With the food strapped to my basket, we zipped back to the houseboat. Miss Gloria fed the cats while I dished out our dinner. Then we sat out on the deck, watching the twilight fade into night, watching the pinks go to gray. When we'd inhaled every bite of the crispy vegetables with tofu and the spicy noodles, Miss Gloria retreated to the living room to catch her nightly dose of *Jeopardy!* and I stayed outside, thinking.

First, I reviewed what Tony had told the new pirate performers about the guy who'd been beaten up for stealing from other people's acts. I'd seen this undercurrent many times before on this island: Competition was fierce among restaurants, among shops, among bars, among artists, among writers. Each vendor scrambled to get attention from the tourists and thereby make a living selling whatever they had to offer. The murdered man, Bart, had been in Key West a lifetime in street-performer terms. What if he had insisted on his grandfathered right to the best spot on Mallory Square? What if he'd jumped what other performers might have considered a firm line? Would this be enough to get him killed? Clearly, as I had learned from the conflict I witnessed in the city commission meeting, performance at Sunset was a serious business.

I got out my computer, fired it up, and noticed I'd missed a Skype call from my mother. I dialed her number.

Her face appeared on my screen, looking haggard and tired. "Oh good, it's you," she said. "We are so sick of staring at each other—we were hoping you would call." She adjusted the position of her iPad so that Sam came into view. He, too, looked pale, his face drawn as though he'd suffered, which he probably had—in more ways than one.

"Tell us what you've been up to—we're sure it's more interesting than what we have to tell you," Mom said.

"Miss Gloria and I took a spin around Mallory Square right before Sunset, remember?" We'd talked about this only a couple of hours earlier—could be the strain of caregiving was turning her brains to mush.

"Oh, I love Sunset," Mom broke in with a mournful wail.

Sam patted her knee and forced a smile. "You'll be back soon, I promise. I could always hire a visiting nurse."

"Don't be ridiculous," my mother snapped. "All they'd do is take your vital signs. They won't actually take care of you. Besides, I want to be here, with you, until you're all squared away. Or at least until there's only one of us left standing." She kissed him on the ear.

"Back to Sunset," I said, gritting my teeth. It was still a little challenging to watch my mother's newish relationship unfold on the screen in front of me. "Of course, Lorenzo wasn't there. We chatted with Tony, who was giving advice to some new performers who didn't seem so thrilled to receive it." I shrugged and described the conversation, hoping to divert them from their problems. "Maybe you two can help me. I've been thinking a lot about competition among the players at Sunset. I mean, how do you even make a living?"

"They're not paid to perform there, right?" Sam asked. "It's all based on tips?"

"I think that's right," I said. "So position is everything. And the quality of your act, too. I wonder if there's ever been a case of copyright infringement between jugglers?" I laughed. "Sam, I'm certain this is not exactly your area of the law, but maybe—"

"He'd love to delve into something like that," Mom said. "What can I do?"

"How about some research on Bart Frontgate?" I suggested. "Who was he before he became a juggler and where did he come from?"

"Done!" said my mother, looking more cheerful already. "What are you doing for Valentine's Day?"

I stiffened. "Nothing. When is it?"

"This weekend," Mom said. "Tomorrow. If you don't have a reservation by now, you probably won't get one. But wait, aren't you going to that new place?"

I groaned. "I don't have a date."

The words "I'll loan you mine" slipped out of Sam's mouth so quickly it stunned us all. Then we started to laugh.

Lorenzo's little white cat crept out from the shadows and I patted my lap, inviting her up. After several reassuring clucks, she made the leap. And launched her rough little kitten purr almost as soon as she'd landed.

"This is Lola," I told Mom and Sam, holding my computer so the cat appeared on the screen. "Lorenzo's new kitten. I'm worried sick about him. Lorenzo, not the cat. He doesn't have a murderous bone in his body, so why would he run?"

"He's panicked about something," Mom said. "We'll figure it out."

Once we'd hung up, I e-mailed Wally. Texting was too blunt of an instrument to do this delicate job.

How's it looking for the weekend? Could you possibly get here tomorrow for floating restaurant? Palamina made a reservation for four. I was thinking of asking Connie and Ray. Then back here for dessert?

I pressed *send* and then began to surf the Internet, looking for information about Lorenzo. It was a serious disadvantage not remembering his real last name. I finally found an old article in *National Geographic* about the charm of the Key West Sunset Celebration. One of the photos illustrating the piece showed Lorenzo at his table. This was back in his turban-and-makeup days, which he'd had to abandon several years ago because of the way the crowds reacted. He felt like a sideshow, he'd told me once—people interrupting the readings he was giving to ask him to pose for photos. No privacy for his customers at all.

Generally, the article was a puff piece about the Sunset as Key West icon, and did not contribute much to solving my mystery. Although it reminded me that Lorenzo's real name was Marvin Smith. There were probably hundreds of men by that name in this country. Then, even though I'd assigned the job to my mother, I Googled Bart Frontgate. He'd made several appearances in the crime column in the *Key West Citizen*—two drunk and disorderly arrests and a petty theft. I imagined that might be fairly typical fare for a street performer, living on the margins of the island's society.

I tried to focus on figuring out a pattern in this history, but the question of whether Wally would come for the weekend kept surfacing in my brain. And if he did, what cake should I serve for dessert? I gave up thinking and called Connie. She'd been my roommate in college and she'd taken me in on her houseboat soon after I'd arrived in Key West and had been summarily dumped by Chad Lutz. She and Ray would be the perfect dinner partners. They knew Wally and liked him. And, it being almost a year since their wedding, their newlywed status had worn off enough that Wally and I wouldn't feel pressured about being out to dinner on Valentine's Day. I spilled all that out in an anxious rush of words when Connie answered the phone.

"Oh, sweetie," she said, "I thought you and Wally were doing so well."

"We were for a while, but he's been distant the last few weeks. I think he's mostly worried about his mother, but I'm afraid to ask. What if it means he's cooled off about me?"

"Better to know that early, I suppose," she said. "I'd love to come but I'm feeling so sick to my stomach."

"But the dinner's twenty-four hours away. I bet you'll be feeling much better," I said. "Please, I need you."

"I can tell this is not the kind of flu that passes by in a day. I'm sorry," she said. "Ray would be thrilled, though. He was disappointed that we had to cancel our reservation at Deuce's." She hollered for him and he came on the line and agreed that he'd meet us tomorrow night at the boat at six thirty.

I went inside to appeal to Miss Gloria. "I only have three now for tomorrow's dinner," I told her. "A trio will be awkward no matter how hard we try to pretend it isn't." I flashed my most piteous and beseeching look.

"No can do," she said, borrowing my turn of phrase. "I've been looking forward to this mah jong party for months."

I sighed and nodded. I couldn't think of another friend who'd accept a last-minute invite on Valentine's Day. Only one avenue remained open: Palamina.

I punched her contact on my phone list. "It's last-minute," I said when she answered. "I didn't mean . . . I don't want to imply that you don't have your own date for Valentine's Day. But if you don't, one of my friends got sick. Would you like to join us at dinner on the floating restaurant?"

"Yes!" She answered without hesitation, sounding genuinely thrilled. "I look forward to seeing you in action."

After we hung up, I started to worry about her watching me while I ordered and took notes on the food. I scolded myself for worrying: I was a pro. I knew how to eat and write a review.

Then my thoughts seesawed back to the cake and which recipe would rise to the occasion of the after-party. Though some people might find this a sacrilege, Wally was not a fan of chocolate. And I tried to cook with whatever's in season in South Florida. Raspberries were not on that list in February, but I'd seen a couple of boxes at Fausto's market this morning. They were organic and outrageously priced, but plump and soft red. I could imagine them folded into a cream cheese icing with powdered sugar, turning a luscious pink color as they released their juices into the creamy frosting. I could make the cake tonight and finish up with the frosting tomorrow.

But would this cake transmit the message that I cared a lot, but without any pressure, and that it was for Valentine's Day, but no declaration intended, nor anything expected in return? Would it send the message of love and care, without appearing needy, too sweet, or clichéd?

This, I realized, was a lot to ask of any cake.

8

A hulking braised lamb shank in midwinter was more blunt than focused, while a lukewarm pork chop that was probably never going to get off the ground didn't get much aerodynamic lift from the mushy, oily mass of pine nuts and raisins on top.
        —Pete Wells, "Stepping Into the
        Role of the Ringmaster,"
        The New York Times

The next night, Wally swung by our houseboat half an hour before the reservation. His hair was still damp from the shower, his cheeks a little gaunt, his eyes tired. Without thinking, I flung my arms around him and squeezed. Then Miss Gloria burst out of her cabin, dressed in a red sweat suit with hearts sprinkled across the chest, and demanded her due.

"You look fabulous," Wally told her when she finally released him, touching the white curls she had worn tightly wound in rollers all day. And then the headband with hearts on coiled wires that bobbed endearingly when she moved. "Who's the lucky guy?"

"Oh, you!" She slapped his arm. "It's just the mah jong ladies. Our Valentine's Day tournament: Busy minds and hands don't get lonely, you know. But Hayley sure has something for you." She smacked her lips and tipped her bobbling hearts toward the kitchen, where the glorious pink cake studded with raspberries waited in the fridge.

He looked distraught. "Oh my god. It never even crossed my mind to get you anything."

"It's a cake—that's all," I said, smiling to cover my disappointment. Even though I told anyone who would listen that Valentine's Day is a trumped-up Hallmark holiday designed to put pressure on single people and struggling couples, some buried piece of me still yearned to be part of the lunacy. "We'll have some after dinner. From what I've seen on their online menu, the desserts at this restaurant tend toward bean-paste confections."

"Ugh!" said Miss Gloria. She pinched her nose and then reached over to squeeze Wally's wrist. "Thank goodness this girl is thinking ahead."

Wally grinned. "Can we give you a lift?" he asked her.

"Oh no," she said. "I'm picking up two of the ladies. I'm the only one in our crowd who's still allowed on the road at night."

"God help us all," I said, pressing my palms together like a prayer.

Ray arrived just then, cutting off my rant that driving at night should be reserved for younger rods and cones, which wouldn't have made a dent in her denial anyway. Simple truth: Nagging seldom changes anyone's opinions. We all started up the dock to the parking lot, where Wally had left his beater Jeep.

"You be extra-careful!" I hollered to Miss Gloria, and slid into the backseat, which had barely enough room for a small person, certainly not for Ray.

"What kind of food are we eating tonight?" Ray asked as we pulled out onto Palm Avenue. "I didn't even think to wonder. I guess that goes to show that I have a very open palate."

"Or no palate at all," Wally added with a laugh. "Hayley says your wife has the stomach flu?"

Ray glanced at him and then back at me, a curious smile on his face. "I thought you might have figured this out already. It looks like she's pregnant. Morning sickness, except for her it seems to be morning, noon, and night. Not a lot of fun."

"Oh my god, Connie's pregnant?" I squealed and threw my arms around his neck from the backseat. "I can't believe she didn't tell me."

"She wanted to tell you in person, not over the phone. And now she'll have my head because I blurted it out before she could. Honestly, we're scared to death."

"Total idiots manage to raise kids okay," Wally started.

"Thanks, man," said Ray, punching him in the shoulder.

"I didn't mean it like that." Wally laughed. "I think you'll be super parents."

"You will," I said. "You'll be the best dad. And Connie will be an amazing mother. What fun!" I pulled out my phone to text Connie a message so full of exclamation points she might have found it hard to read. Wally pulled into the parking garage on Caroline Street and we started to walk toward the bight.

Half a block ahead, I spotted Palamina waiting for us, dressed in a stylish black maxi-dress covered with gold shooting stars that made her look even thinner than she actually was. I waved at her and picked up my pace. "So glad you could make it," I said when I reached her, not sure whether to hug her or shake her hand. I did neither, my arms swinging awkwardly by my sides. Palamina kissed Wally's cheek and shook Ray's hand, congratulating him after I blurted out the unnecessary details of his status as father-to-be.

"Shall we head in?" Wally asked.

We strolled up the dock, past the Hindu sailing vessel and a luxury yacht. A wide-plank walkway led us from the dock to the floating restaurant, which bobbed as we stepped aboard. I paused for a minute to admire the reverse view of the harbor—the lights twinkling from Schooner Wharf and Edel's Bistro and all the other restaurants lining the dock. And behind them, the lights of the brand-new exquisite and pricey Marker resort. Locals had some concerns about how this place would fit in with the scruffy, down-home establishments along the harbor. All that remained to be seen.

A man dressed in a white shirt and black pants emerged from the cabin onto the deck. "Can I help you?"

"Reservation for four in the name of Wells," said three of us at once.

Ray—the only one who hadn't answered—raised his eyebrows and grinned, as we trooped behind him. "Lots of chiefs in this crowd."

Inside the cabin, we paused to adjust to the dim lighting, and the host seated us at a low table surrounded by cushions arranged on the polished wood floor. I pulled out my phone and jotted a note: *Some tables inaccessible to diners with disabilities—ask to be seated at regular tables in bow.* A waiter wearing a short black kimono over black pants presented the menus, followed by fruity drinks topped with little pink paper umbrellas.

"Our liquor license is in process," he said. "So the cocktails are on the house, along with a complimentary glass of sake or beer with dinner. I'll leave you with the menus, but please note that our special appetizer tonight is a traditional cold bento box, with two kinds of tofu including the Kyoto yudofu, the tuna and salmon roe sushi, and our edamame and daikon radish salad. We also have a few servings of puffer fish sashimi. If you decide you're interested, we will tell you the price. Oh, and Chef is also serving one special entrée tonight: flambéed grouper served in a nest of locally sourced seaweed." He bowed and backed away.

"The puffer fish?" Ray asked. "Isn't that the one that's poisonous if the chef isn't perfectly skilled?"

"Don't worry." I snickered. "They aren't going to want to poison someone during their first week open." I made some suggestions about what we should order, explaining to Palamina that I try to cover all the bases in my reviews, from the sure-bet crowd-pleasers to offbeat dishes that might demonstrate a chef's imagination and potential.

We all studied the menu, and from the long pause in the conversation, I suspected that they were having as much difficulty sorting through the options as I was.

"I can't figure out what kind of food this is. The appetizers definitely sounded Japanese, but the entrées are sort of trying to be everything for everyone," said Ray. "I'll taste whatever you order. Since you're the expert. You know I am not a fan of tofu." He grinned. "But if you say it's good, I'll eat it."

"Man, what a sport," said Wally. "If you're going to eat tofu, I guess I will man up and eat it, too."

"You guys rock." I turned to face Palamina, who still had her head buried in the large menu. "Anything in particular you want to be sure to try?"

She grimaced. "So many choices. If it was me writing, that's where I'd start the review," she said. "What does it say about a restaurant when the menu is two feet long?" She handed her copy to me. "I went on a business trip to Tokyo and Kyoto about five years ago. I remember loving the shabu-shabu. And of course any kind of sashimi or sushi works for me. Except for that puffer thing."

The waiter approached the table again and I smiled up at him. "If you don't mind, I'll order for my friends."

He folded into a formal bow that didn't quite mesh with his sun-bleached hair and tan face. "So you are the Japanese expert."

"Not exactly," I said, "but apparently I'm in charge for tonight. We would like to try your specialty, the cold bento box. And then we'll have several small plates, the chicken yakitori, the vegetable tempura, the beginners' introduction to sashimi and sushi, the buckwheat soba noodles with bonito flakes and mountain vegetables. And the shabu-shabu sampler. Anything I left out that might be a specialty of the chef?"

"Grouper fish flambé, of course," he said. "The owners caught the grouper themselves last night. And we went out with Chef early this morning and gathered the seaweed from Smathers Beach."

I had to bite my lip to keep from snickering: hard to

picture the restaurant staff moving among the early spring break revelers, scooping up seaweed.

"Okay, we'll try that, too."

"That's a lot of food," Palamina said. "Are you sure?"

I nodded and continued to focus on the waiter. "And for our landlubbers, how about a hamburger all the way with truffled fries and the Maryland chicken. And the vegetarian pad thai and an order of Vietnamese spring rolls." I settled back into my chair, realizing how ordering in front of Palamina made me feel tense—as tight as one of the Cat Man's felines on a high wire. Almost as if I was auditioning for my job all over again. "I know it seems like more than we can eat, but I take leftovers home or give them to my homeless buddies," I explained to her while attempting to uncrick my stiff neck. "The main thing is to try a fair sample of the menu. The budget doesn't allow for multiple visits. Or at least it didn't under Ava."

"I see your point," she said. Though she didn't sound convinced. "I'm glad to hear you're thinking about the budget."

After selecting complimentary beer and sake to go with the dinner, Wally and Palamina began to talk shop about future financial planning for the e-zine. Ray and I wandered out to the deck to admire the night again. Across the harbor, the lights of the restaurants winked, reflecting a swash of stars in the sky. The air smelled like salt and fresh fish, with a dash of diesel fumes to keep us moored in reality. I suspected we were both thinking of the last time I was here with him—I'd been shot and in serious shock. I plucked at the rubber band on my wrist, which Eric had suggested might distract me from unpleasant recurrent memories.

"Your new boss is a little intimidating," said Ray, his eyebrows drawing together in concern.

"She's not so bad," I said, leaning on the railing and looking over the side. Gray shapes glided through the water underneath the boat. "You should've been around when Ava Faulkner was in charge. Palamina is a walk in the park compared to that witch."

He grinned. "I'm glad to hear it. When you first moved down here, you were anxious about everything. I think you've developed more of a backbone."

"It wouldn't take much to improve from those days, would it?" I asked with a snort of laughter. We strolled around the outside of the restaurant and headed back into the dining area.

Ray held up his phone. "I'm going to give Connie a buzz, make sure she doesn't need me."

I ducked into the ladies' room to freshen up.

On the way back out, I heard Wally's voice rise over the rumble of conversation from the other diners.

"Can I speak frankly? Hayley's reviews are the one thing you don't have to micromanage at *Key Zest*. She's improved one hundred percent since she started, especially since getting that monkey Ava off her back."

"What did I say?" asked Palamina, all surprised innocence.

"Nothing direct, but I get the sense that Ava's distrust of Hayley may have taken root in you."

I felt my face grow hot and I froze, not wanting to show up at the table immediately and let on that I'd overheard their discussion. Wally was putting my submerged fears into words. I tensed for the worst.

"Not at all," said Palamina. "I was only trying to make a few suggestions. Keep in mind that you may not be in the most—how can I put this?—unbiased position." Her voice remained pleasant but firm. "Hayley is adorable and eager. But she's young and a bit impulsive—don't you think? I worry about her decision making, that she loses her focus."

"Did you know that Paul Woolston of the *Times* reads her stuff every week? He loves what she does," Wally said. "He told me that not only does she understand food; she understands why people eat it. What they crave and what they tend to turn away from—and the psychology behind those decisions. And that's unusual in a food critic. Particularly a critic who's not working in the rarified stratosphere of a major newspaper in a big city."

Palamina shrugged, the expression on her face neutral. "We'll have to see how it goes, right?"

I retreated farther into the hallway that led to the ladies' room and counted to a hundred. Then I adjusted my shirt, ran my fingers through my hair, and marched back to our table.

"I am so looking forward to this dinner," I said brightly, then took a swig of the sake that had been left near my place setting. My eyes burned as the alcohol seared my throat and I choked and spluttered. Ray returned from calling Connie and slapped me on the back. "Watch it there, maestro."

The first course was delivered and we began to eat.

"Have they solved the murder yet?" Ray asked. "Spooky that the body washed up right near Tarpon Pier. Is your friend the tarot card reader really involved?"

Wally shot me a warning look, which I read as, "Stay out of it." A man with a round, pleasant face and a close-cropped salt-and-pepper beard approached the table, a woman with lovely silvery curls following him. They waited for us to finish our discussion.

"I'm sure he had nothing to do with it," I said. "And I won't stand by and watch him get blamed for something he didn't do. That's all I'll say." I cracked a tight smile at the man standing by.

"Good evening, folks," the man said. "Thanks for coming out this evening."

I recognized his smooth baritone voice from the city commission meeting—this was the owner of the restaurant, Edwin Mastin. He'd gotten a haircut for opening night.

"We are the owners, Olivia and Edwin Mastin," he said. Olivia waved and beamed.

"We'd love your feedback, both good and not so good," Edwin assured us. "With a new restaurant, there are always things that can be improved."

"You must have spent some time in Japan," I said. "You don't see shabu-shabu on a menu very often. Or puffer."

"We won't have that on the menu regularly, but our chef insisted that we carry it for the opening and my wife agreed," he said with a friendly smile. He patted her on the back. "She's the Japanese expert. I would have been fine with fried fish and steamed shrimp, but she convinced me that our town needed something different."

"I thought Key West could use something a little more challenging," Olivia said. "We've got plenty of seafood restaurants on the island already."

He waved his arm at the bustling dining room. "I believe she was right. Again. Although I see you've chosen some of my favorites, too." They moved aside so the waiter could deliver our main courses, including the landlubber dishes I'd ordered.

"Your waiter mentioned that you not only run the restaurant, but you catch the fish as well?" Ray asked.

Edwin smiled. "Unfortunately we're getting too busy to spend as much time on the water as we'd like. We'll leave you to enjoy your meal." He hesitated. "I couldn't help overhearing—another murder is a real shame for this island. That kind of publicity hurts all of our businesses. So I can only hope the police wrap this up soon."

"Me, too," I said, "me, too."

Once the Mastins had moved on to the next table, I asked Palamina, "How did your meeting with Commissioner Greenleigh go?"

She made a face. "I really got nothing of substance. It was like a puff piece in a magazine, only in person."

I nodded, trying to look sympathetic. But feeling a tiny bit of pleasure that she had run into the buzz saw that could be Key West politics.

We powered through most of the food, especially enjoying the process of cooking the thin slices of beef in a pot of simmering broth. When Wally insisted that his lips started tingling after tasting the tiniest bite of puffer, none of the rest of us tried it. We ordered one bean cake just to say we'd sampled dessert; then I collected the check.

We saw Palamina off, and the three of us returned to Houseboat Row. "Come in for cake?" I asked Ray.

"I'd better get going. But I'd love to take a piece to go for Connie."

I rushed into our galley, cut two pieces of raspberry

cake, wrapped them in foil, and sent him off. "Are you hungry now?" I asked Wally. "Or should we wait on dessert?"

He patted his stomach. "Let's wait a bit." He sat on the couch and tapped the seat beside him. All three of the cats leaped up and nuzzled his hand.

"Scram, you guys." I scraped them off the upholstery, then sat, and he circled his arms around me and leaned in for a long kiss, which turned into another, and another.

"I've been looking forward to that," he said with a smile. "Missing you." He brushed a curl away from my forehead, leaving me tingling from my head to my toes. After a few more kisses, the conversation with Palamina, and Lorenzo's dilemma, and my mother's unhappiness, all floated away. I even began to forget that I had a senior citizen roommate.

The screen door banged and Miss Gloria burst into the living room. We leaped apart, straightening our clothing and our hair. I was sure my cheeks were flaming red; I felt like a teenager caught necking with a boy in the living room by my parents.

When I had collected myself, I looked up and noticed the contraption on Miss G's head that had replaced her bobbing hearts. A black band circled the crown and her forehead, and a webbing of straps crisscrossed her white hair to hold the band in place. Attached to all that was something that looked like a small pair of binoculars.

"Good gravy, what are you wearing?" I asked.

At the same time Wally said, "What in the world are you doing in those glasses? You look like a sea creature."

"Night vision goggles," she said with a smirk. "Hayley kept nagging me about how well I could see, and my sons did, too. And so I started to believe them, even got a little worried about driving at night. But it turns out there's no need in the world to be concerned. Because these are amazing." She slipped the contraption off her head and handed it to Wally. "Try them out—you'll see."

"Where did you get them?" Wally asked as he peered through the lenses.

"They were in a bag of cat food," she said. She picked up Lola and began to rub her ears.

"Come on, like a prize in a Cracker Jack box?" he asked. "Publix or Winn-Dixie?"

"Hayley brought the bag from Lorenzo's place—for Lola." She giggled, ignoring my warning eye bulge. She handed the white cat to me, took the glasses from Wally, and snapped them into place, resembling for all the world a miniature creature from another planet. Looking puzzled, Wally turned to me.

"Lorenzo asked me to take care of his kitty for a couple of days," I explained. "Yesterday I went to his place to pick up the cat and some of her cat food."

"I reached into the bag to feed the cat, and presto," said Miss Gloria, "came out with these." She patted her head.

"What in the world would he need night vision goggles for?" Wally asked. "Does he play paintball?"

"He doesn't strike me as a paintball kind of guy," Miss Gloria said, giggling again. She swung around to peer out of our side window. "He's totally nonviolent. Look, I can see right into the neighbor's bedroom. Mr. Renhart is having a nightcap."

"Stop that." I scrambled off the couch and tapped Miss Gloria's shoulder. "Come on, someone's going to call the police and report a Peeping Tom."

"Oh, wait," said Wally, rubbing his chin with his fingers. "I just read in the paper this week that the cops think the cemetery burglar is using goggles during his robberies."

"No way. You can't think Lorenzo robbed all those homes," I said indignantly.

"What, then? Why hide those glasses in a bag of cat food?" he asked, his tone even. "Why have them at all? I think you should turn these in to the cops."

"They could have nothing to do with anything," I protested. I took the goggles from Miss Gloria and placed them on the counter.

Wally got to his feet, too. "So your friend is hiding criminal evidence in his pantry and you don't see anything fishy?"

"Criminal evidence? There must be dozens of reasons why a person would need night vision goggles. And more reasons why he might have concealed them in the pantry."

I just didn't know what they were.

When it became clear to me that Wally was acting like a turkey, and clear to Wally that I wasn't prepared to call the police, he left without a piece of cake or a good night kiss. Then Miss Gloria retired to her bed, leaving nothing but me and the cats. I sure didn't want to spend the night ruminating about the way the evening had ended with Wally, with him angry and me annoyed, and every bit of sexy warmth ebbed away. One thing might help a little.

I snapped Eric's rubber band around my wrist and went into the galley to cut a mammoth-sized piece of raspberry cake. As I ate, my thoughts kept wandering back to Lorenzo.

Where had he gone in such a hurry? How much did I really know about him? Why would someone hate him enough to set him up for murder? And most perplexing of all, why did he have night vision goggles stored in Lola's cat food?

9

But the next day, I pressed an ice bag to my head and lapped at my café Cubano like one of Hemingway's dazed polydactyl cats.

—Norman Van Aken,
No Experience Necessary

The three cats woke me up earlier than I would have preferred, prancing across the bed and playing a vigorous game of leapfrog that ended in attacking my toes through the quilt. When I rolled over and buried my head under the pillow, Evinrude pinned the little white kitty down and batted her until she screamed.

"Knock it off, Evinrude!" I yelped once I had identified the perpetrator. "Good gravy, you're the senior animal here. You're supposed to be setting an example." He walked up to the head of the bed, purring and tail twitching, and then tapped my cheek with one paw.

"Okay," I grumbled. "Give me one more minute."

Halfway through that minute, the memory of how last night had ended flooded my brain. A sickening weight of disappointment settled into my gut. I needed to get over myself. Maybe fixing a big breakfast would help. I threw on my most cheerful fluffy pink bathrobe and shuffled out to the galley, cats filing behind me. Miss Gloria had left a note on the kitchen table.

> *Gone up the finger to have coffee and muffins with Mrs. Dubisson. Terribly sorry if I caused trouble with Wally over those silly glasses. Love, Miss G.*

Well, she had caused trouble, but maybe it was a case of pulling the curtain on a devastating fault in my relationship with Wally. Maybe— I needed to eat first before examining the grim details.

I gave the cats each a ration of kibble, then pulled two eggs out of the refrigerator, along with a bar of good cheddar and a quarter stick of butter. Then I rustled through the freezer until I found several pieces of whole-grain wheat bread from the Old Town Bakery. I chopped up half a small onion and soon had it sizzling in the butter, while NPR fed me the day's news. Once the whipped eggs were starting to solidify in the hot butter, I scraped the cheddar into the middle of the omelet and folded it over. The toast popped out of the toaster, a lovely medium brown, and I buttered that, too. Then I poured a big mug of Miss Gloria's coffee and took my breakfast out to the deck. The bigger cats trotted after me, looking hopeful, and Lola fell in behind them. It wasn't taking long for her to adjust to her new surroundings, the in-house pecking order, and the feline routines.

As I ate, I tried to convince myself that the argument last night hadn't sounded the death knell for me and Wally. It wasn't only that he was disappointed in me. I was disappointed in his reaction, too. If he didn't understand how important it was to stand up for your friends, what did that mean for our future? Nothing good.

I used the last corner of toast to soak up a leftover bit of melted cheese, then put the plate down for the cats to lick. As I sipped on the coffee, Schnootie, the next-door neighbor's gray schnauzer, burst out of their boat and began to bark furiously at my felines. Mrs. Renhart hurried out of the cabin and snatched up the little dog.

"Sorry, Hayley," she said. "One day maybe she'll get used to them."

I shrugged and smiled. "I bet she will." Which I didn't believe, really. She would be a senior citizen confined to her doggie bed and she'd still woof her fool head off at any resident cats.

"It's one of those days when I'm just glad to be alive," my neighbor crooned. She buried her face in the dog's fur. "And having a silver beastie makes it even better." She grabbed the dog's paw and waved at me, and then at Evinrude, and went back into her boat.

I straightened my shoulders, trying to shrug off my gloominess. It *was* a great day to be alive. And I was luckier than most. And I would not let a silly argument with Wally ruin that truth. After all, hadn't he stood up for me with Palamina at the restaurant before I got back to our table? Whether our friendship turned into something more serious or not, I could be perfectly happy continuing to live here with Miss Gloria. I had a job I loved, on an island I loved, surrounded by people I cared about, and they cared back. I wasn't dead like Bart Frontgate or scared to death like Lorenzo.

A text came in from Connie. *I see you out there in your pj's. Come down for a second coffee?*

I dropped my dishes in the kitchen sink, threw on jeans and a T-shirt, and trotted up the finger to join Connie. She was waiting on the upper deck with a full pot of coffee. I felt my eyes filling unexpectedly with tears as I threw my arms around her.

"Congratulations! I am so happy for you."

After a long hug she pushed me away, her hands still gripping my arms. "I'm sorry you found out about the baby from Ray. I wanted to tell you in the worst way, and I knew you'd want to know. I knew that. But after the miscarriage last fall . . ." Her voice trailed off and she wiped her eyes with a tissue. "I can't even explain it; it was like losing something so precious, but something that I never quite had in my possession. Does that make sense?"

I nodded. "I think so."

"It felt like the most piercing pain, but nobody else could really see it. I know it isn't exactly like losing a child, but it felt like that. I just couldn't talk about it until we were pretty sure I was past the most dangerous weeks."

"I understand completely," I said. "That was awful. And this time must feel so scary, even though you're bursting with happiness."

She settled back into her beach chair, a crooked smile on her face. "I know I'm driving Ray crazy with these ups and downs. One day I can't get enough of a certain food, and the next day it makes me sick to my stomach. One day I'm euphoric and the next, inconsolable." She grinned wider. "I don't know whether we're going to make it through this or not."

"Of course you will," I said, sitting down beside her and pouring another cup of coffee. "You're an old-fashioned pregnant woman—that's all."

"By the way, the raspberry cake was amazing," said Connie. "I ate my piece and Ray's, too. He didn't dare make a fuss once he saw me go after it. So little agrees with me right now." She put her hand on my knee and squeezed. "Hey, how did it go with Wally last night?"

"He got mad at me and stalked out."

She groaned. "Mad about what?"

So I explained about the goggles and how Miss Gloria had found them in the cat food, and how the cat food came from Lorenzo's pantry, and how it looked for all the world like he was hiding them. And if he was hiding them, why? And the only thing we could come up with was something to do with either burglary or murder. And both of them were awful. And he'd run away, which only made him look totally guilty.

"Mr. Moral Fiber, of course, thinks I should run the goggles down to the police department, turn my friend in."

"This island is in a weird place right now," said Connie, rubbing the slight swell of her stomach protectively. "And I don't think it's only my hormones. From everything I read in the paper, the city government officials are fighting with each other. And the tourists are struggling with the locals. And the locals are snarking at each other and at the homeless. I'm sure there have always been problems, but doesn't it seem more tense than usual?"

"Maybe too many people crammed into too few square inches," I said. "Maybe it always feels this way in the high season and we just don't remember."

"What does Lorenzo say about what happened?" Connie asked.

I sighed. "The trouble is, he's disappeared completely. I haven't talked to him since we had brunch with Eric at Firefly on Friday. And he ran out of there like somebody threatened him. And maybe they have. When I went over to get his kitty, the only thing I really found out was his neighbor said he left in a pink taxi-cab. Carrying a train case." I smiled in spite of myself—that luggage was so Lorenzo.

"Oh," said Connie, her face lighting up. "I know the dispatcher who works the afternoon shift at the pink taxi place. I'm sure he's not supposed to tell me anything about his customers."

"Could you try?"

She punched the number into her cell phone and asked to speak to Theo. "Hey, buddy," she said, "it's Connie Arp. We have a friend who's in a spot of trouble. Well, actually it's more than a spot. We think he's in physical danger. He was picked up at"—she rattled off Lorenzo's address as I fed it to her—"sometime Friday afternoon. Could you possibly check and find out where your cabbie dropped him off? It's really important or I wouldn't ask you to break the rules." She listened for a minute, then thanked the man and hung up. "The cabbie took him to the Key West ferry terminal. Right about the time he would've been boarding the Vomit Comet en route to Fort Myers."

"You're a national treasure," I said to Connie. Then I sprang up and started for the stairs. "I'll talk to you later. If you can think of anything you want to eat, anytime, text me, and I'll make it for you and bring it over."

"Since you asked, do you have a recipe for baklava?"

"Of course!"

Her thank-you followed me down the dock.

10

Wally flashed a smile, tight as the rubber
band around a bouquet of broccoli.
                    —Lucy Burdette, *Death with*
                              All the Trimmings

The so-called Vomit Comet is a high-speed passenger
ferry that travels from Key West to Fort Myers and back
twice a day. It was nicknamed for the effects it often has
on its customers during cold, dark voyages. I wasn't
looking forward to taking the trip, but I would do it if
there was good reason. Like now.

I grabbed my backpack and sprinted down the dock
to my scooter. The questions circled wildly in my mind.
What would Lorenzo be doing in Fort Myers? And in
the bigger picture, what was he running from? Although
locals complained about the traffic and angst that came
along with the tourist high season, they counted on
business being brisk enough to fill their bank accounts
and cover the slower times. In other words, Lorenzo
wouldn't give up his slot at the Sunset Celebration for
a minor problem.

Which brought me back to the most worrisome

question: What was his relationship with Bart Front-gate, if any? And if he had no personal relationship with the dead man, who had one? One lousy enough that it ended in a grisly murder? Murder was not a casual act, as I'd seen too clearly in several deaths over the past few years. It was an extreme end to extreme rage or revenge or conflict over love turned sour.

I buzzed down Southard Street dodging delivery trucks, wobbly tourists on bicycles, and irritable locals. I shouted a quick hello to Kevin McChesney, a carpenter and builder who was unloading stacks of wood and carrying them to a large white Conch house at the corner of Elizabeth. We are pretty much out of land on this little island, so people with enough money focus on snatching up properties that can be rebuilt or refurbished or, very occasionally, when the gods of the Historic Architectural Review Commission smile down on them, knocked flat so they can start from scratch. I took a right into the back parking lot of the pink stucco public library. Along with flying the flag of literacy and literature, the library serves as a gathering place for folks who don't have access to the Internet. Or sometimes to air-conditioning or even indoor plumbing.

To the right of the circulation desk and down the small hallway, I found the Florida history room, glassed off from the rest of the library. It had a cool, hushed feel. The walls were lined with shelves of old books and binders with hand-lettered labels on them. A lanky white-haired man, his back bent like the gentle sway of a question mark, looked up and blinked behind thick glasses.

"Good morning," I said. "I'm hoping you can help me with a few questions. I'm writing a piece about the history of the Sunset Celebration on Mallory Square. I was hoping to get some background from you."

"Modern history, then," he said, then included a faint smile. "Not ancient. Suppose I give you the basic outline in a nutshell, and then I can direct you to a few resources for further reading." One silver eyebrow arched.

"That would be amazing," I said. "Perfect."

"In the very old days, there was no formal Sunset Celebration. But in the 1960s, when the so-called hippies came to town, they would congregate on that land to watch the sun go down." He pursed his lips. "And do whatever they were doing to amplify their enjoyment of the situation. Of course, there was no pier back then. There were no cruise ships."

"That's hard to imagine," I said, just to keep the flow of information coming.

"According to our records, the first ship docked in 1969. But the pier as we know it was not built until 1984. The city wisely at that point decided there needed to be some regulation of the Sunset events. The area had grown into sort of a flea market, with all kinds of people selling all kinds of things. I imagine there was a lot more going on than what is recorded here in my history room." He chuckled, tipping his chin at the bookshelves. Then he swept his glasses off and began to polish the lenses with a big white handkerchief.

"About the same time that the city was getting concerned, the adjoining businesses were, too. They put a lot of pressure on regulating the activities at Sunset. Some of the performers got together and formed what we recognize now as the Artistic Performance Preservation Society."

"Which has been in the news a lot lately," I said. "For unfortunate reasons. Do you know if any of those first performers are still involved with the Mallory Square events?"

He slid his glasses back on. "Bart Frontgate was one of the earliest. Sadly, though he had enormous potential, he never quite got his life on track."

"Do you have any idea where Bart Frontgate came from?" I asked.

"Oh, his family has been on the island forever," said the librarian.

"He was a local?" I asked. "I had no idea."

"Sure, his family owns a couple of businesses in town, and they have a rather large plot at the cemetery. If you ever get over there, take a look. The stonework is magnificent. I suppose he'll be buried there. I'm not sure what his relationship with his parents had been like since he changed his name."

That tidbit perked me up. "He changed his name?"

"The family name was Gates," he said.

A guilty expression passed over his face; he looked as though he wished he had not mentioned Frontgate. Or his family. A man of history, not gossip.

Then he stood up and shuffled through some papers on his desk. "You feel free to look around. The Key West historical documents are over to your right." He waved at a shelf across the room and disappeared through a door at the back corner.

I was dismissed. I spent another half an hour perusing the materials in the Key West department, which largely confirmed the short history the librarian had given me. I found multiple mentions of Bart Frontgate's family, aka the Gateses. His father had run for a position on the city commission as well as the mosquito control board and the school board. Though the elections were close, he had not won any of them. His mother had performed in productions at various venues over the island and was generally assessed by critics as enthusiastic if not supremely talented. They were frequent contributors to local fund-raising events, as evidenced in many society-page photos. I then Googled their names and made a note of their home address in Casa Marina, while realizing that a few days after their son's murder might not be the best time for a visit.

The tall librarian had returned to the pile of books and papers on his desk while I read, so I approached his island refuge again. "May I ask one more question? Do you recall whether the tarot card reader, Lorenzo, has been in town for a while?"

"Can't help with that one," he said, his expression flat. "I eschew the occult."

Cased closed, clearly. I thanked him, packed up my stuff, and returned to my scooter.

As soon as I got back to the boat, I parked myself on the living room couch and texted my mother. She phoned me right back.

"I thought you'd never call," my mother said. I ignored the yearning in her voice. I assumed it had to do with her feeling trapped by the winter weather and Sam's broken hip—neither of which I could help. The best I could do was try to keep her entertained. And involved.

"I have lots of news to share. First of all, Connie's pregnant."

My mother yelped with excitement. "I am thrilled for her. I can't wait to go shopping! I'll call her as soon as we hang up. Boy or girl? What names are they considering?"

"I didn't ask any of that," I said.

She sighed. "Send a girl to do a woman's job . . . What else?"

"Connie found out that Lorenzo took the passenger ferry to Fort Myers yesterday. Whatever that means."

"What it means," my mother said, her voice electric with the thrill of a dog on the hunt, "is that he went to see his mom."

"And you know that because . . . ?"

"Because you assigned me to do research about Bart Frontgate. But I actually worked on Lorenzo's background first, and I discovered that his mother retired there to a little golf neighborhood called Seven Lakes several years ago. I was able to track down her phone number. I called her," she admitted sheepishly, "but she hung up on me as soon as I mentioned her son. I suspect you'd have better luck talking with her in person."

"Mom," I said. "You weren't supposed to do anything with your information—"

"I know that. I just figured, mother to mother, she might be willing to talk."

"I wonder if Lorenzo's there hiding out. He won't answer my texts or calls or e-mail. I tried again this morning."

"I don't think the boat runs very often," said my mother. I could hear her keyboard clacking in the background. "Here's the schedule. The ferry leaves in an hour, with one returning early tomorrow. And another, late tonight. Want me to make you a reservation at a hotel for the night? It might be hard to find something this time of year."

"No, thanks," I said. "Can't stay overnight. I have too much to do. Have to get lunch at Azur tomorrow and then write up my article."

"Speaking of that," Mom said. "How did things go last night at Sake? Did you like the food? And how about the date?"

I had to give her credit for holding back on asking about Wally until the end of our conversation. Although I gave myself credit for putting Connie's news first to distract her from her own daughter's lackluster romance.

"Well, the food was—how should I say this—interesting. The bento box dishes were kind of weird and a little slimy. I didn't go wild for either of the specials. When Wally's lips started to numb up after the first nibble of puffer, we called it a day. Although it's possible that was all in his head. He's not much of a foodie." I laughed. "However, the chef did a couple of tempura dishes, which were fantastic. But how can you go wrong frying Key West pink shrimp? They seated us on cushions at a low table, which I don't think will be popular with the creaky-knees set."

"They'll be cutting out a lot of snowbirds if they don't have some normal tables," Mom agreed. "What else?"

"We liked the landlubber specials. The burger reminded me of B.O.'s Fish Wagon—absolutely enormous, and loaded with fried onions and dripping cheese and mustard and mayo, the works."

"I'm practically drooling," said my mother. "Is it time for lunch yet? Sam won't let me cook much because he's expending so few calories. He's afraid we'll turn into chubby little bears. And it's quite likely, isn't it?" She sighed with disappointment. "I sure will be happy when he's on the mend and we can get back to normal."

"You're through the worst of it," I said. "Send me some links about anything interesting you discovered about Lorenzo, okay? I'm going to pack a little bag just in case I get stuck in Fort Myers."

"Is there anything new from Lieutenant Torrence?" she asked. "Have you checked in with him?"

"Not today. I was hoping he'd call me if he had anything, but now that you mention it, why would he? I'm like a pesky moth fluttering against his lampshade."

Mom laughed. "Oh, wait," she said. "Before you hang up. At the risk of being nosy, you didn't tell me about Wally. How did that go? How did he like the cake?"

I took the easier question first. "He left without eating any cake." And then I explained about the goggles that Miss Gloria had found in the bag of cat food. "Wally got mad because he thought I should tell that to Torrence right away. I guess he thinks it implicates Lorenzo somehow and that it shows bad judgment if I protect him." I couldn't bear to tell her that I'd overheard Palamina warning Wally about my judgment while we were in the restaurant. That felt lousy enough without sharing it with my mother.

"Implicates him in what?" she asked.

"I don't know, the cemetery burglaries? The murder? I don't know."

My computer dinged and I saw that she had sent me several links relating to Lorenzo and his family. "I gotta run now, Mom," I said. "I'll let you know what I find out in Fort Myers."

"Take a Dramamine before you board the boat, honey," she warned me. "You know our side of the family is famous for weak stomachs. We're designed for eating— not for sailing."

As I hung up, I heard Miss Gloria clatter in from the dock and greet each of the cats, with a special nugget of affection for little Lola.

"How is Mrs. Dubisson?" I asked as I emerged from the cabin into the bright midday light.

"She's great. How could things not be great living in paradise in February?" She flung her arms open. "I'm sorry about the business with the goggles," she said again, and then scooped Lola into her arms. "I'm sorry if I caused trouble with Wally."

I shrugged, summoning a cheerful smile that didn't match what I felt. "If that train has left the station, your little show won't make any difference."

Miss Gloria bit her lip and then nuzzled the white cat, who leaned into her cheek, rumbling a noisy kitten purr. "Did you call the police department?"

"I'm going to call them," I said. "But I'm going to ask for information, not hand it over. We don't know what Lorenzo was doing with those goggles. We don't know anything about them. He could have owned them for years. They might have been a gift from his father from World War II."

"Someone might have put the goggles into his cat food and he didn't know anything about it," she suggested helpfully.

I nodded, though it all sounded far-fetched. "So why would I make trouble by turning them over? I'd rather wait until I speak to Lorenzo. And I'm hoping that will be tonight."

Then I told her about my plan to take the high-speed ferry to Fort Myers and track down Mrs. Smith. "If you can, take care of the cats while I'm away? I'm hoping to be back on the late boat."

"Of course," she said. "I don't have any big plans other than bask in the sun, take a nap, have a simple supper, and watch some TV."

"A perfect cat day," I said, and gave her a little hug.

11

In the end, I didn't take the Dramamine because we
had none in the house, and I didn't have time to get to
the drugstore. I'd have to keep my fingers crossed that
sailing would be smooth. I packed clean underwear
and socks and a toothbrush and my brand-new copy of
Best Food Writing in my backpack along with a hunk of
the raspberry cake and an apple and a peanut butter
and raspberry jam sandwich on whole-grain bread. If I
wasn't sick to my stomach, that should last me the voy-
age. At the last minute, I packed a piece of cake for
Lorenzo's mother, too.

While I waited to board the ferry, I scrolled through
the articles my mother had e-mailed. The first was an
obituary for Lorenzo's father, dated two years earlier:

*Marvin H. Smith, formerly of Woodbridge, Con-
necticut, and recently of Fort Myers, Florida, died late*

*Tuesday. He was born in January 1929 in Danbury,
Connecticut, and lived his entire life in that state until
recently retiring with his wife to Fort Myers. He was
an electrical engineer at the Sikorsky Aircraft Corpo-
ration and worked there until his retirement. He was a
member of the Woodbridge Country Club, an active
member of the Woodbridge exchange committee, and
on the local board of the Boy Scouts of America. He
served both as a deacon and an elder at the Orange
Presbyterian Church. He is survived by Marion, his
wife of forty years, and his son, Marvin H. Smith Jr.,
of Key West, Florida. A memorial service is planned for
a later date. In lieu of flowers, the family requests that
donations be sent to the Woodbridge hospice.*

All in all, a short and bloodless recording of a man's
life. The paragraph did not tell me much about him,
though I could read the subtext: Having a son who was
a tarot card reader residing in Key West would be for-
eign to his experience. How had his relationship with
Lorenzo changed over the years? His mother would
know.

After hearing the first boarding announcement, I
walked onto the boat and made the call I'd been dread-
ing. Torrence answered right away.

"Wondering whether you've arrested anyone in
Frontgate's murder."

"Not yet," Torrence said. "Getting closer, though.
Did you have something to add?"

"Don't you think it's a little unlikely that Lorenzo
would have wrapped up the murder weapon and stuffed
it into his own cart? Right where the cops would find
it? He's a smart man. And that would be a dumb move."

"Who said anything about his cart?" Torrence said. After a short silence, he added, "The weapon was wrapped in his tablecloth and thrown in the Dumpster. Right down the road from the cemetery and not that far from where the dead man was recovered, as a matter of fact." It sounded like he was tapping his pen on the phone.

"How did Frontgate's body get into the water, anyway?" I asked. "Lorenzo certainly doesn't own a boat."

"It's nice you want to stick up for your friend," Torrence said, "but as usual, there's a lot you don't know."

"You're beginning to sound a lot like Bransford," I said, "and that's not a compliment." I hung up in a huff.

The ferry pulled away from the dock. In spite of the reruns of *Three's Company* blasting on the TV in the lounge, I hunkered down inside to keep my mind off the chop of the water and the hours at sea ahead of me. I worked on the review of For Goodness' Sake, trying to keep my description balanced but accurate. I crafted a paragraph about the ongoing zoning dispute—Palamina could cut it if she didn't like it, but I refused to be cornered and deflated by her low expectations. Then I jotted down a series of questions that I hoped to ask Lorenzo's mother, Mrs. Smith. First, assuming she'd let me in. And second, assuming she'd talk at all. My mother was extremely persuasive—if she hadn't gotten anywhere, I might not, either.

With great relief, I noticed that the shoreline began to twinkle with the lights of Naples and a slew of golf and beach communities that had sprung up to the north and south of the city. There was a line of taxicabs waiting as we disembarked from the ferry at Fort Myers Beach. I managed to snag the fourth one. Once settled in the backseat, I read off the address of Mrs. Smith's condominium in Seven Lakes.

"According to my map app, it's right across the road from the Bell Tower mall, and also the Outback restaurant."

"I know the area," he said, turning up his sports-talk radio as we wheeled off. It wasn't even baseball season, but he was listening to a station playing classic-game reruns. If listening to baseball was agony, listening to a baseball game for which you already knew the outcome had to be worse.

The streets of Fort Myers Beach had only a smattering of tourists on them. Nine p.m. The witching hour in South Florida. Different from Key West, where the action would just be getting rolling on Duval Street. After twenty minutes on the road, we pulled off the busy four-lane highway into a driveway that led to a property containing older-looking boxy condos. A small gatehouse with a retractable arm guarded the entrance. The taxi driver pulled up so I could speak with the guard, a uniformed man with a fireplug shape.

"I'm visiting Mrs. Marvin Smith," I said. "I am her niece." He nodded and grinned, exposing several missing teeth, and went back into the guardhouse.

"I have a feeling she forgot to let you know that I was coming," I called after him, flashing my most brilliant smile.

"Not to worry—I'll phone her," he said.

"Please don't call; it's a big surprise. I've been telling her for two years that I'd visit her—ever since I moved down to Key West from Jersey. But this week is her birthday. Seventy-five, can you believe it?" I fished my driver's license with the Key West address out of my purse and waved it in front of him—as if that proved anything. "I really wanted to surprise her."

He looked at my license, then peered into the backseat of the cab, studying me, my backpack, my absence of luggage and birthday gifts. The whole time I grinned like a monkey. After a long hesitation, he returned to the booth, raised the bar, and waved us through. "Tell her happy birthday for me!"

The closer we got to the building where Lorenzo's mother lived, the more anxious I felt. I had yet to see anyone who looked under seventy, which by itself was not a problem. But the scathing and suspicious looks that were thrown at the cab by a few dog walkers worried me.

"Here you go, ma'am," said the cabbie, turning his baseball game play-by-play down so he could arrange payment.

I hopped out of the cab, paid the driver, adding a little tip, and slammed the door. Nothing to do but forge ahead. Rather than take the elevator, I climbed the set of concrete stairs that wound around the building's exterior, gathering my thoughts, trying to visualize how to approach the crucial door-answering moment without having it slammed in my face, and hoping in my heart of hearts that Lorenzo would actually answer.

On the third floor, I went down the long outer hallway, which was open to the outdoors. Everything about the place looked as though it would need some serious work in the next few years—the paint on the walls almost ready to peel, the metal fence rusting and wobbly, the screen doors on each apartment hanging just a little bit loose. When I reached number 310, I took a deep breath and tapped on the door.

A small woman with dark curls painted with streaks of gray cracked the inside door open, leaving the screen latched between us. She had deep violet eyes and high cheekbones. She looked a little frightened, but when she saw me, the fear shifted to a determined expression I'd often seen on Lorenzo's face. I would have recognized that expression anywhere.

"How can I help you?" she asked, her voice not welcoming. "My husband is just inside watching TV."

That fib, I was sure, was meant to scare off any frightening accomplices.

I tried a big smile. "I'm sorry that I didn't warn you ahead of time, but I'm a friend of Lorenzo's. Is he here?" I tried to peer around her, down the darkened hallway, where the television screen flickered.

Her eyes got wide. "A friend from where?"

"Key West," I said. "He's my favorite tarot card reader in all the world. Except for when I get the Tower. I keep drawing that darn card and your unflappable son keeps telling me I have to learn to work with chaos." I flashed another smile but she did not respond. "I take it he's not here. I'd really love to talk with you for a minute. We could go out if you're more comfortable with that." I dropped my voice lower, so curious neighbors would not overhear. "But I'm very worried about him running from the police. Of course he didn't kill that man, but it makes him look guilty. You know?"

Lorenzo's mother's face was stony, except for the uncertainty that flickered in her eyes, as though she was on the verge of calling security and having me thrown out. Had she even heard about the murder accusation? I had to talk faster, convince her I was on the right side. Lorenzo's side.

"Honest to god, I'm his friend. And I really care about him and I'm worried about him. He called me to pick up his kitty. Lola. She's staying on our houseboat with our two cats. It was not love at first sight between them, but now she's folded right into the pack. I'm afraid she may have some bad feline habits when he picks her up again."

Her mouth relaxed a little. "He told me about Lola."

I smiled. "She's the sweetest little thing. But listen, I'm worried sick about him, but I said that already. He must have told you that the police think he might have killed the man who was murdered earlier this week in Key West. Apparently there's some evidence pointing that way. And you can understand that him disappearing—well, it makes him look bad."

The woman's lips began to tremble and her eyes looked moist. She backed away from the screen door and motioned to me to enter. "I'm sick about all of this, too," she said and led me into a dark living room with white carpet that had seen a lot of foot traffic. Two La-Z-Boy chairs upholstered in tropical prints faced the television—an old model, not a new flat-screen. A PBS mystery flickered on the screen. On the table between the chairs sat an old-fashioned keyboard, unattached to any computer or iPad or any other modern device. She saw me looking at the keyboard and gave a faint smile.

"WebTV. We're probably the last subscribers in the world. But I never got used to the computer and Marvin Senior said he spent too much time staring at a screen at work to want to take it up at home, too. He was a stubborn man. And Marvin Junior took that from him. Can I get you a cup of tea? The water's hot—I was about to pour when you knocked. Chamomile okay?"

"Lovely. Thanks," I said as she waved me to one of the lounge chairs. She returned shortly with two cups of tea in bone china with silver around the rims, and flicked off the television. I stirred a cube of white sugar into my cup and took a sip of tea, which tasted a bit like sweetened dishwater. I settled the cup into the saucer.

"Is this wedding china?"

She nodded and flashed a sad smile.

"Did Lorenzo ever mention the name Bart Frontgate?" I asked. "That's the man who was killed."

She shook her head, her lips tense again. "Nothing like that."

She was scared to death, and I was pushing too hard. "What can you tell me about why he left Key West in such a hurry?" I asked in a gentle voice. "Was he concerned about something? Why was he here?"

"I don't know anything about that man, Frontgate, or whatever," she said. "He was worried about a girl. Someone who relied on him."

"That's why he ran?" I asked.

"He ran because he didn't believe the police would look for the real killer. He thought they'd be satisfied with any suspect—even himself, and he had nothing to do with it. Clean up the mess, dump the trash into the bin. Tell the public the mystery was solved. And be done. Let the people think the murder was the result of a drunken brawl and that it probably didn't matter too much who the real killer was. As long as someone was caught and punished."

I noticed a photograph across the room on the table next to the TV, and I got up to investigate. Two men stood together, stiffly, a teenage Lorenzo, or Marvin Junior, as she called him, and a tall blue-eyed man with wide shoulders—most likely his dad.

"That was my husband, Marvin Senior," the woman said. "It may be the only photograph I have of the two of them together."

"They didn't get along?" I asked.

"I'm sad to say they did not," she said. "Marvin Junior hated sports. He didn't mind losing, but he hated the idea of beating someone else. And even more, he couldn't bear hunting and fishing. He wanted no part of hurting other creatures. He was not a boy's boy—you know what I mean?"

I nodded, thinking that issue seemed to cause more trouble between fathers and sons than any other I'd heard of. Men sometimes had an image of what their relationship with a son should be like, and it was hard to give that up and adjust to what was really there.

"My husband resented that Marvin Junior spent so much time with my mother. He never did forgive my mother for getting him started with tarot cards. But she was certain that he was gifted, that he had the sight. And he was so soft and sweet and he preferred the company of his grandmother to the rough-and-tumble boys in the neighborhood."

"She was his respite," I said.

Her eyes glistened with tears. "Marvin Junior adored my mother and he soaked up her attention, and he finally began to understand and accept that he did have an unusual vision." She took a tissue from the box beside her chair and patted her face. "My husband was so relieved when he went off to college. But instead of studying, Marvin stayed up late nights and read cards for people in the common room." She gave a soft laugh. "That didn't do much for his GPA and he finally dropped out."

I replaced the photo and went back to my chair. "Tell me about the girl he worried about. Not a girlfriend?"

She shook her head. "He believed she was in danger. Maybe doing something illegal, too." Her forehead wrinkled with concern. "Nothing feels more important to him than helping people find their way."

"Was it possible he believed this woman killed Frontgate?"

Lorenzo's mother shrugged and covered her face with her hands. "He takes on the problems that people bring to him. He takes them too much to heart. It's like he doesn't have the filter that most people have, a shield to protect himself from other people's heartbreak."

Lorenzo's mother stood up. "I was about to put a frozen dinner in the microwave. Would you like to stay for supper? I know it's late . . . I got caught up in my programs. Or we could go across the street and get a blooming onion at the Outback. Marvin Senior and I used to do that every week and I miss it. But I certainly couldn't order a whole one by myself." She patted her stomach. "I can't handle fried food the way I used to."

Neither sounded at all appealing, even though I was hungry in spite of the snacks I'd packed. And the two pieces of cake I'd eaten—not saving one for her as I'd intended. "Thank you so much for the kind offer. I was hoping to catch the late ferry back to Key West. I'll call a taxi."

"I'll take you," she said. "Give me a minute to freshen up and I'll be right with you." She went into the back bedroom to get ready. I breathed a sigh of relief, pleased to have dodged the bullet of a frozen dinner or an oversized fried onion with mayonnaise-y dipping sauce. Neither of those options would be good company on the long, dark boat ride back to Key West.

Mrs. Smith led me to the elevator and we clunked and lurched to the bottom level and trotted across the parking lot to her car. She gestured to a big old Buick stored under a carport next to a golf cart. The inside of the car seemed to be held together with duct tape. "Don't mind the patch job," she said, grinning as she slipped into the driver's seat. "No way my husband was going to trade this car in. 'Nothing new could be better than what I already have,' he always said. Which I suppose was a good motto for a long marriage." She smiled. "Are you married?"

"Not yet." Which sounded dishonest. "Not even close. Maybe someday. My mom's engaged, though." I mentally clunked my skull for sounding silly. But the subject of marriage seemed to turn my head to mush.

She fired up the car, backed out of the carport, and headed out of the complex, waving to the guard as the arm protecting the driveway swung up. "Wait, how did you get in here?"

"Don't be mad at him," I said. "I was very persuasive. Said you were turning seventy-five and I was here to help celebrate."

"Seventy-five, huh? You added five years to my total." She laughed away my apology, then turned right toward Fort Myers Beach, where the ferry docked. We wound through a series of smaller streets, never setting tire on busy, crazy Route Forty-one.

"You could be a taxi driver yourself," I said with admiration. "You seem to know all the back roads."

"I don't like to make left turns into oncoming traffic," she admitted as she pulled up to the curb.

"Do you know where he's gone?" I asked as I was getting out of the car.

She glanced over, her face quiet, and said nothing. She knew exactly what I was asking. She simply wasn't going to answer. So I traveled four hours each way on a rolling sea for zippedy-do-da-nothing.

12

She had said that the very thought of him made her want to pan-fry her face, but I didn't believe her.

—Jessica Soffer, *Tomorrow There Will Be Apricots*

It was hours after midnight when I finally staggered into our houseboat, feeling queasy and yet ravenous. Evinrude, Sparky, and Lola greeted me at the door. After a quick scratch hello behind three sets of ears, I marched directly to the refrigerator. The cats launched into a chorus of meows. "Shush," I whispered, "you'll wake Miss Gloria."

I poured them each a tiny dollop of milk and rummaged around until I found some cheese, a decent-looking apple, and two pieces of leftover pepperoni pizza that Miss Gloria must have ordered for supper. Standing by the sink, I ate quickly, then noticed a package that had been left on the counter. Miss Gloria had scrawled a note on top.

Valentine's package. You won't believe how cute they are!

I tore open the wrapping, buzzing happily with the thought that maybe Wally had recognized he'd overreacted and dropped off a Valentine's gift after all. But instead of something romantic from him, or even last-minute, day-after holiday chocolates, my mother had sent white flannel pajamas with bright red hearts all over them. Sigh. A second note was clipped to my jammies, also in Miss Gloria's handwriting.

She sent me the same! So cute! I washed and dried and ironed them so we could wear them right away.

I rubbed the fabric between my fingers. They did feel soft and cozy. So I slid them on, brushed my teeth, and fell into bed, determined not to think about Lorenzo's problems. Or my own. Everything would look brighter in the morning. It always did.

A couple of hours later, I woke up with the vague foreboding that I'd heard a noise in the living room. The cats? I could see in the faint graying light that slipped through the slats of my window blinds that Lola was gone from the bed. The other two were splayed across my quilt, ears perked and eyes wide so they looked alert and worried. My heart began to pound. And I was rushed by memories of Miss Gloria's terrible near-death experience last winter.

Miss Gloria. Oh my gosh. What if an intruder had gotten to her again? But having learned my lesson over the past fourteen months, I dialed 911 and whispered my address.

"Stay on the line," the dispatcher said, so I tucked the phone into the pajama chest pocket. Then I grabbed the scrap length of two-by-four that I'd kept at the back of my closet ever since Miss Gloria's fright, and edged my door open.

"Get out! I've called the police!" I shrieked into the living room. "The cops will be here any second."

And as if to underscore how serious I was, the sound of sirens screamed from the direction of the police station across the bight. With the piece of wood poised over my head, I peered into the living room. A tall man in black jeans and a black T-shirt froze, looking terrified, with Lola in his arms. Lorenzo.

Miss Gloria burst out of her cabin, also dressed in my mother's Valentine's Day pajamas and brandishing a wooden rolling pin. "Lordy, lordy," said Miss Gloria. "What in the world is going on? You people could wake the dead."

"Lordy, lordy is right," I said. "The cops are gonna show up any minute. What are you doing here?"

Lorenzo's eyes widened with fear. "I swear I'll tell you all about it, but they can't find me," he said, clutching the white kitty to his chest.

"We've got to hide him," I said to Miss Gloria, my brain still fuzzy with sleep and the shock of being awakened abruptly. "The back deck?"

She shook her head. "That's the first place they'll look. Come here quickly. Leave Lola with Hayley." She grabbed Lorenzo's forearm and hustled him down the hall. Then she flung open the trap door that led to the cubby containing our bilge pump. Last December, we'd installed a new pull and oiled all the hinges so the door worked easily, so that even a small person like her would be able to push it open if she was ever trapped again. "It won't be comfortable, but it won't be for long."

He handed me the kitty and lowered himself into the pit. Then he crouched down, folded himself into a ball, and signaled for us to drop the lid. Because of his height, the door wouldn't quite shut, sticking up a quarter inch above the floorboards around it. Miss Gloria grabbed the heart-shaped rag rug that we kept on the floor in front of the kitchen sink and threw it over the opening. The kitty leaped out of my arms and dashed into the bedroom.

"There. Just don't say a word until we give the all clear," she called down to Lorenzo. "No coughing, no throat clearing, not even a hiccup."

We heard the clomping of boots on our outside deck, and then banging on the door. Miss Gloria and I both scurried over and peered out. Two cops in blue uniforms from the Key West Police Department were waiting, right hands on guns, left hands holding two oversized flashlights. I flicked on the outside deck light and opened the door. A few bugs fluttered into the pool of light.

"You called for help?" asked the bigger man, dark haired and lanky. The other man, smaller and rounder, stood a foot back, his eyes scanning the room behind us and the boats to either side, following his flashlight beam.

"I thought I heard an intruder," I explained. "But it turns out it must have been the cats." I pointed at Evinrude, who lounged full-length on the coffee table, looking appropriately mischievous.

"We'd like to come in and take a look around," said the smaller man.

"Oh, I know what you're thinking," said Miss Gloria. "I bet sometimes people call for help but they're being held hostage. And the hostage taker catches on to what's happened and tells them to answer the door but warns the prisoner: 'If you say one word about us, we'll shoot you in the head.'"

The cops exchanged glances. "Something like that," said the smaller cop, looking from her heart pajamas to mine. "You had an incident here last December, didn't you? Can we come in?"

"Of course," said Miss Gloria. "Maybe we can get you something to eat while you're casing the joint."

I glared at her behind the big man's back. The longer they stayed, the harder it would be for Lorenzo to remain quiet, crammed into that little cubby. And besides, I'd just foraged through the refrigerator and polished off the edibles. There would be very little of interest to an uninvited guest.

Neither one took her up on the offer of snacks, but they began searching through every space on our boat where an intruder might possibly hide, including the tangle of clothing and shoes that constitutes my closet. They finished by flashing their lights on the back deck, all through Miss Gloria's plants, where I'd foolishly imagined that Lorenzo would be safe.

We perched on the living room sofa, waiting for them to reappear. I buried my fidgety fingers in Evinrude's fur. The policemen clomped back down the short hallway, the bigger one tripping on the heart-shaped rug. Miss Gloria leaped up.

"Oh, silly me, we are always stumbling over that, too." She kicked the rug back into place, took his elbow, and marched him safely to the living room.

"I'm sorry we were a bother, Officers," I said. "I'm a friend of Officer Torrence, and he's always telling me,

'Call the police even if you're not sure you need help.' I have a little reputation for trying to do things myself." I pasted on a silly grin and bobbled my head.

"You may very well have had an intruder in here," said the big cop, his face looking fierce. "You ladies need to be more careful about locking your door."

"We need to get the latch fixed," said Miss Gloria, fibbing so quickly my head was spinning. "It just gave out this week. I've called a fellow to come do that and a few other odd jobs. But it's so busy on the island this time of year. They tell you they'll definitely be here and they don't show up. I'll tell him tomorrow that it's urgent."

"We're going to have a look up and down the dock, just to be safe," said the small, round policeman. "It's a good thing that you called. You should always call if there's a question. Trust your instincts. When women don't pay attention or don't want to raise a fuss, that's when they get into trouble."

I nodded vigorously and got up to show them to the door. For ten minutes we watched the flicker of their lights as they went up the finger, illuminating our neighbors' decks with beams of light. Finally, after waving as they passed our boat, they trooped back to their cruiser and drove off on Palm Avenue.

"Sheesh," said Miss Gloria. "I've never known them to be quite so thorough."

We hurried back inside to the hallway, removed the rug, and opened the hatch door. Lorenzo scrambled out. He was drenched in sweat, even his hair soaked into damp rings. And he was trembling.

"Coast is clear," Miss Gloria sang out.

"What in the world is going on?" I asked. "I'll get you a glass of water, and then come sit and tell us." I was beginning to realize that, as much as I wanted to protect Lorenzo, I was sick with apprehension about whether he might have done something terrible. Was this really the right thing—hiding him? I filled a glass with cool tap water and brought it to the living room, determined to squeeze the facts out of him. He was sitting on the couch with Lola on his lap. Miss Gloria was perched next to him, massaging his shoulder, which looked as hard as concrete. Lola sputtered her kitten purr—the only one of us happy and relaxed.

"I went to see your mother last night," I said, handing him the drink. "Might as well get that out on the table."

"I know," he said. "That's why I came. She said you were so worried. I feel bad about all of this."

"She mentioned something about protecting a girl. Supposing we start there."

"Or we could start with those wacky night vision goggles," said Miss Gloria. "Hayley here got into man trouble on account of those."

He cringed, then covered his face with his hands. After a deep breath, he dropped his hands back to Lola, buried his fingers in her fur, and looked at both of us. "It's all the same; it's all part of the same story. This girl—I'm loath to say her name because it was given to me in confidence—she came for a reading and she was very agitated. And I became worried about her, though not necessarily for the reasons she mentioned."

We waited for him to gather his thoughts, each of us with a cat on our lap, Miss Gloria and I in the goofy matching pajamas. "So she came for a reading," I prompted. "On Mallory Square?"

He nodded and took a sip of the water. "I noticed right away that she had an aura of danger around her."

"An aura of danger?" asked Miss Gloria. "What color is that?"

"Red," he said. "Of course. And then after I read her cards, which were very disturbing, she started to talk. She was keyed up, too, like she was on drugs, though I'm not certain that she had taken anything."

"What were the cards like?" I asked.

"Every dangerous combination you can imagine. Past, present, and future. Worse than anything you've ever drawn."

Evinrude dropped off my lap with a thunk and headed into the galley to hunt for stray kibbles. I hugged my knees to my chest. "And that's saying something."

"She kept alluding to the fact that she had done something dangerous, something illegal. And this obviously frightened her but also gave her a rush." He pressed one hand to his cheek and the other to his chest. "I think that's what upset me most. She was feeding off the danger."

"And then what?" asked Ms. Gloria.

"Then I suggested she come back the next night. I suggested that she slow down and think things over before she got too involved. And she did come back, a few more times. I thought we'd really forged a connection and were making some progress." He ruffled the white kitty's fur. "But then she disappeared. When I heard the news the other night about Bart Frontgate's death, I really panicked."

"I'm not following," said Miss Gloria. "Why would you think she'd murdered that man?"

"It's hard to explain. Just that the sense of danger—violence even—was so strong in her cards." He pressed a hand to his forehead. "I couldn't know for sure, of course, but murdering someone would fit with the level of agitation I was seeing."

"But then," I said, "the murder weapon turns up wrapped in your tablecloth."

His expression grew pained. "I couldn't imagine why she would divert the police in my direction, unless she killed him and then panicked. Maybe she chose to shunt the blame off on any reasonable target, even me. Or maybe she worried that I would turn her in. In that case, did she think that if I was in jail, I couldn't hurt her?" He looked so sad. "I would never reveal what she'd said. Since I'd gotten this information in a confidential relationship, I simply couldn't go to the police. What would I possibly say? I didn't know what she'd done or what had happened to her. When I thought of her, that bright red color kept coming to mind—the sense of danger. So I ran."

"That's not a long-term solution, young man," Miss Gloria said, patting his knee. "Why did you put those goggles in the cat food?"

"It won't make much sense to you," he said, keeping his gaze on his lap. "It barely makes sense to me. I got so worried that she'd panicked and done something crazy. So I went to her home."

I felt my eyes widen. "You broke in to her place?"

"I didn't break in; she left the back door unlocked. And there on her kitchen counter were the goggles. And then I got spooked by someone on the sidewalk outside and grabbed them and ran. And when I got home, I said, Marvin Junior, for the love of God, what have you done?"

I couldn't help snickering a little, because his voice sounded exactly like his mother's.

"So I stuffed them in the cat food bag so I could deal

with them later. And then the cops came sniffing around, suggesting I was responsible for Frontgate's death. I swear, I never meant for you two to get involved. I'm so sorry." His voice broke and he fought back tears.

"Well, you can't do much tonight—what there is left of it," said Miss Gloria, patting him again. "I think we should all try to get a couple hours of sleep. I'll bring you a pillow and a blanket and—" She looked at Lorenzo and then the couch. "You'll barely fit here."

"You can have my room," I said.

"Absolutely not," he said. "I'll be fine right here."

"We'll figure the problems out in the morning," Miss Gloria said. "Things are always easier in the morning after a cup of coffee. And maybe Hayley will make us some of those once-in-a-blue-moon pancakes. That will definitely improve our situation."

13

I don't have to tell you I love you. I made you pancakes.
                    —Kathleen Flinn, *Burnt Toast Makes You Sing Good*

I was the first one up in the morning, unusual for me. But Lorenzo's appearance and his worries about his client had churned through my dreams overnight. When it became clear that I wouldn't be able to drop back off for a couple of extra z's, I rolled out of bed. I fed the cats and then headed to the galley to make coffee and begin to collect ingredients for the once-in-a-blue-moon pancakes. These were not the delicate silver dollar pancakes of my youth, but rather a crusty, robust cousin. The kind of food that would stand up and roll out of the room if it didn't approve of the condiments served alongside it. Aunt Jemima fake syrup? *I'm out of here.* Margarine or other fake butter? *Hasta la vista, baby.* These were the kind of pancakes that would stick with a person through a long morning. And I had a feeling our whole day could be a long one.

I measured out the blue cornmeal, coarse like the sand used to make cement, and then added unbleached white flour, baking powder and soda, a little sugar, and salt. Into a glass measuring cup, I poured buttermilk and whipped in eggs and vanilla. Then I mixed both bowls of ingredients together and added a heap of blueberries. The chunk of butter I plopped into my cast-iron frying pan began to pop and sizzle.

Within minutes both Miss Gloria and Lorenzo were up and seated at the kitchen banquette. Lorenzo looked pale and exhausted. I poured them each a cup of coffee and went back to watching the stove.

"How did you sleep?" Miss Gloria asked Lorenzo.

"I didn't do too much sleeping. A lot of worrying," he said.

"We should make a plan, then," Miss Gloria said, slapping the table with her palm. "A plan always helps." All three cats jumped up on the bench and nuzzled Lorenzo.

"A plan sounds good," he said, as he rubbed each cat's head in turn. "But right now it feels impossible to come up with anything sensible."

"You should lie low," I said to Lorenzo as I flipped the first pancakes onto a plate and delivered them to the table with syrup and cinnamon butter. "It won't do any of us any good if you're arrested and thrown in the slammer. I'll talk to Eric while I'm at lunch and get his read on the situation." I squeezed Lorenzo's shoulder, trying to communicate caring—and more confidence than I actually felt. "You didn't really get a chance to see this the other day, but Eric's very empathetic and he can totally be trusted to keep a secret."

"I was also thinking," Miss Gloria said, "that if you didn't kill Bart Frontgate and this girl didn't, either, who did? Can't you tell us who to talk with at Sunset? We didn't have too much luck the other night, but you might have a better idea who we could approach. You know the characters. You understand the action."

"Let's go back to Bart Frontgate for a minute," I said, bringing another steaming stack of blue pancakes to the table. I served Miss Gloria first, then scraped a couple of them onto my plate, where I slathered them with cinnamon-scented butter and doused them in real maple syrup.

I took the first bite—loaded with texture and flavor. "Are they too gritty?" I asked.

"No, fantastic," Lorenzo said, and Miss Gloria, her mouth full, nodded her agreement.

"The only guys we really got to talk to at Sunset were the homeless men," I told Lorenzo. "And some new jugglers dressed like pirates and the man who makes hats. None of them were saying a whole lot. But if you could make some suggestions about who might be in the know, we'd follow up."

Lorenzo laid his fork down on his plate and swallowed hard. "I don't think it's a good idea to send you nosing into people's business. Some of those characters are very rough. And if one of them is a murderer . . ." His voice trailed off. "I don't want any part of putting you two in danger."

"Oh, we wouldn't actually try to arrest anyone," said Miss Gloria with a peal of laughter. "Just gather intel. You know, like undercover spies used to do when they were fighting the KGB."

Lorenzo put a hand to his forehead, glancing from Miss Gloria in her red heart pajamas to me in mine. "It would break my heart if anything happened to either of you."

"Well," said Miss Gloria, "suppose you lay out some cards and see what kind of trouble's in the future? Whether any of us are in danger? Maybe you could get tips from the other side?"

He snorted and began to eat again. "These pancakes are amazing. I love the blue color. And the texture. And that little hint of cinnamon. They make ordinary pancakes look like tissue paper."

"Thanks," I said, grinning. He was distracting us from Miss Gloria's question, but he'd get around to answering when he was ready.

When he'd powered through the remaining hotcakes and a second cup of coffee, he turned back to Miss Gloria, a sad look on his face. "My channels feel completely blocked right now. It happens when I'm scared, I think. I freeze up and forget to keep my heart open to what the universe is saying. And my mind, the place where I usually see things, is just a big white space. Nothing. I tell my clients—choose love instead of fear, and then your path will become clear. But it's so much harder than it sounds."

"We'll think of something," Miss Gloria said. She got up to clear the dishes away and refill our coffee cups for the third time.

"We can do some good old-fashioned sleuthing without getting into trouble," I said. "Especially if you give us some guidance. Who are your friends down there at Mallory Square?" I asked. "Who are the good guys? The guys we could chat with and tell them you'd sent us?"

"The fellow who owns Snorkel the Pig," said Lorenzo. "He's a decent guy. Pretty new to performing. So he's not involved in all the ugly politics that have been going on for years. But on the other hand, will he know anything? I'm not sure."

"What about Dominique the Cat Man?" Miss Gloria asked.

Lorenzo sighed, scraped a stray blueberry onto his fork, and popped it into his mouth. "He's smart because he stays out of the petty machinations of the rest of the Sunset Celebration. Have you noticed that he's always got a spot on the outer perimeter of the madness?" We both nodded. "He's earned it because of the show he puts on."

"He's very entertaining," said Miss Gloria. "And it's wicked hard training cats to do things. We tried with Evinrude and Sparky, and honestly we got nowhere."

"They got a lot of great treats for doing nothing," I agreed.

She wiggled her fingers and clucked her tongue to get Lola the kitty's attention. "Maybe with this new baby girl we'd have better luck."

"I don't know," I said shaking my head. "As far as I can see, Evinrude and Sparky are busy teaching her everything they know. And it's not all good. I saw her out yesterday teasing poor Schnootie to the point of apoplexy."

My cell phone skidded across the counter as it rang, and I got up from the table to answer. Torrence. "Good morning," I said brightly, though I was tempted to send it to voice mail.

"What's this about a break-in on your houseboat last night?" Torrence asked.

"I'm pretty sure it was an overreaction," I said. "You know how you're always telling me not to try to handle things by myself?" I glanced over at Miss Gloria and Lorenzo, feeling sick with guilt. But even more afraid I'd say something odd that would bring him rushing over. "So rather than attack a burglar on my own, I called nine-one-one. But I think it was just the cats banging around. We have a new kitten and they're all acting crazy. As I'm sure you know, your cops didn't find any sign of a break and enter, nor did they find anyone on the finger who shouldn't be here."

"You did the right thing," Torrence said. "Don't let the possibility of embarrassment keep you from doing it again, got it?"

"I got it," I said.

"That's not the only reason I called," said Torrence. He paused for a moment. "I'm hoping you can promise to keep this confidential. But I think you should know, so I'm taking the chance. If—or I should say when—we find your friend Lorenzo, aka Marvin Smith Junior, he will be under arrest for murder. I can't say exactly why; I can only tell you the case is quite clear."

"What do you mean you can't tell me?" I asked. "It's not quite fair to give me that information and no facts to back it up."

Torrence cut me off. "I can't say anything more. I shouldn't have said anything at all. But I'm hoping that you will keep this in mind if you're in touch with your friend. Encourage him to turn himself in. It will go easier for him if he cooperates, and that's not just a television crime show cliché."

"Thank you for calling," I said in a weird, high voice that didn't sound like me. "I'll let you know if I hear anything." And then I hung up and returned to the table, not sure how much to say.

As much as needed and nothing more, I decided. I

took Lorenzo's hand and stared into his eyes, noticing for the first time the wide pupils, surrounded by two concentric rings of rich brown. And then the tired lines webbing from the corners of his eyes that left him looking older than I figured him to be. I thought I knew him, but maybe I didn't. Maybe he had been driven to a heinous personal attack that I could scarcely imagine.

"I need you to tell me the truth. Did you kill that man?"

"No, I did not," Lorenzo said. "I did not." He pulled away from me and rubbed the fingers of both hands together. A washing motion. "But Cheryl Lynn might have killed him."

"Cheryl Lynn is your client?" I asked.

He bit his lip and nodded. "That's where I found the fork." He looked back up at me and then over to Miss Gloria, whose face was frozen with disappointment and dismay.

"What do you mean you found the fork?"

"On her counter," he said. "I cleaned it up and put it at the back of her silverware drawer."

This boggled my mind. "What fork are we talking about? And what the heck was on it?"

He groaned, a long, low noise like an animal in distress. "I don't know exactly. It looked messy. It could have been blood, maybe even from the meat Bart used in his act. But it just as well could have been spaghetti sauce. I told you about how I grabbed the goggles—I wasn't thinking straight. I wanted to help her in case she'd done something awful. So I cleaned it up and hid it in plain sight—with all the other oversized implements in her kitchen."

"But that's tampering with the evidence," I said. "You can't do that—it's against the law."

Lorenzo set his lips in a thin line. He got up and went over to the sink, where he began to rinse our breakfast dishes. "The ants will come if you don't wash that syrup off right away," he said.

"I suppose that lets out going to search her house," Miss Gloria said. "That was my next bright idea. But maybe we could take a quick look before the cops figure out it might be part of the crime scene."

"No, no, no," said Lorenzo, slapping the sponge down on the counter. "I can't believe she did it. And even if she did, it wouldn't have been at her home."

"Then why in the world would she have a bloody murder weapon?" I asked.

"It wasn't bloody, it was—it had something on it . . ."

"This has really gotten bigger than what we can deal with, even for a dear friend. You're changing the story every time we talk. You have to call Torrence yourself and turn yourself in."

"But—" he began.

"There's a murderer loose and you're protecting him. Her, I should say. And meanwhile, you're the main suspect in the investigation, sitting right here at our breakfast table." I pounded on the Formica, more upset than I'd been in a long time.

"What if we look for clues just for today?" he suggested, his voice pleading. "If nothing turns up that points us in the right direction, I'll drive over to the police station and turn myself in."

"You won't drive; I will take you," I said. "It's that or nothing."

The disappointment on his face was plain, but keeping him here any longer, even just the day, felt wrong. I no longer trusted what he said.

"You look tuckered out," Miss Gloria said. "Why don't you grab the first shower? Come on. I'll show you the ropes and get you a clean towel."

Lorenzo followed her to the bathroom while I washed the dishes and cleaned up the ingredients from the blue pancakes. The celebratory euphoria that I'd felt earlier, the kind of good feeling I get from helping a friend, was gone. I wiped the burners of the stove clean and wrapped up the leftover pancakes to store in the freezer for a snack at some future low-blood-sugar moment. I left a message for Eric, reminding him to meet me at Azur at noon, then pulled out a pad of paper and a pen and thought about making a list.

I pictured the Sunset Celebration and how hard it was to get the truth from unusual people with unusual lifestyles who had not a shred of a reason to trust me. Maybe a better idea was to take something irresistible to eat to a local, someone who'd been around town forever and who would've heard whatever there was to know about Bart Frontgate.

I heard the patter of the water running in our shower and Miss Gloria returned to the kitchen. "I have to take a shift at the cemetery in about an hour," she said. "I'm thinking maybe you should swing by after work and we could go look at this Cheryl Lynn's house."

"I don't think—" I started, but Miss Gloria cut me off.

"She could be dead in there and who would know? Lorenzo didn't look any further once he saw the goggles and the fork. He totally panicked. He swears she's in some kind of trouble, but definitely not murder."

"So what, she stole the murder weapon from somebody else's home and just happened to leave it lying around?" I asked. "If Lorenzo really washed it up and put it in the drawer, how in the world did it get in the Dumpster?"

"Well, maybe she threw it out after he was there," said Miss Gloria. "Or maybe he did and he's afraid to tell us. Anything is possible. And worse comes to worst, I get a ride home—instead of driving myself"— she grinned—"and then we can swing by Mallory Square and see if any of Lorenzo's friends are around."

Lorenzo emerged from the bathroom, his hair wet and his face worried. "I know you don't believe me, and I don't blame you for doubting, but I think Cheryl Lynn is in some very dark trouble. And by trouble, I don't mean she murdered someone."

Either he really believed this, or he'd memorized a couple of lines that he would parrot until he won us over.

"We have to trust him," Miss Gloria said. "His judgment is better than ours—he's psychic."

"And while I was in the shower, I thought over what you said," Lorenzo added. "You're right. If nothing turns up by this evening, I'll go with you to the police station. I shouldn't have hidden the evidence. But you know this yourself: You see something that doesn't belong, that doesn't feel right, and you respond. You just act without thinking."

Not much I could say about that. More than once, he'd seen me shoot off like a pressure cooker with a blocked steam release valve.

"But who is this Cheryl Lynn?" I asked. "Could she possibly have had a reason to take the fork used to stab Mr. Frontgate?"

His face looked even more worried. "Drugs, I suppose. If she was really high, she might steal. That would fit with the craziness I'd seen during her last couple of readings. And that awful red color." He shuddered and Miss Gloria patted his back.

"But maybe it wasn't drugs at all. Maybe it wasn't her. Maybe she just picked the fork up somewhere." He drooped into a chair.

"Oh, come on, what are the chances?" I asked. "Would you pick up a bloody implement?" Silence. Of course he would—he'd done exactly that.

Finally Lorenzo said, "Bart wasn't an evil person."

"How would you describe him?" I asked.

"He didn't think much about the people around him. 'Oblivious' is the best word, I guess. It probably took up all his energy, living on the edge as he liked to do." Lorenzo laughed. "Of course, you don't have to be terribly observant to realize that. He made his living on a high wire, juggling flaming forks."

"Good point," Miss Gloria said.

"And Cheryl Lynn, like I said, she liked the excitement of the edge, too. I could see that all over her cards. But I didn't notice anything that made me think she'd be a danger to others." He dropped his head to his hands and ran his fingers through his curls.

I noticed a few sprigs of silver that I hadn't seen before. Almost as if the last few days' worth of events had aged him beyond his years. "So anybody else at Mallory Square he didn't get along with?" I asked.

"Well, Louis. He's the guy who weaves those hats. They butted heads all the time. But Louis gets on everybody's nerves. But on the other hand, he knew exactly how to push Bart's buttons."

I studied his face. Was he telling us the whole truth now? "One more thing," I said to Lorenzo, determined to ferret out a lie if he'd fed us one. "Why in the world did you wrap that fork in your own tablecloth and then throw it in the Dumpster where anyone could find it? It just sounds dumb. Unless there's something else you're not telling us."

His eyes grew wide. "No, no, I swear I told you everything. I did not remove the fork from the house. I panicked and grabbed it and threw it in her drawer. Then I got out of there and started to ride my bike back home. The cops were stopping everyone who came from the direction of the cemetery. You know how freaked-out they are about catching the thief."

Miss Gloria nodded. "The longer the robberies go on, the more embarrassing it is for the police. Not to mention scary for the neighbors."

"They were stopping tourists, kids, even the iguanas," said Lorenzo.

Miss Gloria giggled, but I was finding it hard to see any of this as funny.

"It was only then that I realized my tablecloth was missing from the cart. I couldn't go back to look for it. And I was so sweaty and nervous, I'm surprised they didn't arrest me right on the spot."

"Which would probably have been for the best," I grumbled. "She may very well have been the murderer—you like to think the best of everyone. And we're the idiots who are hoarding information to keep the cops from solving the problem. If Wally ever gets hold of this drama, I won't have a job or a boyfriend."

"Hayley sounds harsh," said Miss Gloria, reaching around the rounded corner of the table to hug Lorenzo. "She's worried about you; that's all."

I made a face and headed for the shower. Then I spent an hour holed up in my room, tweaking the article about For Goodness' Sake that I'd started on the ferry last night. The mood I was in probably colored

my review, because I didn't find all that much positive
to say. I raved about the burger and the tempura and
the beautiful night on the boat, winding up with a
semihopeful suggestion that seeing as it was early in
the season for this restaurant, things would likely get
better. And that Valentine's Day was probably not the
best night to judge anyone's food. And that I was looking forward to trying dinner there again.

Which I wasn't. There was a major contrast between
this opening night and the one I'd experienced at Edel's
restaurant, Bistro on the Bight, last December. Edel was
the kind of chef who wanted every detail taken care of.
Who wanted every bite memorable. For Goodness'
Sake, on the other hand, gave the impression that good
enough was fine. That the Japanese-style food was a
gimmick because maybe the chef otherwise couldn't
cook.

Then I gathered my things together, stuffed them in
my backpack, and tapped on Miss Gloria's bedroom
door, where we'd agreed that Lorenzo would hide out
for the day.

"I'm going to Azur with Eric," I told him. "And then
Miss Gloria and I will noodle around town a little bit.
You should probably be thinking about how you plan
to word your confession. Because I think that's where
we're headed. To the police station." I frowned. "And
be thinking about exactly why you hid the goggles, and
why you cleaned the bloody fork. Because that's sure
what I'd like to know."

14

After all, life-changing work experiences come and go. But homemade meatballs and red sauce are forever.
— Ann Mah, *Mastering the Art of French Eating*

By the time I reached the tiny parking lot at Azur, I was beginning to dread the lunch with Eric. I was pretty sure the food would be good, and Eric's company is always welcome, but it would be painful holding so much back from him.

He was waiting inside by a big potted palm, the waiters bustling around him, preparing for the lunchtime rush. After we'd bussed cheeks, the host led us to a table on the porch. As with many places in Key West, the restaurant made the most of a small space on a busy street, ending up with a spot that looked cozy and tropical. Before the host could slip away, I ordered a basket of eggplant chips with fleur de sel and rosemary honey, along with Mediterranean mussels and tater tots bravas with salsa diablo. We refused his offer of bread: We couldn't afford the empty calories, no matter how fresh it was.

"You seem tense," Eric said right away with his head cocked, looking puzzled.

"You're onto me," I said, trying to force a smile. "As usual I'm worried about my job. And where things are headed with Wally. It must get old listening to the same old, same old stories." I tried to keep my voice light and solid like a wall that his curiosity could bounce off. Luckily, he was professional enough to get the message and to respect my privacy.

"Have you heard anything from Lorenzo?"

"Not a word," I said, crossing my fingers under the table. Childish, but I hated lying to my dear friend.

"And your mom?" Eric asked.

"Going crazy." I grinned. "Her baseline anxiety is pretty high, as you know. She's taking awfully good care of Sam, but I think she can't wait to get back down here."

The waiter delivered our pre-meal nibbles, followed soon by the main dishes I'd ordered. Eric sampled the gnocchi bathed in short ribs sauce and pronounced them amazing. "It's kind of cool that they cook winter dishes even when it's eighty degrees here."

"This would really go over big in New Jersey, wouldn't it?" I asked. "I think they're getting another ice storm tonight, or so my mother said." I paused for a minute to jot some notes about the food in my iPhone. "Have you ever had one of the Mallory Square street performers in your therapy practice?"

He looked up, surprised. "Where'd that come from?"

"I've been thinking a lot about Lorenzo. And that got me to thinking about the other folks who appear for Sunset every night and what their lives are like. And what their psychology is like. Even the homeless guys are a little easier for me to wrap my head around than those performers."

"I haven't ever treated one," said Eric. "I would guess there's a fair amount of alcohol and drug abuse. Those performers have to get themselves ramped up every night. And this is not like a Broadway show or big-name concert where they're being paid regardless of how they perform. These guys rely on the hat being passed."

"And there's nothing much to bind them together as a group," I said, "so it doesn't surprise me that they've had trouble negotiating a new contract with the city. It's more like a bunch of individuals fighting to make their way than a real functioning community."

"You're thinking about Frontgate's murder again."

I nodded. "It can't be Lorenzo. He's too kind, too gentle." I felt a spurt of sadness. Because who knew what lurked underneath that kindhearted exterior? "I am so hoping it doesn't turn out to be him."

After we'd tasted all the dishes I ordered, we asked the waiter to wrap up the leftovers for Eric to take home to Bill and the dogs. "You didn't have much of an appetite," the waiter said as he cleared the nearly full plates.

"The eyes-bigger-than-stomach problem," I said. "But the food was wonderful."

The truth was I didn't have an appetite. Which had something to do with the blue moon pancakes sitting heavy in my gut, and something to do with the over-sized secret hiding out in Miss Gloria's bedroom.

"What are you up to the rest of the day?" Eric asked. "I hope you're not having to eat dinner out, too."

"Probably not. Haven't thought that far ahead. I'm

going to buzz over to the cemetery. Miss Gloria is being trained as a tour guide and she wants me to be one of her guinea pigs. I went the other day and she's having so much fun with it." Somebody else wouldn't have noticed the change in my voice.

"It must be hard, though, with her being in her eighties," Eric said. "Hard not to think about mortality."

I nodded, throat constricted, wiping my face with a white linen napkin to cover the tears that had filled my eyes. "I realize that any of us could go at any moment, but some are closer to the last curtain call than others."

Eric patted my hand. "We're due to shake off the blues and schedule a martini night at Virgilio's. Or a beer at the Green Parrot," Eric said. "I'll check the list of bands coming this weekend and text you what looks good."

We strolled out into the blanket of warmth radiating from the sidewalk and I headed south and east on my scooter toward the cemetery. Miss Gloria doesn't carry a cell phone regularly, and she wasn't standing outside the sexton's house as we'd agreed earlier. So I parked and went in. Jane Newhagen, her boss, was poring over handwritten records that had been spread across a long table. She looked up with a big smile.

"Your roommate is out memorizing gravestones and the stories that go with them. She's amazing. Most people her age would be content to sit in a rocking chair in front of the television, but she's the most enthusiastic new guide we have."

"She's amazing, all right," I said. "Can you point me in her direction?"

"Better yet, I'll show you the way," said Jane. She got up from the table, straightened a few stacks of records, and followed me out into the bright sun, locking the door behind her. "The sexton is giving a talk to the new class of Key West Ambassadors," she said, noticing me watch her lock up. "Most people wouldn't do any damage in here, but there's always the one who might wander by and decide my vintage paperwork would make a good souvenir." Her eyebrows raised, she shrugged. "We're all a little on edge with the cemetery burglar business."

"What's the latest on that?" I asked.

"There hasn't been anything new in the last few days," she said. "The police have been working with the homeowners association—folks who live around the cemetery. And they're sending out regular e-mails to keep people informed."

"More like keep them from freaking out?" I asked, and we both laughed. "I'd be happy to hear any family stories you don't mind telling me as we walk," I said. "Until Miss Gloria came to work here, I never really thought of how much is buried in the cemetery." I snickered. "I mean I know there are bodies."

"But there's history," she said. "So much wonderful history." She waved at a worn stone that was listing to the left. "This is Sofronia Bradley Hall. Her claim to fame is that her husband was a game warden who was murdered because he was trying to protect endangered birds from poachers. They were killing birds to grab feathers for women's hats."

"That's awful," I said. "Not being married to a hero, like Sofronia, I'm going to have to do something important to get included in your history."

She chuckled and pointed at another set of stones, which looked familiar.

"Oh my gosh, that's the murder-suicide grave. Miss

Gloria told me about them the other day. I think it's horrible that they're buried together."

Jane shrugged. "Probably that was arranged in happier times. The story goes that they were fighting, probably drinking, and he shot her and then finished himself off by drinking carbolic acid."

"So he punished himself," I said. As we continued to walk, the diminutive shape of Miss Gloria emerged. She was standing in front of the wedding cake monument, where six layers of crumbling concrete were settled on a brick base. On the short end of the cake, a white marble marker was etched with the initials WWR and MMR.

Miss Gloria said, "If I do well enough in the stock market the next few years, I'm going to make a donation to renovate this grave site. It's so gorgeous—it's criminal to let it fall apart like this."

"Donations gladly accepted," said Jane, swishing her ankle-length skirt.

I left the two of them chatting about what the grave site might look like if it was updated, and wandered two plots over to the Gates family plot. On the far side, behind a black iron fence, I spotted another family plot by the name of Mastin. I called over to Jane. "Is this is the same family as the fellow who just opened the floating restaurant?"

"Yep, that's the one," she said. "They've been around this island forever, too."

"How do you score a plot in this cemetery?" asked Miss Gloria.

"Not that you're going to need one anytime soon," I scolded her.

"Of course not," she said. "Of course not. But planning ahead saves your family a lot of trouble when the time finally comes."

"Unless you're willing to join the others in the condos," Jane said, pointing across the cemetery to a group of cement crypts near Olivia Street, "getting buried here is not that easy. Obviously there isn't any free land around for expansion. But sometimes a family will sell their property because they've moved away from Key West. Or maybe their ancestors thought everyone would want to be buried here, but they're planning something else. That's how I got my plot."

"We'd love to see it," said Miss Gloria.

"Sure," Jane said, and beckoned us to follow down the main path.

I smiled automatically, but I didn't really want a tour. The whole cemetery thing was creeping me out. Even when I tried to think of it as fascinating history, the present realities of age and inevitability crept into my mind.

So I stayed behind to study the names in the Gates family compound, thinking that somewhere in here must be a hint about Bart Frontgate's life, and from there, his death. As I leaned against the metal fence that separated this plot from the one next to it, a sudden flash of movement drew my attention. A scaly three-foot creature with spikes running down its back and a third eye disappeared into a sinkhole under a flat crypt. I screamed. The two ladies came running. "What's wrong?" asked Miss Gloria, her chest heaving and voice aquiver.

"I swear a giant lizard slithered under that crypt." I pointed to a hole under the slab where he'd disappeared.

"It's the darn iguanas," Jane said. "They wouldn't harm you; they're mostly herbivorous. You probably scared him more than he scared you."

"I doubt that." I felt my heart beating so hard I could almost see my shirt move. "They don't smell so good, either."

Jane grinned and shrugged. "They like it here because it's quiet and they can lie in the sun on the gravestones and soak up the heat."

"And then they keep house under the graves?" I asked, taking a few steps away from the gaping hole under the crypt cover. "That's kind of gross."

"Hayley's not a cemetery person," said Miss Gloria, cracking a grin. "I'm going to get her out of here. But I'll see you tomorrow." She linked her hand through my arm as we marched down the path. "I'm not leaving until we've at least looked at the outside of that girl's house. Maybe she's home and she can answer all our questions."

15

Miss Gloria and I mounted the scooter and drove two blocks to Cheryl Lynn's address. The house looked quiet and abandoned. The trash can and recycling box were empty, tipped over in the driveway, and the small yard's grass was longer than that of the houses around it.

"We should probably tap on the door before we go blasting in," said Miss Gloria.

"Of course we should," I said, though I hadn't exactly thought of that. We left the scooter on the street and scuttled up to the door.

Miss Gloria knocked lightly. We listened: no footsteps, no radio or TV, no scrabbling of a dog's feet on the wood floors. Hard to say whether we were being watched by any of the neighbors. The homes on either side looked slightly run-down, not the kind of neighborhood where houses had been renovated and resold to wealthy outsiders by profit-hungry contractors. Not yet, anyway.

"Let's go around the back," said Miss Gloria. "That's how Lorenzo got in. He said it wasn't locked. But I wonder if he locked it behind him."

"I thought we were just looking." I planted my hands on my hips.

"We are." She pushed her way past a pale gray palmetto and some overgrown philodendron, her feet crunching on the oystershell pathway. I followed. A wind chime made of broken glass bottlenecks spun and jingled as we went by. There was a pocket pool in the backyard, with only a green scum of water at the bottom, overrun by weeds.

"Whatever she's up to, she hasn't been doing much yard work," said Miss Gloria. "That's one big advantage of life on a houseboat. No lawn maintenance is expected."

"Yeah, but you'd be out there trimming if you did have a yard. You'd never let things go like this. Your little back porch looks a thousand times better than this yard."

"Either she's wrapped up in something else, or she's a renter and not responsible, or she doesn't care."

"Or she's on drugs and doesn't see it," I added.

We stepped up onto a small, weathered deck, furnished with one cheap plastic green chair. I held Miss Gloria back and peered through the door's window.

Then I tapped on the glass. After a few minutes, I said, "She's not here."

"Or she can't answer." Miss Gloria reached around me and rattled the doorknob. The door swung open. "I consider that an invitation," she said, a wicked grin on her lips.

"Just don't touch anything," I said. "Torrence would kill me if he knew we were in here."

"We are checking on a friend," said Miss Gloria as she barged past me into the kitchen.

Once inside, my nose wrinkled up, matching the grimace on Miss Gloria's face.

"Kind of stinks in here, doesn't it?" she asked. "Like no one's emptied the garbage in a long while."

The air in the house felt hot and close, and I was sure that didn't help. I grabbed a paper towel from the roll on the counter and opened the cabinet under the sink. Sure enough, the garbage was filled to overflowing. At the top of the bag, I saw onion skins and an empty package of bacon. Without digging any further, I closed the door and checked out the sink. A frying pan shimmered with grease, and on top of that were stacked coffee cups, plastic water glasses, a plate with streaks of egg stuck to it, and dirty silverware. A stream of ants filed from the sink to a crack in the Formica, and then into the silverware drawer, which hung open at an awkward angle. The fork Lorenzo had insisted that he'd placed at the back of the drawer was not there.

"I don't think she's been here in a while," I told Miss Gloria. "Let's take a quick look around and then go on to Sunset." Miss Gloria pattered up the stairs to the second floor and I took a sweep around the living room, which appeared messy without being dirty, except for the full ashtray that contained cigarette butts and several marijuana cigarette roaches.

"Come look what I found." Miss Gloria's voice reverberated down the wooden stairwell. I trotted up the stairs and into the bedroom, which took up the entire second-floor space and had probably been recovered from an attic. If it had felt hot downstairs, it was a 450-degree oven up here. Using the sleeve of her sweater, Miss Gloria opened the top drawer of the dresser. It was crammed to the top of the wood with jewelry, men's watches, and a pile of iPads and iPhones.

"I swear, she *is* the cemetery burglar," I said. "The question is how to get Torrence and his guys in here to discover this without telling them we made it here first."

"There's another question," said Miss Gloria. "Where's this girl run off to? And why and why and why?" She pointed to each of the piles of items in turn.

We closed the drawer behind us and returned down the stairs and out the back door, as we had come. Then we slunk through the overgrown bushes and out into the sunlight and my scooter. I buckled on my helmet. "That would certainly explain the goggles. And unfortunately means that Wally was right. The fork is still a mystery."

"I've got a full-blown case of the creeps," said Miss Gloria.

"And I have just the tonic for that," I said with a big smile, trying to appear more cheerful than I felt. "Dominique and his flying house cats."

"Wheeeee!" she said as she vaulted onto the back of the scooter, looking more like eight than eighty years old. "I love that man!"

We buzzed down the island to Mallory Square and parked near the Waterfront Playhouse. At the end of the pier near the water, tourists were streaming onto an oversized cruise ship that piped calypso music over all of Mallory Square. I wondered how many of them were relieved to climb back on the mother ship and how many wished they could stay on our quirky island. Quite possibly, the ones who'd stayed in the lower Duval Street quadrant were happy to leave. Confining a visit to Key West to those bars and tacky souvenir shops doesn't give the kindest impression of the city.

A few of the Sunset Celebration performers had begun to stretch out their black ropes to mark off their territory and get ready for the night ahead. We crossed over the tiny bridge, past the aquarium, and then passed the trolley bar, where the bartender was making a big container of mojito mix. A second cruise ship was starting to chug away from the pier. Directly in front of the Westin, in the shade of the departing ship, the Cat Man was unloading his equipment and cages of cats.

"Dominique!" cried Miss Gloria.

He whirled around, poised to launch into his usual wacky routine, consisting of jittery movements, French words, and demonic laughs. But when he saw it was her, he opened his arms and ran over for a hug. He held her at arm's length.

"How are you, my dear? You look even better than usual."

She blushed and blinked her eyes and drew me forward. "This is my roommate, Hayley Snow. She's watched you a million times, but I'm not sure you've met."

I shook his hand, grinning from ear to ear. "We are

such big fans of your show and your cats. We've tried to teach our own kitties a few tricks, but we don't have the touch."

"Are you purrrrfectly in tune with the universe?" he asked with a crazy cackling giggle.

"Working on it," I said, snickering back. "On a more serious note, we were wondering if you'd heard any news about Bart's murder."

He shook his head, eyes narrowing. "That situation is a very sad comment on the status of the island and the Sunset Celebration. We all know who did it, but proving it—that's the problem."

"You know who did it?" asked Miss Gloria.

"But of course," he said brushing his silver curls away from his face. "The demon cocaine."

I sighed. "But the demon cocaine couldn't have stabbed Frontgate in the chest."

"So true. But his dealer could have. Or a dissatisfied customer." Then he noticed a family studying his display of Cat Man T-shirts, which hung on a rope near the cat cages. "Excuse me? I have zee customers." And he twirled away, kicking up his heels to show off his yellow cat kneesocks.

Miss Gloria and I rounded the corner back to the main part of Mallory Square, which was starting to bustle with performers and tourists. The cruise ship had pulled away from the pier, leaving only eddies in the water, and probably trash on Duval, to mark its presence. The section of the pavement that had been reserved in earlier days for Bart's impromptu memorial now housed a father-and-son team of zombie jugglers. I jogged over to flag down the older of the two.

"I take it they've released Mr. Frontgate's plot?"

The man stared at me, one cheek twitching. "It wasn't doing him any good, now, was it?" he asked. "And it was a downer for the tourists. And we were next on the waiting list." He jutted out his chin, as if to say he'd take me on if necessary. "So sad. But for once, the city commission got things right." He guffawed and turned back to his props. Fifty feet away we noticed Louis, the palm-hat weaver, screaming at another man. Hard not to notice him, really, and a crowd was gathering—some of them probably not sure whether this was a show, and others ready to egg them on, regardless.

Twenty yards or so away from Louis, another familiar figure moved toward the fight, wearing a not-quite-familiar costume. This fellow reminded me of Bransford, though, with the chiseled chin and bulging biceps. But this man was wearing sunglasses and tight jeans and walking a small brown-and-black dog, possibly a combination of miniature pinscher and Italian greyhound. The dog lunged from left to right, jerking his neck each time he darted to the end of his leash. No way that was Bransford.

Then Miss Gloria spotted him. "Isn't that your detective friend?"

"A forced acquaintance, more like. And that can't be him—he doesn't do pets. If he did have a dog, it would be a German shepherd attack dog or a combat-trained pit bull."

As I finished speaking, the little dog lurched at Louis, the palm-hat weaver. Louis kicked at the animal, yelping, "Get away from me, you nasty little cretin."

The Bransford look-alike let the leash go and charged at Louis, yanking his hands behind him and dropping him to the cement with a knee to the back. He glanced over and saw us. "Could you get the damn dog, please?" he hollered.

"It *is* the detective!" Miss Gloria cried.

I snatched the little animal up and tried to calm him as he shivered and quaked. "It's okay, honey," I said softly. "Daddy's just a little bit of a hothead."

Bransford dragged the weaver to his feet and barked into his ear. "How would you like to be taken to the police station and charged as a public nuisance? Maybe we could add open container in a public area to that. And how about this: suspect in a murder?"

"No way in hell I murdered that butthole," said Louis. "You ask the fortune-teller who really did it. He'll tell you it weren't me. And how would you like an accusation of police brutality, Mr. Thinks He's a Big Shot detective cop?"

Bransford took a shuddering breath and let the man's arms go.

There had been lots of noise in the past year—both on this island and off—when police were accused of carrying out their work more vigorously than the public believed was necessary. Even Bransford had to realize this was an ongoing and sensitive issue.

"You touch that dog one more time and I swear"—he bared his teeth—"I swear I will wring your skinny neck. Get out of here. And wipe that smile off your stupid lips. I don't want to see you back in the square tonight."

Louis shuffled off, muttering furiously. Bransford straightened his shirt and his sunglasses and came over to me and Miss Gloria to retrieve the dog. He nuzzled the animal's neck and whispered something I couldn't hear.

"Where did you get this guy?" I asked, stroking the

dog's shiny fur. "Are you supposed to be incognito? Did they tell you to carry a pet in order to look more approachable?"

Bransford glared and set the dog back on the pavement.

"I think it's probably his own pet dog, don't you?" Miss Gloria said. "They look very close. Very emotionally connected."

"Thank you, Miss Gloria," said the detective. "It is my dog. His name is Ziggy Stardust and I got him at the pound. Last benefit I worked."

"You volunteer at the pound?"

My mind whirled as I watched Bransford tip his chin and stalk off toward the water, the little dog trotting behind him. Did I know who *anyone* really was?

16

*Personally, I'd hate to think my last meal
was a plate of lettuce.*
                         —Roberta Isleib, *Preaching
                                    to the Corpse*

No way we'd be able to gather any more information
with Bransford watching our every move. And to be
honest, something about Louis really frightened me. Besides, it was close to sunset—time for Lorenzo to come
clean with the cops, and then let them mop up the con-
fusion. We forded against the tide of sunscreen-and-
beer-smelling crowds who pushed toward the water.

"I need to stop in the restroom again," Miss Gloria
said. "I never did have a camel's bladder, but now that
I'm middle-aged, it's the size of a thimble." She cackled
at her own joke.

"Fine. I'll be over looking at the Memorial Sculpture
Garden." I pointed to the garden, close to the road,
which was studded with busts of Key West notables
and shaded by dignified coconut palms. I walked
through the wrought-iron gate and began to browse.

Hemingway was here, and Harry Truman, and cigar magnate Eduardo Gato. Bart Frontgate's family was represented by his grandfather, William Gates, a sailing ship captain. Jackson Mastin, one of the original shopkeepers on the island, had been sculpted wearing a butcher's apron and a welcoming smile. I could see the resemblance to Edwin, the owner of For Goodness' Sake. And this reminded me that the Mastin family had a plot in the cemetery adjoining the Gates family's. Maybe he'd be a good person to chat with about Bart's early history on the island.

When Miss Gloria returned, we buzzed on home to the marina. Schnootie began to woof as soon as our sneakers hit the dock; her barking swooped into a crescendo as we got closer. Mrs. Renhart tried to shush her, without effect, then called out from her deck: "I think you have a gentleman in your boat—Schnootie warned me, and then I saw his shadow through your blinds. I almost called the police. I'm a little jumpy after last night. But then I thought, maybe it's Hayley's new beau. And wouldn't that be embarrassing?" Her last words tilted higher, inviting us to spill the dirt.

"That's my guest," said Miss Gloria with a regal smile. "Never too old to say never, right?"

We took advantage of Mrs. Renhart's openmouthed astonishment to retreat into our cabin. Lorenzo was waiting with a cup of coffee at the kitchen table. His hair stuck up at all angles and he had purple-and-yellow half-moons the color of old bruises under his eyes.

"Did you find anything?" he asked. "I'd offer you coffee, but your coffeemaker flummoxed me, so it's cold and bitter. Not recommended." He shrugged helplessly, a husk of the man he usually was.

"I'll make you a fresh cup," I said, and then put the

kettle on to boil. We wouldn't need a whole pot; I'd make him a nice, strong cup of drip coffee.

We sat at the banquette on either side of him. "We went to her house," Miss Gloria started. Then stopped. "Never mind coffee. Anybody for cheese and crackers and a tiny sip of beer?"

"Sounds good to me," I said. Lorenzo shrugged. While she rummaged through the refrigerator, I told him what we'd seen and found. "Cheryl Lynn obviously hasn't been there in some days. But we can't think of any explanation for all the stuff squirreled away except for this: She *is* the cemetery burglar." I patted his hand because he looked so immediately distraught. "That would explain the night vision goggles, too," I added softly.

"I was afraid of something like that," he said. "But I didn't paw through her bureau drawers."

Miss Gloria flushed the color of beets.

"For one thing, I probably didn't want to know. And I felt I couldn't disclose her secrets, as they were only my hunches. The more I saw, the harder it would be to hold everything in." He drew in a big breath and straightened his shoulders. "After you ladies have a bite to eat, maybe you'll run me over to the police station. Unless I confess what I know, I can't see another way the police will get this information. It's not fair for you to take the heat."

Miss Gloria returned to the table with a plate of Ritz crackers and a small slab of blue cheese from the Restaurant Store. I retrieved a bottle of Key West pale ale from the fridge and divided it among three glasses. Enough for courage, but no so much we'd turn up tipsy at the KWPD.

"Speaking of the cops," Miss Gloria said, "we ran

into Detective Bransford at Sunset. He was trying to go incognito with a little dog and skintight jeans. You should have seen Hayley's eyes goggle out. She couldn't stop looking at his arms. They are like sculpted marble, even I have to admit."

"Did not!" I said in an outraged voice, slapping her hand. She just smiled.

"I've been holding else something back," Lorenzo said, fixing his gaze on my face. "About you. I keep wondering whether to say something or keep it to myself and leave it for you to discover."

"You have to tell me. Now you have no choice!"

He pushed his little glass of beer away and fiddled with the coffee cup. "It's about Wally. And you. And Chad Lutz. I see you needing a strong partner. Someone who will insist on bringing out the best in you. Challenge you." He pursed his lips together, puffed a bit of air. "Not sure either of those men can do it. That's all."

"Lutz is nothing but a bad memory," I protested, waving the thought away with my fingers. "But Wally does challenge me. He goes over everything I write and insists that I make it better."

"Professionally, yes," said Lorenzo, touching his palm to my cheek.

"I don't want to hear this right now," I said, pulling away from him, clamping my hands over my ears.

"It does raise a question, though," said Miss Gloria. "If Wally is the right man, why is it taking so long for you two to get together?"

"His mom's been so sick; you know that," I said, grinding my jaw and refusing to admit there was any truth to this bomb. Refusing to think about why this felt like a funeral and a balloon ride all mixed up together. "And everything at *Key Zest* has been in upheaval. I'm going to text Torrence and tell him we're bringing you in."

We drove over to the police department in Miss Gloria's lumbering sedan in dead silence. I parked in front of the big pink stucco building and turned to face Lorenzo in the backseat. "We're going with you."

"You don't need to," he said.

"But we want to," said Miss Gloria. "Are you planning to tell them about the fork?"

"I think I have to."

She nodded gravely.

Lieutenant Torrence was waiting for us at the fountain. "I appreciate you coming in," he said, swinging the heavy glass door open. "We'll go up to the conference room, where we can chat. The others are waiting."

He led us down the hallway to the back of the building, where the elevator was located. We all four loaded on and stood facing the door, not saying a word, our worried expressions reflected in the polished metal.

"Straight down the hallway," said Torrence. "Hayley will remember."

I took off ahead of the others, striding the length of the hall to the conference room that overlooked the parking lot. Bransford was there, along with the chief of police, who looked somber and stoic. He must be sick to death of having accusations of incompetence leveled at his police force in the local paper and the locally based blogs.

"Have a seat," Torrence said as he closed the door behind us.

We sank into office chairs. Down the hall, we heard a series of sharp yips coming from the direction of Bransford's office. He must not have had time to drop

Ziggy off. I still couldn't believe he had a dog. And such a cute one. I would not look at him, not even once, I decided, as I felt a surge of heat sweep up my neck to my face.

Both the police chief and Detective Bransford crossed their arms over their chests.

"Hayley said—" Torrence began. "Wait. I don't think you all know each other. Let me back up and make introductions," he added, glancing at the three of us. "This is Detective Nathan Bransford; I suspect you already know him. And our police chief." He turned back to the cop side of the table. "And here we have Hayley Snow, resident food critic; her roommate, Miss Gloria; and our tarot card reader, Lorenzo Smith."

Lorenzo nodded formally at each of the men.

"Please go ahead," Torrence told Lorenzo.

"I did not kill Bart Frontgate," said Lorenzo in a low voice. "On that let's be clear. But I believe I have information about your cemetery burglar. And possibly some information bearing on the murder case."

"We'd like permission to record your confession," said Bransford, holding up a small recorder.

"He's not confessing," I said brusquely. "He said he didn't do anything. Did you not hear that?"

"As you like," said Bransford, not looking at me. "Do we have your okay to record?" he asked Lorenzo.

Lorenzo nodded. "Cheryl Lynn Dickenson is one of my clients," he began. "She has visited me on and off, but more recently it was more often. I'd say half a dozen times over the last few weeks. I grew very worried about what I saw in her cards and also the way she was behaving during the readings."

"Describe her behavior," said Bransford.

"Erratic," said Lorenzo. "Jumpy. Edgy but excited."

He heaved a great sigh. "So when she did not return as she promised several days ago, I went looking for her at her home. I knocked. No answer, so I went round the back. As the door was open, I went in." His expression hardened. "That might be illegal if you did it, but I went as a loving and concerned friend."

And then Lorenzo described how he found the fork in his client's kitchen, and then panicked, thinking he needed to protect a fragile being. So he rinsed it off and returned it to the back of her silverware drawer.

"The implement was bloody?" Bransford asked.

Lorenzo nodded, but then held a finger up. "Well, I wouldn't say bloody, but it wasn't clean."

"Exactly where was the fork?" Torrence asked.

Lorenzo fidgeted. "On the counter."

And then the fibbing came in. I watched his face carefully to see if he'd give us away.

"But I also saw that she had a drawer upstairs in her bedroom full of goods that looked like the things you've been describing in the crime reports," he said.

"Such as?" asked Torrence.

"Such as men's watches and some cash. And iPhones and iPods and mini iPads." He hung his head. "She also had a pair of night vision goggles, which I took with me and hid in my cat food bag. I can't really explain that." He glanced over at Miss Gloria and she nodded her support.

"You can't explain that? Why in the name of god didn't you call the police?" asked Bransford through gritted teeth. The police chief sat, watching all of this unfold, his neck cords pulsing with tension.

"Men like you won't understand this," said Lorenzo, "but my readings suggested she was in trouble. The constellation of her cards worried me deeply. Several times the Devil turned up in combination with the Tower. And I began to see her surrounded with a bright red aura. And that image got stronger and so powerful, those minutes I was in her home. I was afraid for her life and all I could think was to protect her."

"You're right," said Bransford. "We don't understand that. Because a normal person would consider the fact that this woman was a thief, best case. And in the worse case, a murderer."

Lorenzo shook his head. "I don't believe that."

"See, the police department can't operate on the basis of woo-woo hunches," Bransford said. He waited a moment. "Can you explain how the bloody fork got into the Dumpster where our officers recovered it later that same evening? Wrapped in your tablecloth?" Emphasis on the words *bloody* and *your*. He was such a bully. And poor Lorenzo was shrinking into his chair.

"I can't explain that. After I left her home, I pedaled home on Olivia Street," said Lorenzo, his voice a whisper. "Officers were stopping people at the corner of Eisenhower, but I was too upset to talk to anyone. I could only think things would get worse if they learned I'd been in her home. How would I ever explain?"

And now the heads of all three policemen were nodding.

"Help us understand your relationship to Bart Frontgate," said the detective. "There are video cameras on Mallory Square; you must know this. We saw you fighting with him just last week."

Lorenzo turned practically purple and fluttered his eyes. "Everybody fought with him—he was a most annoying man."

"What was *your* disagreement about?"

Lorenzo folded his hands on the table. "He was harassing one of my clients."

"Cheryl Lynn Dickenson?" Torrence asked.

Lorenzo nodded.

Bransford again: "So you were worried about her and went to her home. Is it possible that you wanted to save her, and this incident with stabbing Bart happened by accident? Is it possible that you blacked out and don't remember the sequence of events? A neighbor saw you leaving her home right before the fork was discovered."

"That's preposterous," I said. "You're fishing now."

"Then how did I drag his body to the bight?" asked Lorenzo, his eyes blazing. "And I can tell you right now, I do not own a boat."

"A very good question," said Bransford. "And I don't recall mentioning a boat." He looked at the other two cops and then back at us. "We are going to place your friend under arrest. Thank you for delivering him. Say your good-byes and the lieutenant will escort you out."

"But he told you everything—he didn't do anything wrong," Miss Gloria protested.

I squeezed her hand. "We need to go. He'll be okay. They won't do anything awful to him, because they know we'd investigate and scream bloody murder." I wished I'd used a different description. "Detective Bransford sounds like a tyrant, but this department knows better than to let him run the whole show." I glared at Bransford and then said to Miss Gloria, "We can be more useful if we go home and find him a lawyer."

"Call my mother, too?" Lorenzo asked. "Tell her

where I am. She won't be surprised. But please, she doesn't need the gory details."

We both hugged Lorenzo, and then Lieutenant Torrence ushered us to the ground floor and out into the night. "I promise I'll call you with any news I can share," he said. "It feels lousy, I know, but you did the right thing."

"You're right, it feels lousy," I said, my voice cool and unfriendly.

"What's on your calendar for tomorrow?" I asked Miss Gloria on the way home. Just to make conversation, because she must have been feeling as flattened with exhaustion and disappointment as I was. I would not soon forget the haunted look in Lorenzo's eyes as we left him with the phalanx of cops.

"Now that I know my way around the cemetery pretty well, I've started studying the meaning of the symbols on the gravestones," she said, her face brightening. "I'll be the only guide who can give a tour on that subject. Would you come over tomorrow for half an hour to listen to my talk? I know you don't like the cemetery as much as I do."

"You got that right," I said. "We'll be spending enough time in a cemetery for the rest of eternity. Why start early?" I forced a laugh.

Once we were settled back on the boat, I called Wally to tell him my article would be a day late because of Lorenzo's situation. I vaguely hoped he'd be bubbling with warmth or even offer to come over or take me out for a bite to eat or a nightcap—anything, really, that would demonstrate the spark that Lorenzo inferred was missing. But instead, he seemed distracted and distant.

"I'm glad the right thing was done," he said after

hearing my story. "Don't forget the staff meeting tomorrow. You can bring the piece then."

"I wouldn't," I said. "I was thinking about interviewing the owner of the floating restaurant before I write that review up—maybe ask him about what the permit process was like and get a statement from him about his exemption from the restaurant statutes. What do you think?"

"Maybe," he said. "We'll talk with Palamina about it tomorrow."

"I'm sorry about the other night," I said, staving off the end of the conversation. "You were right on that. And you missed the most amazing cake."

"I'm sure it was delicious," he said. "Have a good night." And hung up.

Then I called Eric, feeling really blue. "Lorenzo needs a lawyer," I said flatly. "The cops have him."

Once I had gotten the name of the lawyer Eric had used last year, and given him a brief rundown on the day's activities, I considered calling Mom. She'd be sick about Lorenzo's arrest. And then she'd ask about Wally. And talking about the coldness that had permeated the conversation with him would only make it feel more real. I'd phone her tomorrow.

17

The flat-footed key lime pie should be re-paired or replaced, and the poached fruit in a moat of sparkling wine was a little too Ladies Who Lunch for me.
— Pete Wells, "Expressing Himself with Joy," *The New York Times*

The next day dawned crisp and slightly brisk, with enough sun that the mercury would probably hit eighty by noon. There had been no news from Lorenzo, but I didn't expect any. I could picture him in his orange jumpsuit behind bars at the jail, a target for derision and bullying from other more seasoned and hardened inmates. Hopefully Eric's lawyer would manage an arraignment sometime today and extract him out of that awful prison.

I texted the owner of the floating restaurant, telling him I'd like to meet with him that morning to take a few photos before the review went live, and that I would love to chat with him for a few follow-up questions if he was available.

I had no idea what might be going on with Wally, but at least I could keep my i's dotted and t's crossed on the business side of things. Palamina had said she wanted photos, so she'd get them. Still, it seemed wrong to wait for her stamp of approval on every idea I had. This regime wasn't turning out to be that much of an improvement on the last.

Edwin Mastin texted me right back with a resounding *yes*. The truth is, most people in the business of selling something are desperate for publicity. I thought of an old advertising slogan: "Even bad publicity is good publicity." Or was it the best publicity is bad publicity? It didn't matter: He was eager to talk to me and maybe I could slip a few questions in about how well he knew the Gates family and Bart's history on the island while I was at it.

He was waiting for me on the dock in front of For Goodness' Sake, along with his wife. I snapped a few photos so I wouldn't be caught in a lie about the purpose of my visit. "Good morning," I called brightly.

"And it is a beauty." Edwin grinned. "But then it's almost always a good morning on this island." He pointed to three chairs set up on the deck with a primo view of the harbor, facing toward Edel's restaurant, the Bistro on the Bight. "I thought we should take advantage of the weather and chat out here."

"I hope you don't mind that I've joined you," said Olivia in a wistful voice.

"Of course not," I said.

We took our places and Edwin signaled for a man in a long white apron to bring us coffee—café con leche in white china cups with anchors drawn in the foam, and a small bowl of brown sugar cubes.

"Such a wonderful setting and such service," I said,

tipping my face toward the sun. "This is almost too pretty to drink." I dropped two cubes in my coffee, stirred, and took a sip. "That's delicious. Thank you."

"So how did you like your meal the other night?" Edwin asked after a few minutes of small talk. He reached over to put a firm hand on my elbow. "And don't feel you have to sugarcoat it. We know we have things to work on."

Olivia nodded gravely. "We want this place to be the best it can be."

I hemmed a little, then decided honesty was best. "First let me say I'm not a huge fan of Japanese food. I'm afraid I was ruined by years at the local Japanese steakhouse—anything too authentic seems odd. And I'll say that in the review and talk about how I try not to let my personal preferences color my opinions."

Edwin shook his head with a wry smile and took his wife's hand, her long, delicate fingers disappearing into his meaty fist. "But that's not really possible, is it?" she asked.

"Not really," I said, smiling at her. "We loved the burger; that was probably our favorite. Not so crazy about the bento box."

"We're taking that off the menu," she said. "Though we've had experience with authentic Japanese food, we shouldn't overreach."

"People don't necessarily visit Key West to have their palates stretched," said Edwin. "But we figured we'd start casting the net wide and then close in on the choices that people enjoyed most."

I nodded, though if I'd had a restaurant, I would have done it the other way around—start smaller, with perfectly executed dishes, and then try some more experimental food. But it wasn't my place. So I went on to describe the dishes we enjoyed, and which others, not so much. Edwin jotted a few phrases into his phone as I talked. This was not normal food-critic protocol, discussing a review ahead of time with the owners. Far from it—it probably bordered on unprofessional. But this wasn't a normal situation, either. Lorenzo was in jail, accused of murder. And I would go to whatever lengths it took to help clear his name.

"I was walking through the cemetery the other day," I said, looking at Edwin, "and I could see that you've come from one of the original Key West families. So you probably have some perspective about the ups and downs on this island."

"I don't know about perspective," he said. "But we sure have been here forever."

"Forever," Olivia echoed. "Sometimes I think it's past time we left—started somewhere fresh."

"Sounds like you have a question?" Edwin asked.

"One of my friends is implicated in the Bart Frontgate matter. I wondered if you had any thoughts about what happened or why Bart was killed."

Edwin plucked at his shirt, scraping off a splatter of something that resembled mustard. He looked up and smiled. "Sorry. I was helping the chef this morning and I should've put on an apron."

"I tell him that every time," said Olivia fondly, brushing at his collar. "But does he ever listen?"

"Frontgate has always been an enigma," Edwin said. "He wanted to be a star, but he never wanted to really work through channels." He rubbed his chin, gazing across the water. "I don't think he realized that he'd never achieve rock-star status as a street performer at Sunset." He looked back at me. "You probably know he insisted on that primo spot on the square."

I nodded. "I saw the memorial after they found his body in the water—with all the notes and flowers. Although by yesterday, already a new set of performers had taken over his section."

"It's valuable real estate. All real estate is valuable by definition on an island. Because it's finite. I bet we've got more real estate agents per square inch than anyplace else in America. All squabbling over the same high-end homes. Why should it be different with performers?"

"Or restaurants," I said, my eyebrows arcing.

"Touché." He laughed.

"But as you were saying," I said.

"He was not a nice man," said Olivia.

Edwin patted her back. "Agreed. As I was saying, he was a robber, really. I heard from my friend Rick—the guy who performs with Snorkel the Pig—that he put in an order for a Vietnamese potbelly himself. That's the best example I have. He sees how someone else is succeeding and tries to snatch it away from them. Or saw, I should say. The whole thing is very sad. But what else could you expect from a group of people who teeter on the edge of sanity?"

Which seemed a little harsh from one local to another, but why would I expect them all to pull together? "Enough about Bart. Last thing I wanted to ask was about the process of getting approval for a floating restaurant. I've seen quite a few articles protesting the food trucks, but not so much publicity about your concept."

"Her highness excepted," Olivia said, ducking her chin at Edel's place across the harbor. "We haven't gotten ten complaints because we've worked hard at doing everything by the book. Health inspections, workers' compensation—all that good stuff."

"The only thing we've skirted—and I can say this to you because it's not a secret—is the Historical Architecture Review Board," Edwin said as he shrugged. "Ms. Waugh would have skipped that, too, if there had been any way to work it out."

After I wrapped things up with the Mastins, I motored over to the *Key Zest* office. Only Danielle had arrived, which surprised me.

"Wally and Palamina had a business coffee this morning with the chamber of commerce," she informed me. "But they'll be back by ten for the meeting."

I grabbed a glazed doughnut from the platter on her desk and went down to my office nook to work. I tweaked the rough draft of "Paradise Lunched," summarizing the food from my visit to Firefly—which seemed like weeks ago—and yesterday's outing at Azur. Then I roughed in the section on the Vegetarian Café. I'd had lunch there with Lorenzo last week, so at least for this draft version, I could visualize and write up a few of the dishes we'd actually eaten. The bartender and the waitress had been so happy to see Lorenzo. They delivered extra artichokes on his pizza and a plate of sweet potato fries on the house. The memory made me heavy with sadness, rather than hungry, as I might have expected.

After finishing that work, I e-mailed the whole thing to Wally and Palamina. Then I thought about what Mastin had said regarding Bart and the other performing artists living on the edge of reality. Key West is definitely a place of flux, and in flux tempers can rise. But considering what I'd heard from the Florida history librarian, hadn't that always been so? Wasn't there always some new group discovering paradise and wanting to grasp it and keep it for themselves?

Twenty minutes later, my shoulders tensed reflexively as I heard Wally and Palamina come in. And then Danielle called down the hall to say the meeting was starting. I joined them in Wally's office, which appeared to be the office of both Wally and Palamina at this point. WallyandPalamina: one word, like a wedding couple's Web site. I pushed away a flicker of jealousy. The two of them were positively bubbling about the chamber of commerce meeting.

"I don't know why we never thought of this before," said Wally. He smiled at Palamina. "Brilliant idea: They loved us."

"They did love us," she agreed. "Because they are all about celebrating the city of Key West and drawing in new people, and so are we." She raised her hands over her head and waved them from side to side. "Wheeee!" Then she cleared her throat. "But back to business. Hayley, tell us about your articles for this week's issue."

"I'm just about finished with 'Paradise Lunched,' which by the way is a brilliant title; thank you," I told Palamina. Buttering her up couldn't hurt. Right? She certainly liked it when Wally called her brilliant. "I sent you the draft. If I have time, I'll make one more stop at the Vegetarian Café, although I could practically recite what's on the menu without going." I grinned at Wally, who'd eaten there with me more than once. His return smile was barely there. "And I've made good progress on For Goodness' Sake. In fact, I stopped by for an impromptu visit this morning just to chat with the owners about what it's like setting up a floating restaurant." I paused and bit my lip. "I kind of had to tell them about what I'm putting in the review, but that won't change what I was going to say. Not much, anyway."

"Hmm," said Palamina, nibbling on her own lip. "That's not what Paul Woolston would do, I don't think."

The restaurant critic for the *New York Times*. Invoking his name in a critical comment gave it much more heft than it would have otherwise.

She wrinkled her forehead and looked at Wally. "Do you feel it's okay to run it if she's contaminated the facts?"

"I don't think 'contaminated' is quite fair or accurate," I protested.

"It will be fine," Wally said. "Hayley has good judgment in these things, and if we don't like it there's always a red pencil."

They snickered together and went on with the agenda, Wally and Palamina clicking through the bullet points. Even Danielle was full of ideas. She'd been working on the e-zine's Pinterest boards and was especially proud of one called "Key West, the Character."

"Take lots of photos when you're out doing research," Palamina told me. "Danielle can use some help in this area." I nodded and scribbled a note to myself. Team player. Buck up, cheer up, and take pix. WallyPalaminaDanielleHayley. I'd be all over it.

"You're so quiet, Hayley," said Danielle. "Everything okay?"

"Stomach's a little queasy after last night. Probably got a bad clam."

"Where did you eat?" Her carefully shaped brows drew together with concern.

"It's a metaphor," I said, and smiled with hearty reassurance. "I'll be fine."

When the meeting had concluded, everyone full of excitement except perhaps for me, Danielle excused herself to run to a doctor's appointment, and Palamina hurried off for her meeting with one of the city commissioners.

"Could I have a word with you?" Wally asked as I started toward my office cubby.

"Sure," I said, and sat back down in the chair where Palamina had been sitting. My chair, before she came on board.

He got up and closed the door behind me. "I'd like to put something out there. It's not written in stone, but I thought I should tell you where I am."

My stomach clenched up and I knotted my hands together, trying to keep a neutral expression. Something rotten was coming. "Sure, I always want to hear what you're thinking."

He nodded and tweaked his lips into something resembling a smile. "I think we should call off the personal relationship between us right now. Concentrate on business."

"Oh my god," I burst out before I could think. "Are you seeing Palamina?"

"Oh, Hayley." He reached across the desk and took my hands and squeezed. "Of course I'm not seeing anyone else. Certainly not Palamina. That's not it at all." He sat back in his chair. "I just feel like now is not the time for us. *Key Zest* could really be on the cusp of something special. I feel more excited about our magazine than I ever have. And I want you to be part of the team. And I don't think our relationship and *Key Zest* can work together. Surely you see it, too?"

How could I answer? I obviously couldn't beg him to reconsider and not drop me like a steaming spud. And besides, all the things between us that we hadn't addressed were flashing through my mind. His mother sick, mine very much alive and needy. My job hanging on Palamina's approval, his secure. And the balance of power that could never be quite right between us, with me as employee and him as boss. And the heat between us fading like a tableside flambé.

And, I had to admit, I loved him as a boss: funny, insightful, brimming with new angles and appreciation for my work and my humor. As a boyfriend, he hadn't really stepped up.

"I see it," I said. "I'm just sad about it. That's all." And then I got up and walked out.

18

You can put your boots in the oven, but
that doesn't make them biscuits.
                    —Traditional Southern saying

Walking down the short hall to my office, I could hardly
catch my breath. I snatched up my backpack and hurried down the stairs, fast enough that my friend Cory
in the real estate office below couldn't flag me down for
a chat. As I ran, I thought about where I might go and
not run into a bunch of people I knew, and then be
forced to make pleasant chitchat about anything at all.

The West Martello Tower gardens on the Atlantic
Ocean came to mind. This is one of the most peaceful
spots on the island, with an amazing display of tropical
foliage overlooking a small beach and then the long
turquoise stretch of the Atlantic Ocean. The surrounding beaches and streets would be teeming with visitors,
but I should be able to find a solitary spot in this garden. I buzzed over on my scooter and at the entry to the
fort, pushed past a small group of elderly tourists and
into the thickly planted recesses of the grounds.

Barely registering the blooming orchids and the grand old trees and the weathered brick remains of the fort overlooking the Atlantic, I sat on one of the stone benches for a while, trying to inhale the calm and push thoughts about Wally and Lorenzo out of my head. A phone call came in from my mother, but I let it go to voice mail.

Half an hour later, feeling a little more normal and collected, I bit the bullet and called Mom to explain what had gone on with Lorenzo the night before.

After a string of worried questions, most of which I couldn't answer, she asked, "Where are you now? Make sure you give that sweet Wally a hug for me and tell him I asked about his mother."

"Will do, but I'm taking my coffee break at West Martello garden," I said. "Say, you and Sam should put this place on your list of possibilities for your wedding. They have the cutest little gazebo overlooking the water. But it's pretty inside, too, all red brick with tons of orchids, in case you hit bad weather on your big day."

"I am a million miles from wedding planning," my mother said. "At this point in our lives, we'll be thrilled to make it to the grocery store. I suspect you and Wally will get to the altar well before we do."

"Doubtful."

She shifted into doting and psychic mother mode. "Oh, sweetie. What's going on?"

"Nothing really." I sighed. "Literally nothing. I'm pretty sure I've been dumped, but so nicely that I can't be sure. I'll let you know as soon as I figure that out." Obviously, I had been dumped. But it seemed better all around to ease her into this news.

She uttered some reassurances that neither of us believed, and then more credit to her, she signed off rather than quiz me about the details of what had just happened. We hung up and I left the calm of the garden to head over to the cemetery—a different and less comfortable kind of quiet.

I waited for Miss Gloria at the sexton's office as we'd planned. The cemetery is larger than you might imagine, crisscrossed by a grid of roads covering a big city block. So no point in striking off to hunt for her; there was nothing to do but wait. I texted her in case she'd brought her phone and tried not to think about what had happened in the staff meeting. I inhaled the scent of freshly cut grass, listened for the sound of a leaf blower in the distance, and felt the sun beat down on my head.

But my inner child wanted to scream, "I've been dumped—it's not fair!" over and over and over. I pushed the thoughts away again, this time trying one of Lorenzo's techniques—something he would suggest to his clients while he was shuffling his deck of cards. A meditation of gratitude.

"Think of all the people in your life for whom you are grateful," he'd say, "and notice them one by one in your mind."

My mother. My father and stepmother. Mom's boyfriend, Sam. My stepbrother, Rory. Miss Gloria. My friends Connie and Ray. Wally.

Tears immediately welled up in my eyes. Before I could start bawling and embarrass myself in public, I spotted Miss Gloria making her way down the path that led to the office.

"Sorry I'm late," she called, breathless. "I was having a little chat with Jane about reconstruction of some of the monuments and where my money could be best used if I leave them some funds in my will."

I groaned. "That gloomy thinking again."

"No," she said, "it's thinking ahead. Everyone should do it, even a young sprite like you."

"I can barely keep track of what's on my plate in the here and now, never mind the hereafter," I said, giving her a little squeeze as we began to walk. "So tell me what you've learned."

"It's very cool," she said, her white curls bobbing with energy. "Almost like reading Lorenzo's tarot cards. You can kind of tell what was on people's minds, and how they felt about the deceased person, and how well they had worked through the grief about the death. The saddest monuments are erected after a child has been lost. The carved lambs and cherubs."

"Terrible," I said. "I can't imagine."

"The saddest one in the whole cemetery may be the angel facing the cherub across a plot of stones. Do you remember seeing that?"

I shook my head. "Maybe you'll take me by."

"The angel sits on Mary Navarro's tomb. She was only forty-four when she went. But her daughter died four years earlier, at the age of nine. So the tomb reads, 'To the sacred memory of a brokenhearted mother.'"

"That's brutal," I said, following her down a worn path shielded by shade trees and bristling with bromeliads. How I wished she'd taken a normal volunteer job, like helping with the Friends of the Library's book sale or the animal shelter or even showing off gold coins and other treasure at the Mel Fisher Museum, for heaven's sake.

"I was sad when my sweet Gordon died," Miss Gloria went on, "but he had a good life and we had a good, long marriage. But a baby, oh my. That child never had a chance to figure out the first thing about life. Who she should be and where she might go." She whirled around, narrowed her eyes, and took my hand. "Imagine what your mother would have missed, never seeing the woman you turned out to be. What a talented and loving person you are. I feel that way and I'm not your mother. I'm your roommate." She dabbed her eyes with a tissue and swung out ahead of me. "Come on, I'll show you the angel."

This was turning out to be a very emotional day.

After she described the meaning of the sculptures and engravings on half a dozen monuments, we approached the double family plot where I'd seen the iguana yesterday. The gamey smell seemed to have grown stronger, strong enough to make me gag.

"Something smells awful," I said. "And this heat isn't helping."

"Iguana poop," said Miss Gloria.

"It would have to be one of heck of a big reptile, a lot bigger than the one that scared me yesterday. Do you smell it? It's like something died here." I covered my nose with my hand. "Unless a whole pack of the darn things moved in overnight."

"It does smell funky," said Miss Gloria, pinching her nostrils together.

I pointed to the crypt, close to ground level, where the cement had heaved, leaving the opening.

"Maybe I should call Jane over to check it out," Miss Gloria said.

"I'll run up and get her," I said.

"It'll be faster if I text her," said Miss Gloria. She

whipped her phone out of a voluminous pocket and tip-tapped furiously on the keyboard with a little stylus. Within minutes, Jane arrived at the grave and Miss Gloria explained that it appeared the odor under the tomb had gotten stronger.

"I saw our gravediggers and that nice stone mason, Isaac, working on the other side of the cemetery about an hour ago," Miss Gloria said to Jane. "Can we ask them to come over and see if they can push the cover off this crypt?"

Jane laughed. "Nothing's quite that simple around here. We certainly can't dig up a grave without the owner's permission."

"But what if the owner is dead?" I asked. "Isn't that how it works by definition? The owner of the plot dies and gets buried?"

"No, it's the living family's property. But I brought a flashlight," Jane said, pulling a black light out of her backpack. "Before we make a big fuss, let's take a look and see if we see anything."

We crept closer to the grave and she shone the beam into the crevice. A large green iguana darted out of the hole, causing us all to screech in unison and leap backward. I tripped over the wrought-iron gate and crashed to the ground.

"Are you all right?" Miss Gloria asked.

I did a quick body scan and brushed the dirt off my palms. "I'm fine—I don't like those animals. Not up close, anyway."

Jane tapped a hand to her chest. "That got my heart racing." She grinned. "So we definitely have an iguana infestation. I can call the nuisance animal patrol and see if they'll put out some traps." She squinted and rubbed her forehead. "But you're right; I've never known them to smell this bad."

The cherub statue that Miss Gloria had described to me earlier flashed to mind. As the odor mushroomed, so did my imagination. I thought about the child-sized statue Miss Gloria had shown me. And then how when I was kid, I liked to hide out in small spaces that felt like private little caves. I studied the hole—was it possible that a small child could have crawled in and gotten trapped? I blurted out, "What if a kid hid in there and—"

"Don't even say it." Miss Gloria held up her hand.

"That's it, I'm calling Lieutenant Torrence," I said. "This is creeping me out. Maybe he'll be willing to bring some officers over to take a look. Would that do the trick? Can you open a grave if the police suspect there's a child in jeopardy?"

"You can call," Jane agreed with some reluctance. "It can't hurt to have them look. The sexton's out of town until tomorrow. I'll let know him what's up. And I'll run back to the office and get the owner's name and number. When the cops get here, if they need to do more than look, they'll be able to call for permission to open the vault." She started off toward the office, then turned to face us again. "Miss G, if you don't mind, see if you can track Isaac down? It wouldn't hurt to get his opinion about what it would take for the guys to open things up."

As Miss Gloria headed along the path to find Isaac the mason, I called Torrence and explained the issue.

"Do you have any idea how busy we are here?" he said in a short voice. "I cannot possibly come to the cemetery. Every single one of my officers is out on patrol. Not just on patrol—actively working situations."

"Have you had any reports of missing children?"

The silence on his end told me the answer. "I can see if Bransford has fifteen minutes."

I groaned.

"It's him or nobody."

"Him, then." He might not believe I'd stumbled on a police emergency, but I felt it in every cell of my body. We could not, and should not, handle this ourselves. Someone with proper authority had to investigate.

Miss Gloria returned with a wizened black man, as thin as a rail, with ropy arms and of uncertain age—somewhere between fifty and ninety. "This is Mr. Isaac," she explained. "And this is my roommate, Hayley."

"Nice to meet you," we said in unison.

Miss Gloria and I perched on the cement-block wall opposite the in-ground crypt and watched as Isaac poked around the bottom edges of the grave. "Nothing obvious is wrong here," he said. "Other than the iguana markings, it doesn't appear that anyone's been digging. But it does smell worse than Mount Trashmore." The Stock Island dump. He wrinkled his nose.

Within minutes, I saw a police SUV bump onto the sidewalk near the north entrance to the cemetery. Bransford got out and strode toward us. "This better be good," he said when he arrived.

Before I could answer, Jane steamed back from the office, two city workers in tan uniforms huffing behind her. "The grave belongs to the Mastin family. They bought this plot some years ago when the first one filled up. They haven't had the need to replace the old grave, so they just left it as it was. Edwin is on the way over from his restaurant, but he said go ahead and open it up if you feel it's absolutely necessary."

"Who the hell knows whether any of this is necessary," Bransford grumbled.

Isaac moved forward to chip a little cement that had been used for previous makeshift repairs. Then he helped the city workers slide the heavy lid off the grave. Once they had settled it on the grass, Isaac and the head worker crouched down and peered into the hole.

"There's not a damn thing here," said the worker, adding under his breath, "As if we didn't have enough to do already."

Bransford borrowed one of their shovels and poked around the interior, dislodging a brown animal even bigger than the green one that had frightened us earlier. The animal puffed up his head, hissing and bobbing as he bounded out of the grave. Bransford leaped back, yelping an obscenity. I stumbled away from the grave site and stationed myself across the road to avoid anything else with four legs and scales scrambling in my direction.

Edwin Mastin pedaled up on his bike, his face red and his shirt collar damp from the ride over.

"What's the story? Is there a problem with my property?"

"Nothing but damn iguanas here," said Isaac, who now stood by the wrought-iron fence.

"Sorry to have troubled you for no reason," said Bransford. He brushed his hands off on his pants and then waved Mastin closer. "We jumped the gun on opening things up. Seems like your plot is going to need some work."

"It was time we did some repairs anyway," Mastin said, his big hands on his hips, looking down at the hole.

I leaned against a crypt designed to stack three deceased family members, one on top of another, watching the men try to put the grave back together. I decided that the leaf-blower noise I'd heard earlier was more likely a wood chipper; probably one of the local landscaping companies trimming and grinding up palm fronds. The flat gray clouds scudding above the horizon made the sky look more painted than real.

Gradually the terrible odor I'd smelled earlier registered again, this time even stronger. I stood up straight and turned to peer at the multilayer crypt. The top layer had an opening, a couple of inches wide. There seemed to be scrape marks around the square seams. The edges of the block did not quite line up, almost as if it had been removed but then shoved back into place in a hurry. On closer inspection, the left seam was damp. Could that possibly be a whisper of blond hair sticking through the crack?

I crouched to the ground, took a couple of shuddering breaths, and tried to convince myself I was just jumpy. This was a cemetery, after all. People were buried here. Bodies belonged here. And some of the funeral parlors on the island probably had a better handle on the fine points of embalming than others.

Should I speak up again or leave it alone? Even from thirty feet away, I could see the annoyance creasing Bransford's face. In the end, I heaved myself up from the cement block I perched on and crossed the road closer to him.

"Excuse me?"

"Yes?" he asked, his voice icy with challenge.

"I wouldn't blame you if you don't believe me, but something's very wrong over there. Two seconds, can I show you?" I started back to the crypt, hoping he'd follow. "The smell is coming from that grave. And someone's been working on the cement. And I'm afraid that there's hair—"

He jogged around in front of me to look at what I'd found. "Don't touch it," he said. "Move away right now."

19

Bransford whistled to get the attention of the city workers, who had finished piecing together the lid on the
other crypt and reloading it onto the grave. They were
heading toward the Frances Street entrance of the cemetery. As they ambled back to the grave site, Bransford
called over to Jane and Isaac.

"Would you consider it normal for something to
leak from one of these containers?"

"Absolutely not," they said in unison, and hurried
over to join us. Bransford extracted a small flashlight
from his belt and began to shine it around the cracks of
the tomb. Jane took her bigger light out and shone it on
the stone too.

"Do you see what I was saying?" I asked as his gaze

approached the section where I'd seen the dampness. In the light, it almost looked like drips.

"I see it," he said brusquely, moving his body in front of the structure like a human shield. "All of you stand back and stay where you are."

"We weren't going anywhere," I muttered. "We're not all idiots." No wonder all those raging anticop letters ended up in the paper. He treated civilians like enemies. I watched the beam of his flashlight pause and hover over the inches on the left side where I'd imagined I'd seen the hair. The blond strands glinted in his light. He took a few steps away and whipped out his phone.

"I need backup at the cemetery. Now. Possible four-one-nine."

Which I knew—from keeping too much company with cops—meant "dead human body." Common enough in a cemetery, but the dispatcher must have had the sense not to make a bad joke and point that out.

Bransford described our location, and in the distance, a siren wailed in astonishingly quick response. Within minutes, our area of the cemetery was swarming with cops. Torrence roared up last and did not even look at me as he stormed over to Bransford.

"I didn't do a thing wrong," I said as he passed by. "You won't find my fingerprints on that tomb. Everything by the book." He ignored me completely.

Edwin Mastin rolled his bike over to stand with me. "What in the world is going on now?"

"We're not sure," I said. "But the terrible odor I thought was coming from the grave site in your plot seems to be located here"—I gestured at the stone edifice—"and the cops seem to be preparing for the worst."

He scratched his head. "Meaning what exactly?"

"Something's stuffed in there that doesn't belong." I lifted my chin toward the grave. "I think there may be an extra body in that tomb. Something newer than the burial date engraved on the stone."

He frowned as he glanced around at the gawkers who had clustered behind us, standing on graves and leaning on gravestones. "I know this place is a big draw for tourists, but sideshows like this make the idea of closing the cemetery to anyone who doesn't have relatives buried here seem appealing."

We stood watching with Miss Gloria while the police talked with Jane and Isaac. Then the city workers were waved over and they set about discussing how to pry the front cover away without disturbing either the grave or its contents.

By this time, a crowd was pushing closer to the crypt. There were tourists in flip-flops and shorts and crop tops, a small gaggle of elderly women who had been tracing grave etchings in the Jewish corner of the cemetery, and even a couple of homeless men carrying ragged packs. The uniformed cops began to herd everyone back, barking at the gawkers to get off the graves nearest the crypt. As fast as the police pushed them back, the rubberneckers wormed closer in.

Using tools that looked like oversized chisels, Bransford, Isaac, and one of the city workers pried the front cover off the crypt. I didn't know whether to protect my ears against the loud scraping of metal against stone or shield my nose from the odor that mushroomed from the crypt, stronger and stronger. But when the square of stone had been removed, I wished I had covered my eyes. I would never be able to unsee the collapsing face of the woman who had been stuffed inside; the rats' nest of blond curls, the blurry tattoo circling her upper arm, the black rope dangling from her neck. And worst of all, the bugs. Everywhere bugs scuttling to hide from the sudden light.

"Don't even look." I tried to spin Miss Gloria around. But her gaze was focused on Edwin Mastin, whose face had turned into a slack-jawed mask of horror.

"It's Cheryl Lynn," he gasped, and then rushed forward. At the last moment, he was repelled by a wall of blue. Torrence grabbed his arm and towed him back.

"You need to get away, sir," he said gruffly.

"It's my goddaughter," the restaurant owner said to Torrence. "Oh my god, it's Cheryl Lynn." He dropped to his knees and began to sob.

As the presence of the decaying body and the distraught man registered, the police grew deadly serious about clearing the area. The tourists and the homeless men were escorted out of the cemetery and the iron gates clanged shut, closed to any further traffic. Pictures were taken, yellow crime scene tape unfurled, and I was cut out of the pack as a witness.

"Either wait for me at the sexton's office or get a cab home," I called to Miss Gloria. "I don't think I'll be long. I don't really have anything to tell them." Although I knew from past interactions, the amount of information a person thought she had did not always correspond to the length of time spent getting interrogated.

Bransford and a lady cop pulled me aside.

"Why don't you take a seat?" the cop asked, and pointed to the cement-block wall surrounding a group of small marble stones. A vase of faded plastic roses stood sentry alongside a miniature American flag.

"I'm fine," I said, gritting my teeth against the queasiness of my stomach and legs that felt like cooked noodles.

"Did you know there was an extra body in that tomb?" the cop asked.

I swiveled to look at Bransford, my eyes narrowing. "Of course I didn't know that. But I could smell something terrible. I explained that to the detective here, but it took him a while to believe me."

"That's not exactly how it went. First we had the employees dig up another tomb at her suggestion," he explained to the lady cop. "It wasn't like we weren't doing anything about what she reported. But she's not always a credible witness."

"I tell you what I notice," I said in a soft, fierce voice. "And I can't help it if I notice a lot. And I can't just close my eyes and ignore things. How long might it have been before you guys found this body?"

"How do you know Edwin Mastin?" the lady cop asked me, pointing at the distraught restaurant owner who was now talking to Lieutenant Torrence.

"I don't really know him well," I said. "I've interviewed him for an article I'm writing about his restaurant. And we had dinner at his place the other night. It's that new boat on the harbor." I was grateful to have something else to focus on, even if it was a foodie rant. "The menu is kind of pseudo-Japanese—they're still finding their way with the right mix of dishes—"

"Thank you, Hayley," Bransford cut in. "We can't be sure about the identity of the victim until the medical examiner has a chance to confirm it. But do you know this person named Cheryl Lynn?"

I did a quick mental assessment, trying to figure out how much to say. I knew of her, but I didn't know her. That was the truth. And that's what I told them. "Lorenzo knows her, as I'm sure you're aware," I added. "He had some suspicions that she was the cemetery burglar." Oh lordy, he had told them this bit of news, hadn't he? I couldn't remember what had happened when. Had I just thrown him under the bus?

"This would explain why there haven't been any new reports this week," muttered the cop to Bransford. And to me, she said, "We will probably need to talk to you again."

"Detective Bransford has all my contact information," I told her, not looking at him.

As I stalked away, Lieutenant Torrence beckoned me over. "I'm sorry you had to see that," he said.

"I'll get over it," I answered in a breezy voice, though I wasn't at all sure I would.

"Your friend Lorenzo was released from jail this morning," he added. "There was a concern about him being a flight risk, but he's got a good lawyer and someone posted a whopping bond. And this is unusual, but the barrister promised that Lorenzo would stay with you until the trial date. Eric Altman assured them this arrangement would work. I wouldn't be surprised if he's waiting there now."

"That's fine," I said and mustered a cheerful smile. It seemed weird that they'd send him to our place, but I'd do anything to help. He would be devastated by the news about Cheryl Lynn. I knew he'd take her death as a personal failure. "We're happy to have him."

"The thing is, this"—Torrence waved at the cluster of policemen still gathered around Cheryl Lynn's body—"changes everything. All the money in the world isn't going to spring him from jail this time."

"Thanks," I said, and reeled away to find Miss Gloria.

20

The next morning my roommate made us pancakes, and we three ate them while she tried to deduce what had happened. None of us really knew.
                    —Linnie Greene, "Crossing a
                    Threshold and Not Looking Back,"
                          The New York Times

By the time Miss Gloria and I had parked in the Tarpon Pier lot and trudged up to our houseboat, Eric had arrived with Lorenzo. Lorenzo hugged us like a starved man would embrace a sack lunch. He was probably famished, if the chow at the Stock Island prison was anything like that in Miss Gloria's favorite TV show, *Orange Is the New Black*. We settled everyone into the kitchen banquette and I put on water for coffee. Miss Gloria took out a bag of oatmeal-raisin cookies that we stashed in the freezer for emergencies and loaded them onto a plate. Neither one of us said a word.

Eric narrowed his eyes as I brought mugs of coffee

to the table. "You two don't look so good. Like there's been a death in the family."

Miss Gloria gulped. "There sort of was."

They both looked worried now. I perched next to Lorenzo and took his hand with both of mine. "We've had some terrible news. Cheryl Lynn was murdered."

"And her body was stuffed into an empty crypt in the cemetery," Miss Gloria added.

His hands flew to his mouth and a couple of tears squeezed out of his eyes and started to run down his cheeks. "Oh my god," he said. "I wasn't wrong about the red. I'd never seen a color that strong." He got up and strode out to the back deck, the screen door banging behind him. He crouched down among the potted herbs and tomatoes, his face in his hands, making low noises like an animal in pain. The three of us remaining exchanged glances, and then Miss Gloria hurried after him.

"What can we do for you?" she asked through the screen. "Do you want some company?"

He shook his head. "Maybe in a bit."

"Let's give him some privacy," Eric said in a low voice. "Maybe sit out in the sun until he's ready to talk?" Miss Gloria nodded and followed him out to the front deck with the cats. Only Lola stayed behind, rubbing her face on the back door screen, watching Lorenzo mourn.

"I'll be here in the kitchen," I called after Eric. Though I hardly needed to tell him that—everyone knows that cooking is how I handle stress. Heading to my short shelf of cookbooks, I pulled out my recipe for hazelnut fudge. This was an easy recipe, simple to make yet bursting with flavor. It didn't need baking, just a couple of hours in the refrigerator. And if Lorenzo stayed here for a while, we would need it later. It was the kind of treat that said, "You deserve this lump of sweetness. We love you. We're so, so, so sorry." Half-frozen oatmeal-raisin cookies simply couldn't do the same job. They couldn't shoulder the same emotional load as organic hazelnut fudge sprinkled with pink sea salt.

From the front deck, I could hear the murmur of Miss Gloria's and Eric's voices as I warmed the chocolate hazelnut mixture with butter, sweetened condensed milk, and chocolate chips in the top of my double boiler. Every few minutes, snatches of their conversation floated in—Miss Gloria's description of a symbolic cemetery ornament, her amazement about the mass of police gathered around the tomb, and her sadness about the way Edwin Mastin had broken down after seeing his goddaughter.

Finally the back door squeaked and Lorenzo returned to the kitchen from the small deck where he'd been sitting. "If you don't mind," he said, "I'd like to hear the whole story."

"Absolutely. Could you please stir this for a moment?" I asked, holding out a wooden spoon coated in chocolate. "I'll get the others."

I came back to the galley with Miss Gloria and Eric and got them settled at the kitchen table. Then we told the two men exactly what had happened in the cemetery earlier. I described the iguana's nest, the terrible odor, and how the workers had removed the cover of the low crypt but found nothing.

"I backed away to watch from a distance," I said, "because Bransford was there and he was so darn cranky. I was leaning against this triple-decker crypt and the smell was overwhelming." I wrinkled my nose, reminding myself not to be too graphic, for Lorenzo's sake.

"But then I saw something leaking and some blond hair and so I called the police over. Bransford, of course, didn't want to believe me. But it was pretty clear there was something wrong with that crypt. So they pried the cover off and found the woman. I wouldn't have known her"—I stopped myself from saying she was virtually unrecognizable because of the shape she was in—"because I don't know her. But Edwin Mastin was there. His family owns the plot where the first tomb was dug up and they needed his permission to open the crypt. This time around, the cops didn't ask anyone. As you can imagine, Edwin was just sick when he recognized Cheryl Lynn."

"Cheryl Lynn was his goddaughter?" Eric asked.

Lorenzo nodded. "I don't think they're related by blood, but I believe she was a close friend of his daughter years ago, before she died. I think he tried to take her in and look after her a little, as a replacement. The problem is, she had been wild for a number of years." He looked terribly sad. "There wasn't anything Mastin could've done to save her from herself."

"And the same goes for you," I said reaching for his hand again. "We know you feel responsible. You tried to help her—but she wasn't ready to change." I exchanged glances with Miss Gloria, and we both looked at Lorenzo. "You need to tell Eric the rest."

After a moment, Lorenzo told him about Cheryl Lynn's house, taking the fork, and hiding it back in a drawer. Following a few minutes of dead silence, he looked up from his neatly folded hands to Eric. Eric's face had changed from sympathetic to angry as Lorenzo told the story.

"Why? Why would you put yourself out there like that for some woman you barely knew?"

Lorenzo said, "I would think that you of all people would understand the power of empathy."

"But tampering with the evidence was illegal. Why would you threaten your own reputation and a murder investigation?"

Lorenzo looked pained. "First of all, I wasn't certain it was a murder investigation. Second, surely psychologists have ethical boundaries. You can't run around spilling what your clients have told you. It's the same in my profession."

"But in this case, you were lying to the cops to protect someone who was involved in dangerous, illegal activities. And now she's dead."

Lorenzo heaved an agonized sigh. "You have to understand that I have Chiron in my ninth house."

"What the heck does that mean?" asked Miss Gloria.

"Chiron, also called Pegasus the wounded warrior, is strong in my chart."

Eric said, "So you can heal others, but not yourself."

Lorenzo nodded, his eyes unfocused as he looked across the living room to the cats grooming each other on Miss Gloria's reclining chair. "My emotional work will last a lifetime. My birth mother was an addict. I was taken away from her at one and a half and eventually adopted by the Smiths."

"Oh," I said, shocked by this news. Though it answered some questions. Like why he was so desperate to help this troubled woman. And the lack of physical resemblance to his parents. "I wondered why you didn't look like your dad. Like either one of them, really. Though that can happen in any family. And you have your mom's sweetness—"

"That's it!" Lorenzo knocked his fist on the table and sprang up. "I'm going to find the bastard who killed her."

Eric grabbed his forearm. "You can't," he said firmly, looking him straight in the eyes. "Lieutenant Torrence said you need to stay here with these ladies. That was part of the deal that your lawyer negotiated."

"I can't just sit still." Lorenzo's face crumpled. "I feel sick about all this. I should have pushed her harder to get help."

"There's no one who knows better than our psychologist friend," said Miss Gloria, "people can't get help until they're ready to be helped. You can't make someone change. Am I not right?" she asked Eric.

He grinned and blew her a kiss. "You are right. So if you can't go darting around the island looking for clues," said Eric to Lorenzo, "what you can do is help us think through what might've happened. Like who is this Cheryl Lynn? And how was she related to Bart Frontgate, if at all? And who wanted them both dead? Are there two murderers on the loose or did one person kill them both?"

"Two murders by two separate people is too much of a coincidence," said Lorenzo. He tilted his head and turned to me. "Did you say there was a rope? What did it look like?"

"Yes. It was black." I shrugged. "Thick."

"Thick like the ropes they use to mark off performance spaces at Mallory Square?"

"I'd say so." I glanced at Miss Gloria and she bobbed her head with confirmation.

"Crap," said Lorenzo, sinking lower into the banquette.

"How long do you suppose she had been dead?" Eric asked.

"At least a day. Probably longer. I'm no expert on body decomposition," I started, then closed my eyes against the memory of the insects, crawling, creeping, swarming.

"How high above the ground was the crypt?" Eric asked.

I looked at Miss Gloria. "Would you say four or five feet?"

She nodded, touched her hand to her chin. "Four sounds about right. Up to here on me. But why would someone hoist the body up and stuff it into the crypt? They went to a lot of trouble."

"The cemetery part makes sense to me," I said. "It's already full of bodies. So you might imagine no one would be looking for a fresh one. But the murderer didn't think about how it would smell."

"It had to be someone strong; Cheryl Lynn was not a small woman," said Lorenzo. "She was short but solid."

Eric nodded. "Someone strong. Or more than one person. Or someone made strong by drugs."

"Maybe it's too obvious," I said, "but I think we have to assume that the murderer could be one of the performers at Mallory Square. The thick rope around Cheryl Lynn's neck—that can't be a coincidence. And Bart Frontgate—he was the poster child for making trouble at the Sunset Celebration. Somehow he pulled her into something dangerous, and they both died as a result."

Lorenzo nodded his head vigorously. "I'm the best bet for talking with folks at the pier. They know me.

They're more likely to tell me the truth about what's going on. You ladies have already tried and you didn't get much out of them."

Eric held both hands open. "That may be so, but you can't go. Hayley and I will. We'll talk to Snorkel's father and anyone else you suggest. But you need to stay here with Miss Gloria."

Miss Gloria suddenly sat up straighter. "Mrs. Dubisson said something about calling hours at the Smokin' Tuna Saloon for Bart Frontgate this evening. Maybe you could swing back by after Sunset and talk to his family or friends."

"If he had any friends," Lorenzo grumbled.

I changed quickly into a pair of black capri pants, my best sequined sneakers, and a plain white T-shirt. This could pass as suitable garb both for the Sunset Celebration and for a wake at the Smokin' Tuna. I gave Miss Gloria instructions for defrosting spaghetti sauce with meatballs and told her I would text when we were on the way home so she could put the pasta water on. We hopped into Eric's hand-painted Mustang and headed down island.

21

The ephemera may include a frozen disc of dashi, intensely marine under tongues of sea urchin imprinted with yuzo kosho, a flare-up of citrus and chile . . . and day-boat scallop with green tomato Cryovaced to amplify its tang, anchoring a shallow whey broth steeped with kombu and bonito flakes.
—Ligaya Mishan, "Small on Space, Big on Flavors," *The New York Times*

As soon as I clicked my seat buckle and leaned back against Eric's leather seat, the exhaustion struck me. "I feel like a sack of flour," I said to Eric. "Pounds and pounds of King Arthur whole wheat. Not the white whole wheat, either; the heavy stuff."

He laughed. "I'm not surprised. You're doing a lot of worrying. And racing around the island like a crazy woman. And besides that, Lorenzo's troubles are real."

"What's your sense of his future?" I asked him. "Did you get any insight from the lawyer?"

"He couldn't tell me anything confidential," said

Eric, rubbing the side of his cheek with his thumb. "He had to fight to get him released. His mother mortgaged everything she owned to come up with the bond, including her retirement account. And if he's charged with this new murder, no amount of dollars will set him free."

I groaned. "I can't wait until this is over. And I mean over in a good way, not Lorenzo back in jail."

My smartphone chirped and Lorenzo's name came up on the screen. As if he had sensed that we were talking about him. Which I totally and completely believed. I accepted the call and put him on speakerphone. "I'm driving with Eric so I'll put you on speaker. What's up?"

"I remembered something else," he said. "While I was in jail, I did a few readings because two of the other guests recognized me from Sunset. And they told me some things about Bart Frontgate that I hadn't known."

"Like what?" I asked.

"Like he was feuding with Louis, the hat guy."

"What, Louis wanted his spot?" Eric asked. "I hadn't heard that he had any juggling talents."

"Not juggling," Lorenzo said. "Louis has been feuding with him for a long, long time."

I glanced over at Eric and shrugged my shoulders. This new information was too vague to be of much use, as far as I could tell. "Keep thinking," I told Lorenzo. "We'll be home soon."

Once Eric had shimmied into a tiny parking space at the end of Caroline Street, we made a beeline across Mallory Square to the home away from home of Snorkel the Pig. The pig's father, Rick, was dressed in a white shirt and a plaid vest and what appeared to be a golf cap, and his trim, prickly white beard matched the spiky hair of the pig. We joined the tourists who had gathered around to watch their act. After some introductory patter about how a fiftysomething man came to be performing with a pig in Key West, he began the show.

"Up, pig!" he shouted, and the pig stood on his hind legs and strutted several feet. The crowd whooped with delight. Then the pig turned in circles as his father sang "Old MacDonald Had a Farm" and ended the show by serpentining through Rick's legs, a move they had certainly seen the Cat Man do.

Rick and the pig bowed together. "Snorkel and I thank you for your patronage," Rick said, and then reminded the audience that Snorkel's well-being relied on the generosity of his patrons.

A number of children rushed forward to stuff dollar bills into a can with the pig's likeness pasted on the outside. Photos were taken with Snorkel and his dad and the visitors, for which another dollar was charged. When the last of the fans had cleared away, Eric and I moved forward.

"We met two weeks ago," I reminded Rick. "Hello, Snorkel; hello, Rick. We love your show." I reached out to stroke the cute dark patch on the pig's nose, remembering at the last minute that he didn't like his face touched. I clasped my hands together and managed a smile. "We were wondering if you've heard anything more about the death of Bart Frontgate."

He frowned, looking at me first, then Eric. And I realized my interrogation technique was less than smooth. "I don't understand why you're involved. Is this part of the official investigation? Are you deputies or something?"

"We're friends of Lorenzo Smith—that's all. And he suggested we talk with you," Eric said with a reassuring smile, holding his hand out for the man to shake.

"How is Lorenzo?" Rick asked, setting the diminutive pig down on the pavement and shaking our hands. "It doesn't seem right without him here. The vibes feel wonky, like something awful is about to happen and we're all unsafe." His face looked serious, as though he really meant this.

"He's out of jail," said Eric. "So that's a good thing. But there's some solid evidence that points to him as the guilty party."

Rick shook his head. "He's not a murdering kind of guy. He's not like most of the guys around here, who wouldn't hesitate to act on their rage." He flashed a lopsided grin. "Once he's mulled things over, he's able to let his anger go like balloons in the wind. I admire that in him."

"Has he been especially angry lately?" I asked.

Rick shook his head. "I'm sorry I can't help more, but I really don't have anything to add."

My heart sank so hard that I realized how heavily I'd been counting on him knowing something crucial. "There's been another death," I said to him. "A woman who may have associated with Bart. Does that sound familiar?"

"What did she look like?" he asked.

The image of the dead woman's face flashed through my mind, and I clenched my eyes and fists tight to fight a sudden wave of nausea.

"Deep breath," said Eric, touching my back.

I blew out the air caught in my throat, the way Leigh instructed me to do when I picked up a heavy weight at the gym. "On the short side, with blond hair, wavy.

Dark blue eyes, maybe even violet." How fast did a dead person's eyes change color? I shook that horrifying thought off, too. "Maybe a little chunky." Then another memory hit me. "She had a tattoo circling her upper arm."

He rubbed his chin, nodding. "Cheryl Lynn. The tattoo was from a song. 'I used to disregard regret, but there are some things that I can't forget.' She was trouble. If you didn't just tell me she was already dead, I might have said that she killed him. It wasn't a murder-suicide, was it? Now, that would fit."

"No." I shook my head. "No way that could have happened. But you're saying there was no love lost between them?"

"Sick love," he said with a grimace.

"Can you tell us more?" Eric asked.

"They were together, but not. Because of his act—you know, the daredevil-on-tightrope routine—he could pretty much have his pick of loose tourist ladies. The ones who came down to the island for a wild adventure. What happens in Key West stays in Key West. Or so these people seem to think," he added, then reached down to stroke his pig. Snorkel nuzzled him with his enormous pink snout and Rick fed him a treat.

"So what, she'd get jealous and pissed off?" I asked.

He nodded. "Exactly. There was a screaming fight about two weeks ago in the sculpture garden." He pointed down the alley past the Waterfront Playhouse. "She had the loudest, craziest voice and she went on and on. Almost like a two-year-old's tantrum."

"She was mad about another girl?" I prodded.

"A girl and maybe some stuff he was supposed to sell and give her half." He shrugged. "I don't know. It was so ugly and the noise was bothering Snorkel, so I went out the other way."

Eric handed him a business card. "Call us if you think of anything else?"

We started to leave, but I turned back. "One more question," I asked, "about Bart Frontgate's forks. Were they like regular barbecue forks? Like something you'd buy from Kmart or Home Depot in the household goods department?"

"Oh no," said Rick. "He had them specially designed. I don't know where he got the metal part, but he had the handles hand milled. They had to be just the right weight for the juggling act. So he didn't end up miscalculating his tosses and stabbing himself. Or any of the spectators." He laughed and slid his phone from a back pocket. "Here, I have a photo." He showed us a picture of Bart, tall, swarthy, and very much alive, holding a fork in both hands and grinning proudly. As Rick had said, the handle was a thing of beauty, heavy wood inlaid with what looked like ivory. "I think he had them made at a gallery up on White Street. Harrison. The artist makes spear guns in his regular business."

We said good-bye and walked the two blocks to the farewell party for Bart Frontgate. Neither Eric nor I had ever visited the Smokin' Tuna Saloon, a large outside/inside bar off an alley that was sandwiched between Greene and Caroline streets and not far from Mallory Square.

"Never in the world would we have found this place if we didn't have the address. In fact," I said to Eric, "I've never attended calling hours at a bar. I hope it's less grim than standing in line at the funeral home."

I remembered standing for hours next to my mother to greet my grandmother's mourners. I could still picture fresh tears on the cheeks of her elderly friends, and on my mother's friends' faces, and shimmering in the eyes of a few friends of mine. By the end of the night we'd been completely cried out, both numb and exhausted. I wasn't convinced that getting drunk on top of all that sadness would be an improvement.

"I don't think Key West does a lot with funeral homes," Eric said. "Strange that they scheduled this event right during the Sunset Celebration. Though I suppose that's going to keep the undesirable attendees away. The people who didn't really know him but might come to do some grisly people watching. Or score free drinks."

As we walked down the alley to the bar, the odors of garbage and fermented alcohol assaulted us. Once inside the entrance gate, we each snagged a glass of white wine from a passing waitress and moved to the back wall to look over the crowd. I spotted a man who was a dead ringer for Bart, only some thirty years older. "That has to be his father," I said. "I'm going over to give him my condolences."

When the couple who had been talking to the elder Mr. Gates moved away, I stepped in with my hand outstretched. "I'm Hayley Snow," I said. "I didn't know your son well"—not at all but I wouldn't tell him that—"but I enjoyed his act at the pier many, many times. I am so very sorry for your loss."

"Thank you," he said, and squeezed my hand between his, staggering a little as he did. "Shank you." The man was absolutely smashed.

I fell quiet for a moment, mentally scrambling for

what to say. A minister's words from a funeral that I'd attended a while ago in the Episcopalian church on Duval Street flooded my mind and I spit them out. "It's so wrong when a young person goes like this. Well, I mean murder is always wrong. But I mean a young person's death—it's not fair. Your son had so much potential. So many years to enjoy life and make his mark." I stopped blathering to give him a chance to respond.

Mr. Gates looked at me with a puzzled expression on his face. "Make his mark?" he asked, his voice growing louder. "Would he ever have managed that?"

A woman in a black dress, with droopy eyes and very red lips, came over and took his arm. "Thish is Hayley Mills," he told her. "Thish is Bart's mother, my wife."

"Snow," I said, with an automatic smile. "I'm so very sorry."

"Other people before Bart made terrible mistakes and bounced back," she told him. "Who would've thought Senator Kennedy could go from Chappaquiddick to the Senate? And President Clinton, he fell into a ridiculous scandal and came out more popular than ever."

Mr. Gates squared his shoulders, as though she might have convinced him of this truth.

"No telling what Bart might have done, had he been given the chance," I said wagging my head sadly. The woman nodded with me.

Mr. Gates picked up the glass of beer that he'd set on the bar when he greeted me. The bartender had filled it to the brim while we talked. "The hard truth was, Bart never could own up to his mistakes. How in the world was he supposed to move beyond them?"

The woman's eyes filled with tears. "That's cruel. He

would have gotten around to that," she said. "The way those others did."

I was trying to figure out how to ask what Bart's mistake had been, when the woman grabbed her husband's arm, murmuring her thanks, and pulled him away to greet some other mourners.

"How did that go?" Eric asked when I returned to his position against the wall.

I made a face and held my hand up, fingers an inch apart. "Bart's mother seems to be under the impression that their son was just this close to leaving a legacy like President Clinton or Senator Kennedy. His father's not so sure."

By the time we got back to Houseboat Row, starving and worn as thin as a strand of angel hair pasta, I could smell the garlicky-tomato scent of my spaghetti sauce wafting all the way up the finger. Miss Gloria met us on the deck and announced that she'd been fielding texts from her mah jong friends ever since we'd left. News had spread like full-moon floodwaters through Key West that another death had occurred, this one in the cemetery. The residents who lived in that section of Old Town were frantic, and the police department had received hundreds of anxious calls.

"There's a special meeting called for seven thirty tomorrow night at the Old City Hall," she said. "Everyone will be there. The city commissioners will be in attendance along with the police chief and other officers. Of course they want to reassure the citizens," added Miss Gloria. "But I don't see how that's going to happen unless they've got the real murderer behind bars. My friends are hysterical—and they are sturdy old ladies."

"I guess we'll have to attend that meeting," I said with a sigh. "But where's Lorenzo? How's he holding up? Is he resting?"

"They picked him up about half an hour after you left," said Miss Gloria, her gaze not meeting mine. "I didn't see the point of calling you, because his lawyer was here and said he had to go. There wasn't a darned thing you could have done. Apparently the evidence against him is mounting."

22

The long-cherished deposit of ancient schmutz—a spongy mess that you can use day after day and even decade after decade, and whose exigencies you, as a baker, basically can't escape—is called, no kidding, "the mother."

> —Adam Gopnik, "Bread and Women," *The New Yorker*

In the morning, I felt logy from the pile of spaghetti I'd inhaled the night before and discouraged about Lorenzo being taken back to jail. I lay in bed for fifteen minutes trying to piece together what might have happened between Cheryl Lynn and Bart, and how Lorenzo could have been involved. I'd Googled the song that Cheryl Lynn had tattooed on her shoulder—snatches of the melody kept running through my mind. It was a hard-driving rock song about early death, blank stares, yearning for something you can't have, shame, emptiness, and regrets. Definitely not something a happy person would want to ink onto her body. But I'd already gotten the idea from talking to Snorkel's dad and Lorenzo, too, that Cheryl Lynn had been a troubled person.

I finally forced myself out of bed, took a quick shower, and left the houseboat to head toward *Key Zest*. As I fastened my helmet on, my phone rang. It was a Key West number but not one that I recognized. Even though it seemed an unlikely possibility, I couldn't help feeling a surge of hope: Lorenzo had been sprung and needed a ride home.

I pulled the helmet back off and pressed *accept*. "Hello?" I said eagerly.

"Hayley Snow? This is Olivia."

"Olivia?" My hopefulness sagged like a pricked popover. I didn't know an Olivia and I wasn't in the mood for fending off telemarketers.

"Olivia Mastin," she said. "Edwin's wife. From the floating restaurant? I wonder if you would have time for coffee sometime this afternoon."

"I've got an awfully busy day lined up."

"Please," she begged. "I wouldn't ask if it wasn't crucial. I know you don't owe me a thing. But—"

She started to sniffle and my curiosity spiked, along with a little bit of sympathy. Besides, more caffeine and sugar could only help the way I felt this morning.

"I'm on my way to work, but I could meet you right now for fifteen minutes—"

"That's great," she said, cutting me off before I even finished. "Somewhere downtown?"

"Let's say the Glazed Donut in ten minutes."

I left my scooter parked in the lot behind *Key Zest* and walked the few blocks over to Eaton Street. The Glazed Donut shop sits directly next to the Tropic Cinema, although their clientele doesn't much overlap.

Doughnuts in the morning, movies in the evening. I took a seat at the back of the shop after purchasing the doughnut that sang loudest to me, the blood orange bull's-eye doughnut, and a cup of strong Cuban coffee. I bit into the pastry, savoring the tang of the marmalade and an unexpected pocket of orange-scented cream.

Mrs. Mastin hurried in just minutes later, grabbed a coffee, and came over to join me. "Hayley, I really appreciate you meeting with me. I know it was sudden, but I didn't know what else to do." She took a sip of coffee and a moment to regroup, then removed her sunglasses and put them on the table. "Poor Edwin has had such a shock with Cheryl Lynn." Her eyes were glassy with tears that she tried to hold back. And I noticed that they looked puffy and red, as if she'd done a lot of crying.

"I'm very sorry. She was close to your family?"

"Like another daughter," she said. "I understand you were one of the people who found her."

"Yes." I answered with a definiteness that did not invite further questions. The last thing I wanted to do was describe my version of what it had been like to find Cheryl Lynn's remains in the crypt. I didn't want to etch that visual deeper into my brain, nor would she want to hear it.

"Well, anyway," she said, her gaze searching my face, "that's not why I called you. I wanted to talk about your review of For Goodness' Sake. I wonder if you might consider visiting for another meal at our place? On the house, of course."

"I—"

"I'm just afraid that any review less than a rave would put Edwin under." She smoothed a silver curl into her blue headband and waited, a hopeful expression on her face.

I nibbled at the sugar-crusted outer edges of my doughnut, wondering exactly how to phrase the bad news.

"We know the locally sourced seaweed was reaching," she said, adding a forced snicker. "We can do so much better if we stick to the island basics."

"The thing is," I said, wiping my fingers on a napkin, "the review is essentially written. I have to turn it in this morning at the staff meeting. We have a new strict boss who wants everything early. And in fact, this one is already late."

She burst into ragged sobs and I felt my resistance ebbing.

"I can ask," I said, shrugging my shoulders, "but I'm almost sure the answer will be no."

She grabbed my hand and wrung it. "Thank you so much. Thank you."

I stood up, crumpled the napkin, and stuffed it into the coffee cup. "Who is Cheryl's family? Do they live on the island?"

Mrs. Mastin shook her head. "I believe her parents have been deceased for a long time, poor thing. She's been floating around Key West forever, a lost soul."

"Will there be a service?"

Mrs. Mastin shrugged. "I really have no idea. If you check her profile on Facebook, you might find something there."

Which I found bizarre. If she and her husband had been so close to Cheryl Lynn, why in the world wouldn't she know this? I glanced at my watch. "I'm late to my meeting. I'm sorry about your troubles." I left the doughnut store and trotted back over to the *Key Zest* office. As I vaulted up the stairs, I could hear Wally and Palamina bantering in their shared office. Was it my imagination, or did he seem happier since he dumped me?

I tapped on Wally's door and stepped inside.

Palamina glanced at her wrist, decorated with an oversized Minnie Mouse watch. Then she managed a smile. "Now we can officially start the meeting. We've been talking about a new weekly feature. A locals'-eye view of something on the island."

Wally cut in. "We realize that lots of local publications write about Key West food and music and events. Of course we'll continue with that, but we want to step our content up."

Palamina said, "And not just the content. We want the writing to be stunning, too."

First she wanted Buzzfeedable. Now she wanted stunning?

"Then we're thinking of doing a weekly podcast using Google Hangouts that we'll connect with our Facebook page. So readers can match up the personalities with the stories."

My immediate reaction was to wonder how long it would take to lose the ten pounds I'd packed on over the holidays and never managed to shake.

"Danielle had the idea of writing about tropical gardening," Palamina said, her voice approving.

"And don't forget beauty," said Danielle. "In other words, I'll sample the various spas around the island to check out facials and massages." She grinned and patted her cheek.

"Clever girl," I said.

"Any thoughts about what you could add?" Palamina asked me. "Besides your food beat, of course. But not local politics. Wally and I will cover the hard stuff."

Another zinger. Somehow I had to convince her I wasn't an idiot. I creaked through the recesses of my brain like an old Rolodex, with the three of them watching and waiting. "What about a story on the cemetery?" I asked, spilling out the first real thought that came to mind.

"The cemetery?" Palamina asked.

"I'm thinking about the history layered in there. And the way you can get a sense of Key West over the years by looking at the neighborhoods in the graveyard and different styles of stones. And all those complex relationships . . ."

Wally and Palamina exchanged a glance, and then Wally said, "Sounds like it's worth a try. Just nothing too grim."

"Deep, though," added Palamina.

"Deep but not grim," I repeated. "Anything else?"

Palamina glanced at the list on her laptop. "You have your story on For Goodness' Sake ready this morning?"

"One note on that," I said. "I'm kind of thinking we might want to visit the restaurant again before I tweak the review one last time."

Palamina narrowed her eyes and tapped her lip with a pencil. "Why?" she asked. "Do you feel we didn't cover all the bases? Seems to me like we tried most of the items on the menu."

I hemmed and stuttered a little more and finally spit it out. "Mrs. Mastin lobbied me for another visit. Her husband was so distressed about the dead girl we found in the cemetery. He's feeling that loss so deeply and she's concerned that a bad review would finish him off. She says they'll pay for the second meal. They realize that they need to simplify the menu." I widened my eyes, trying to look hopeful, when even to me the explanation sounded lame.

Dead silence for a moment.

"I hate to be blunt," said Palamina, "but that seems like a terrible idea. A terrible precedent to set." Her voice was gentle but firm. "I recall that Ava wanted to accept advertising from restaurants in *Key Zest* in exchange for reviews. And I know you struggled with her on this, how much to allow the restaurant owners and chefs to influence your stories."

She waited until I nodded my agreement.

"And you were right to push back on Ava and maintain your independence as a critic," she said. "We have to try to stay autonomous and transparent, as much as that's possible in a small town."

"Gotcha," I said. "I felt bad for her; that's all. I was letting my heart lead the way when I said I'd ask at this morning's meeting." Which I probably shouldn't have said, as it implied that Palamina had no heart.

When the meeting was finally over I slunk back to my office cubby and e-mailed the story on For Goodness' Sake to Palamina and Wally. Feeling utterly glum—and lonely, too—I texted Miss Gloria to say I'd pick her up and take her to lunch. She texted me right back.

Rain check? Plans with the ladies.

Even my elderly roommate had more going on than I did.

Next I called Lieutenant Torrence. "I've heard that things are looking bad for Lorenzo," I said. "Is there anything new?"

"Nothing," he said.

"I don't believe he has it in his heart to kill someone. Certainly not a second person."

"We can't operate on hunches," said Torrence quietly. "No matter how well-meaning they are."

Dead end there. With lunch with Miss Gloria out of the question, the only thing I could think to do was work. I would write a brilliant article on the cemetery neighborhoods. I had to show Palamina—and Wally, too—that I belonged permanently on the staff of *Key Zest*. And that I could handle any subject under any deadline pressure they might throw at me.

And maybe while I was at it, I could find something in that cemetery that we'd all overlooked. Something that might spring Lorenzo from jail—permanently.

23

*Meat keeps cooking when you take it off
the flame; my mother could turn herself off
in an instant.*
> —Jessica Soffer, *Tomorrow There
> Will Be Apricots*

I puttered slowly across Grinnell Street and took a right
turn on Angela, which runs along the west side of the
cemetery. Two houses over, I spotted two older folks on
their porch, rocking in rocking chairs and sipping
drinks. Their home, a gorgeous eyebrow design built to
keep out the hot sun and trap the sea breezes, was half
a block from the cemetery entrance and only a stone's
throw from Cheryl Lynn's place. I stopped, not exactly
sure what I could extract from them—or what I even
wanted. But if they spent a lot of time watching the
world go by, who knows what they might have seen?

"Terrible business at our cemetery lately," I called to
them. "I'm doing a story on the situation and wondered if you wouldn't mind chatting with me for a bit."

"Not at all," said the woman in a cultured English

accent. "Come up and sit with us. I'm Maureen and this is Brian."

I parked the scooter and scurried up the stairs. "Your home and garden are lovely." I gestured at the stone walkway and manicured plants and a turquoise metal sculpture that I recognized as a John Martini critter, half bird, half fish.

"You'll have to excuse our drinking so early in the day," Maureen said. "But since the murder we don't feel comfortable sitting out at night anymore, so we're starting early." She giggled. "Besides, our granddaughter sent us a monthly subscription to craft beers. I never drank a beer in my life before this. But we have to make a dent in these before the next shipment arrives."

She grinned at her husband, who appeared to be drinking a Budweiser. "He doesn't care much for them," she added with a laugh, "but this chocolate-flavored beer has me hooked. Can I get you one?"

"No, thanks," I said, wondering whether to query them about the cemetery's history or the latest murder. She'd already mentioned the murder, so I went with that. "I work for *Key Zest* magazine. We're doing a story about crime in the city. I thought our readers would like to hear from residents about the psychological effects of the recent crime wave on the neighborhood."

"The burglaries have had us all at sixes and sevens for months, but the murder takes the cake," Brian said. "You can't rule out that it was a vigilante killing."

"A vigilante killing?"

"I'm saying someone might have figured out who the thief was. Someone who was really dratted tired of being afraid. And who then decided to take matters into their own darn hands."

"Watch your language, Brian, darling," his wife

piped up. "We are all so very tired of someone sneaking into our houses and stealing things right off our nightstands while we sleep." Maureen shivered and took another sip of beer. "I've had trouble dropping off to sleep lately, just thinking of someone breaking in."

"But on the other hand, blaming the burglaries on a dead girl wraps things up a little too neatly, maybe, eh?" Brian said.

"We have seen a man hanging around this area lately," said Maureen in a hoarse whisper. "Visiting that dead girl's home. We were the ones who tipped off the cops."

"What did he look like?" I asked, a cloud of dread clogging my throat.

"Tall," she said glancing at her husband for confirmation. He nodded. "With dark curly or wavy hair."

"And glasses," he added. "And the waist on his pants up a little higher than most people wear these days."

The description was a dead ringer for Lorenzo. I gulped and tried to focus on the rest of what she was saying, rather than the miasma of doubt and fear that enveloped me.

"Maybe he was a friend of the woman," I said. "Maybe they were socializing, like normal people. Maybe he had nothing to do with her death."

"Maybe," said Brian. "But we felt we needed to tell the police, let them figure out the facts."

"We moved here," Maureen said, "because everyone told us the neighbors were so quiet at the cemetery." They both snickered—a joke they'd enjoyed before. "Hasn't turned out to be that way, though."

I declined another offer of the chocolate beer, then stood up and said my good-byes. I drove the last half block to the cemetery, parked, and entered through the black metal gate. I wandered up the main drag to the plot where we'd found Cheryl Lynn, drawn like a fly to a rotten carcass. Who was she really?

The sparse grass around the three-tiered crypt had been flattened by the boots of the cops and the rescue crew. Someone had replaced the rectangle of stone behind which Cheryl Lynn had lain, and cemented it in. I watched an ant scurry up the wall, wander in loops around the fresh cement and then around the family's name, written in crabbed script.

This was no random death. It took too much effort to kill a grown woman and then drag her here, open the crypt, and hoist her body inside.

I decided to try Lorenzo's mother again, to see if she'd remembered anything useful. After I dialed her number, she answered on the first ring—not like my generation, who considers the bleat of a phone call highly intrusive. Most of my pals won't even listen to a voice mail, much to their mothers' annoyance. I identified myself.

"Have you heard something?" Her words rushed out. "I am so worried."

"Nothing," I said. "I'm in the cemetery, looking at the crypt where Cheryl Lynn was found. I'm wondering if the place the killer left the body was a random choice or whether it was a statement of some kind. I'm also wondering how someone even got into the cemetery. I'm sure the gates are locked at night."

"Maybe it's like Gramercy Park in New York City," said Lorenzo's mother. "Special people who live nearby and own adjacent property have keys to the garden. It's a very exclusive neighborhood. I used to walk by the park when I visited the city and imagine living there."

She chuckled. "Leave it to Cheryl Lynn to have figured out the angles. She's been in bad trouble over the years, but this is the worst of it, of course."

I felt the jerk of an emotional whiplash. Over the years? My face felt suddenly flushed. "Didn't you tell me Lorenzo only met her recently?"

"Well, I can't be certain," she stammered, sounding completely flustered. "Maybe I'm mixing her up with another of his clients?"

"If you know something, you should tell me. People are getting murdered down here."

A long, loaded silence. "Lorenzo told me that her cousin's death had nearly pushed her around the bend," said Mrs. Smith finally. "And she was getting crazy about it again lately. He was so worried. I begged him to come and live with me. He could find work somewhere here in my town. That island is toxic," she added. "Has he ever talked to you about the current that runs around the outside of Key West?"

"Yes, yes. It sucks you in or spits you out," I said, still trying to picture Lorenzo living in that little retirement community in Fort Myers. I couldn't. "Are you saying that Bart Frontgate was Cheryl Lynn's cousin?"

"Oh no," said Mrs. Smith. "The girl who died years ago was her cousin. Or some relation—I may have it wrong."

I paused again. "How long had he known her? Please tell me the truth here."

His mother said, "Known her? Whoever really knows anyone?"

I waited her out.

"Maybe fifteen years," she said. "But it was all professional."

I waited some more.

"They made a connection because they both lost their parents. He has clients every once in a while where the walls between them come down and his river of loss just flows into theirs. I don't think he ever felt it more strongly than with her. The veil is very thin, if you know what I mean."

"I don't know exactly," I said. "What do you mean?"

"He can be so attuned to other people's sorrow. Sometimes he loses track of his boundaries. I need to go," she said sadly. "My stretch-and-tone class is starting in five minutes."

Once I had retrieved my scooter from where I'd parked outside the sexton's office, my phone rang. It was my father. For once I was relieved to talk to him. He have an outsider's opinion, and he loved being asked for advice. In a matter of minutes I had filled him in on all the goings-on over the last few days.

"I'm so worried about Lorenzo," I added, echoing what Mrs. Smith had said. "He doesn't have a violent bone in his body." Seemed like I'd been trying to tell that to everyone I knew over the last few days.

But my dad took a harsher view. "Honestly, Hayley, it sounds like your friend may have killed two people." I tried to interrupt, but he barreled over me. "You've helped him find a lawyer. You've taken in his pet. That's all you can do, even if you do consider him a friend."

"But he wouldn't have killed Cheryl Lynn," I said. "He was deeply, deeply troubled about her. His mom says she practically grew up with him." Which she hadn't said exactly, but I believed that was the gist of her meaning.

"Sweetheart," Dad said. "I would lie, too, if you were in that much trouble."

I felt prickles of gratefulness but also a swell of despair.

He cleared his throat. "I hate to be this blunt, but . . . let's see, maybe I should use one of your cooking metaphors." He chuckled at his own humor, but I dreaded what was coming. "We saw nothing but a mille-feuille of oddballs and misfits in Key West when we visited last year. I know you love that place, but I'm afraid it will only drag you down. You can always come home, stay with us a few months if you need to."

I said nothing. Moving in with them would feel good for about twenty-four hours. But he meant well.

He finally sighed. "Stay out of trouble—will you please promise me that, Hayley Snow?"

"Okay, Dad," I said quietly. "I'll stay out of trouble. I will."

24

*To eat passionately is to allow the world in;
there can be no hiding or sublimation
when you're chewing a mouthful of food so
good it makes you swoon.*
—Kate Christensen, *Blue Plate Special*

I called Lieutenant Torrence again with yet one more idea. I wouldn't be breaking my promise to my father; I'd be turning information over to the police. "Lorenzo's mother says her son knew Cheryl Lynn for years," I told him. "She said he cared about her. She said that they connected emotionally because they both suffered tragic losses in their childhoods—"

"I do appreciate your loyalty. And your doggedness," said Torrence, cutting me off with a laugh. "You never give up on a friend. But in this case, the loyalty is misplaced." His voice was definite, no room for wiggling.

"I just can't picture Lorenzo as a murderer."

"No one can. And I'm sorry your friend disappointed you. But you know this by now, Hayley: No one looks like a murderer on the outside. Or I should say, the people who look that shady usually aren't," Torrence said. "People have deep recesses that can cause them to behave in terrible ways. And unfortunately, Lorenzo is no exception. Don't you know what you see is not always the truth about what's at the core?"

Of course I knew that. And Bransford had insisted on the same kind of thing. Cops have such a downer view of human nature.

True, Lorenzo's problem was beginning to feel like most situations in Key West. There's a top layer, easy to see and easy to think you understand. But dig a little deeper and you'll find layers and layers and layers. And looking from above, you might have no idea what's bobbing around in those depths. Visitors to Key West think what they see is what they get—all jolly, have a beer, act a little crazy. For example, suppose they slide onto a barstool on Duval Street and settle in for a drink. How would they possibly know its history? How would they know that the owner beat the stuffing out of a tourist just last week because he was saving that same stool for his wife?

They wouldn't.

But in Lorenzo's case, I wasn't convinced that much darkness lay underneath. So I forced myself to think of what else I could do to get at the truth about the two deaths. Could one person have wanted them both gone? Or were they unconnected? And who wanted to frame Lorenzo?

I decided to buzz back over to the library's Florida history room to see if they kept copies of the Key West High School yearbooks. If Bart had been floating around this island that long and Cheryl Lynn had, too, maybe I'd find something that would tie them together. If the yearbooks didn't turn up anything useful, I would try to find the man who'd made Bart Frontgate those special juggling forks—the ones that killed him in the end.

All my leads felt slim, unlikely to lead to a solution. But I wasn't going to give up on Lorenzo until the final door clanged shut on death row in the Florida state penitentiary. I squeezed my eyes shut to push back the tears and parked in the lot behind the Key West library. I made my way down the back hallway and then into the Florida history room. The elderly librarian was puttering at his desk.

"Hello again," I said, my voice brighter than I felt. "Could you please point me toward the Key West High School yearbooks?"

He squinted and huffed a little breath of air. "May I ask for what you're looking?"

"I work for *Key Zest*," I said, annoyed that he would question me. Weren't librarians supposed to be nonjudgmental? But holding back wouldn't help the situation, so like a good reporter, I made up a story. "I'm researching a story on Key West natives. Where our high school graduates imagined they would end up, and how many leave and then return to the island. Or stay on. I thought the yearbooks would be a good place to start."

"We don't keep them here. You might try the high school library. They might keep that kind of record," he said, sounding doubtful. And then muttered, more to himself than to me, "Why in the world a run on high school yearbooks? Hardly worthy of my shelf space."

Feeling discouraged and put off, I hopped back on my scooter and rode up the island to the high school, which sits out on busy, unscenic Flagler Avenue, not far from the strip of grocery stores and the few pitiful big-box stores the island offers. An enormous conch shell had been placed out by the parking area—the high school mascot, of course. A noisy gang of kids burst out of the front door, laughing and tussling with one another, but I wasn't able to move quickly enough to catch the door before it closed behind them. As with most schools these days in the wake of terrifying shootings, the front door was locked. I pressed a button alongside the intercom and explained my mission, including a slight stretcher about an article on the history of cheerleading in Key West High School. Then I held my *Key Zest* press credentials up to the camera.

"I'll send Officer Ryan to escort you in," said the disembodied voice from the speaker on the wall. "Building closes in fifteen minutes."

Within several moments, Officer Ryan appeared at the door with a wide grin on his face. "Hayley Snow," he said, "it's good to see you. Staying out of trouble?"

I smiled back and nodded. He sounded like my father. Surely he had heard about my latest escapades.

"How's your brother doing?" Officer Ryan had been a peach last winter when my stepbrother, Rory, visited with my family—and quickly disappeared into the spring break scene.

"Really well," I said. "Once his father abandoned the ludicrous idea of military school and he and my stepmother started working together, Rory's been thriving. As usual, it's parents who screw things up."

"Hmm, that's kind of a bleak outlook."

I had to laugh—this was the attitude I'd been accus-

ing cops of. "What I mean is, trouble at the top leaks
down and shows up in the kids. You've got a new job
assignment?" I asked, changing the subject. "I hope
you weren't demoted."

He smiled, showing the full range of his dimples.
"Actually, I asked for this—I love working with teenagers. There's still plenty of room for change. And if I can
make a connection now between them and the police
department, it makes our job easier in the future," said
Officer Ryan. "What brings you back to high school?"

I shuddered. "Perish that thought. I wanted to look
through some yearbooks, for an article I'm writing on
the history of the Sunset Celebration." I stopped, hoping that he wouldn't ask me how the Sunset Celebration had anything to do with the high school. And
hoping he didn't compare notes with the woman who'd
buzzed me in, who thought I was writing about cheerleading. Or the Florida history librarian, who'd gotten
an even more convoluted story.

"Come on, follow me. I'll show you the library." He
glanced at his watch. "School closes in less than fifteen
minutes, so hope you can work fast. How is the found-
ing of the Sunset related to this school?"

"It shouldn't take more than fifteen," I hurried to
say. "It's not exactly the Sunset thing, actually. I'm
working on a project about the history of Key West students, how many stay on the island, how many leave,
how many leave and then come back. And the kinds of
trajectories that their work lives take."

All baloney, and from the wide eyes he flashed back,
he pretty much saw through me—that I was making
stuff up as I talked. I had a feeling that if he hadn't
known me already, he would have marched me right
back outside. He led me to a windowless cubby con-

taining a beat-up table and four metal chairs. All the high school publications, including hundreds of yearbooks, were arranged on bookshelves around the outer edges.

"Can I help you look for something?"

"Thanks, but I'll be fine." If I told him what I was looking for, I'd end up spilling the whole story. And then he'd warn me off it, like all the other men in my life.

"Text me if you have any questions or problems," he said. "You still have my phone number? I'll check back before we lock up and make sure you find your way out." He waved and headed down the hall, his radio crackling about a fracas on Duval Street.

Though the books were not perfectly ordered, I found the shelf containing the volumes for the years that Bart would have been in attendance. As I leafed through, the pages released the powerful scent of mildew. Finally I found a photo of Bart Frontgate, aka Bartholomew Gates. As with many school yearbooks, individual photos lauded each senior. And under each portrait was a quotation. Bart's photo was marked by a quote from Alan Wilson Watts: "Man suffers only because he takes seriously what the gods made for fun." I wondered whether he'd chosen that quote to represent himself or whether the yearbook staff had done the choosing.

Candid photos taken at various school events were arranged on the same pages as the senior mug shots. In one photo, taken on the sidelines of a football game, Bart and a second uniformed player had their arms thrown around two girls. Bart and one of those girls were laughing; the other faces I was not able to make out. But the girl laughing with Bart was absolutely a young and beautiful version of Cheryl Lynn. If they hadn't ended their lives as friends—both murdered—they'd started out that way. I searched for Cheryl's photo but found no mention of her; she must have been in a later graduating class than Bart.

Toward the back of the book, another photo had a caption indicating that Bart had been voted "class clown" by his graduating class. As a performer on Mallory Square, he'd pretty much lived up to that moniker, until his life took a darker and murderous turn. Maybe that twist had come only recently, but more likely the darkness had been building up for a while. Hadn't Torrence once told me that victims are most often murdered by people they know? At least now I could be certain that Bart had known Cheryl for many years, though I wasn't any more clear about why either of them had died.

As I flipped through the remaining pages to the section on class highlights and memorials, a staticky announcement crackled over the loudspeaker: The school building was about to be locked up for the night. I pulled out my phone and snapped pictures of the pages on which Bart had appeared, and a few of the pages at the end that I hadn't had time to read.

Eric called as Officer Ryan escorted me out of the building. I waved good-bye to the cop and trotted to my scooter. "Please come for dinner," I begged Eric. "My mind is a train wreck. I need a shrink to sort me out. Not a real shrink," I hastened to add, not wanting him to think I'd broken my long-term embargo on therapy. "But with Lorenzo back in jail . . ." The reality of how bad things looked for Lorenzo punched me hard, and I gulped for air.

"What are you serving?" he asked. "Bill just happens to have a board meeting tonight, so I might be free."

"How about walnut and spinach pesto? We still have some of that fancy Mario Batali Italian pasta that Mom sent for Christmas. And fudge left over from yesterday. And I'm making baklava for Connie, so it should be ready to test by the time you arrive. And salad, with Miss Gloria's little tomatoes and herbs."

"Enough," he said. "I'm coming already. What time?"

I made a quick stop at Fausto's on White Street to load up on butter, walnuts, pistachios, and basil. I'd moved the phyllo dough from the freezer to the fridge last night in preparation for today, and I'd loaded up on local honey at the Artisan Market last week. I didn't mind knocking off work early, because cooking helps me think. And between the rough draft of the article about the cemetery, which I'd promised to Palamina in the morning, Lorenzo's troubles, my father's comments, and my high school expedition, I had a lot to chew on. And lord knows I wasn't really working anyway.

I plopped three sticks of butter in a pan and turned the front burner on low to melt them. Then I pulled my Cuisinart from the pantry shelf to the counter and began to grind walnuts and pistachios with a bit of sugar and cinnamon. When all the ingredients were ready, I unwrapped the phyllo pastry and spread out the first thin sheet in my 9 by 13 inch baking pan. Using a silicone brush, I began to paint the pastry with butter. Then I layered another sheet on top and painted again.

A mille-feuille of oddballs, my father had said.

Maybe he wasn't so wrong about the thousand layers. New visitors to Key West think the action is all about Duval Street. But if they stay long enough, they discover the fabulous art and the music and the food. And if they stay even longer and dig a little further, they find the island history and the conflict between saltwater Conchs (born in Key West) and the freshwater (moved to the island later), all connected by thin lines to the snowbirds. And the tourists float above all of that history. And sometimes the new people act like they discovered the place, like Christopher Columbus thought he discovered Florida and Cuba. As if no one lived there before he showed up. And some of that is reflected in the cemetery, with the way the old established families have elaborate plots, like the Gates family's, near where Cheryl Lynn's body had been discovered.

I pushed my mind away from Cheryl Lynn as I finished painting the pastry, then loaded in layers of crushed nuts and sugar and painted more buttery layers on top. At last I cut the finished baklava into triangles and put the pan in the oven to bake. I had a little time to work before it would emerge, all crisped up, ready to get doused with honey.

I sat down in front of my laptop and thought about the cemetery again and started to jot some notes. No one likes the idea of vanishing after they die, gone and forgotten. People want to be remembered and have their names mentioned, and maybe even have their graves tended by generations in the future. I sat back from the keyboard. Was this the sort of musing that would please Palamina? Maybe I should instead write something about inequality in Key West, how working people who serve the tourists and wealthier residents have trouble affording a place to live. Was this a new trend? I thought a visit to the cemetery would tell me no. Because there, etched in marble and granite and sometimes cement, lay the wealthy neighborhoods, the gated communities, the Jewish and Catholic ghettos, the sacrificial war veterans, and finally, the tiny drawers for the impoverished and the homeless.

The timer in the kitchen dinged and all three cats led the way to the stove. I pulled the fragrant baklava out of the oven and poured honey over the top until it appeared saturated. Then I noodled around the kitchen cleaning up and finally carved out a chunk of the pastry for Connie and Ray. All three cats followed me up the finger to deliver the treat.

"Come on board," Connie yelled from the top deck. "Your mom's on the phone giving me baby and pregnancy advice."

"Cats okay?" Evinrude had lived on this houseboat when we first moved to the island, and he still considered it part of his territory.

"Bring 'em on."

I deposited her baklava on the kitchen counter but then realized she'd probably want to sample it immediately. So I went up the stairs to the outside deck. Evinrude bounded up ahead of the other cats and wound himself in and out of Connie's legs, with a silent meow for emphasis.

"I missed you too, buddy," she said, rubbing his cheeks and tracing the dark M-shaped stripe on his forehead. She rubbed his jowls until his whiskers puffed out and he collapsed beside her, his purr engine rumbling. Then she turned her attention to

Sparky, admiring his shiny coat and wafting her hand along his back and his tail. Only then did she focus on Lola, wiggling her fingers to entice the shy white kitty closer. She was kind that way, always paying attention to the people and animals around her. How lucky her baby would be to have her as a mother. And how happy her own mom would have been to see this moment. My eyes stung with a few tears and I fought to keep them in.

"Take a load off," she said to me, gesturing to the low beach chair beside her. She positioned the iPad so I could see my mother's face.

"Hi, honey. Were your ears burning?" Mom asked. "We were just wondering what was up with Wally."

"Zero," I said, forcing a cheerful voice. "From now on, we've decided it's strictly business. And friends, of course. It's for the best—he's got his hands full. And it's better for my job this way."

My mother went speechless, her lips still moving but nothing coming out.

Connie stared at me and I could feel my lower lip starting to tremble.

"Don't tell me he had the nerve to dump you," she demanded.

"I guess you could put it that way. I think his mother's illness—"

"Is that the baklava?" Connie interrupted, pointing at my package. I nodded and handed it over. She unfolded the foil and showed the glistening pastry to my mother.

"Gorgeous," Mom said. "Your layers are beautiful. And I love the pistachios sprinkled on top. Wish I could taste it."

Connie nibbled on a piece and rolled her eyes to signal her overwhelming approval. "As far as Wally is concerned," she said, licking the honey off one of her fingers, "don't get me started. He's treated you like crap for months, holding you at arm's length like you were an enemy, not a girlfriend. I don't care what problems you're facing; if you're in a relationship with someone, you talk about those issues. His mother is sick and he doesn't seem to want your support. Why doesn't he lean on you? Borrow your shoulder, your ear, take your advice on all that's going on? He doesn't share much about his work dreams, either. And how come he isn't trying to drag you into the sack all the time?"

"Living with Miss Gloria makes it tough," I stammered, blushing, feeling a little sick to my stomach as the truth of Connie's rant began to sink in and take visceral hold.

"He's emotionally stunted—that's why!" she almost shouted.

From her position on the iPad screen, my mother nodded thoughtfully. "This just occurred to me, Hayley, and I wouldn't say this except Connie's already opened the dam."

Connie clapped a hand over her mouth. "I overdid it, didn't I?"

Mom beamed. "Pregnant ladies get a pass for almost everything. Anyway, I think Wally is like your father in some ways. He's solid and dependable, but he lacks passion. And his default position seems to be criticism rather than praise. Even if he changes his mind and begs for you to come back, I worry that he's never going to adore you for who you are."

"In other words, you'd be settling for a lifetime of mediocrity if you choose him," said Connie.

"I can't very well choose him, because I've been dumped." I rolled out of my low beach chair and pushed up to stand. "I need to go make dinner. Eric's coming."

25

By then, she and Rob had developed a relationship that was perfectly nice, but it was like that dreadful carob chocolate. As soon as you tasted it, you knew that it was just a wrong, sad imitation.

—Liane Moriarty,
The Husband's Secret

I returned to my houseboat and by rote began to assemble the spinach-walnut pesto. I hated what Connie had said about my relationship with Wally, but I couldn't find a way to dismiss it, either. It was discouraging to abandon hopes and dreams that I had nurtured with time and energy. On the other hand, if it wasn't going anywhere—and this one obviously wasn't—I'd only waste more time if I obsessed about it. Or even more useless, tried to talk Wally back into connecting with me.

I dumped a clove of garlic into my Cuisinart and chopped it up. Next I added a cup of walnuts and ground those together, feeling unexpected satisfaction in the pulverization of the ingredients. Then I added chunks of fresh Parmesan cheese and crunched that in with the nut mixture, followed by a dollop of good olive oil, and the spinach. The pesto smelled absolutely fragrant and delicious, and just the idea of a plate of pasta doused in this sauce started to make me feel better. And Eric's advice on the Lorenzo situation was bound to help, too. I had begun feeding fresh basil leaves into the food processor when a text came in. Eric.

Rain check? So sorry. I am pining for your pasta. But one of my clients needs emergency session. Speak tomorrow? XO Eric.

I couldn't help feeling instantly blue. But I washed the lettuce and sliced radishes and avocado and Miss Gloria's tiny grape tomatoes, and then mixed up a balsamic vinaigrette, as I had promised Eric. Why should the menu be dumbed down because I was the only one eating? When the pasta was cooked al dente and the piquant pesto stirred in, I loaded a plate full and retreated to the small back deck to eat. An evening breeze had kicked up the water in our little harbor so the houseboat rocked gently and the ropes and cleats clanked from the Renharts' boat next door. A flock of black skimmers soared above me, headed for the concrete piling where they liked to congregate, away from the human madness.

As I ate, I tried to imagine how Bart Frontgate had ended up sloshing in the sloppy water near Route One. Had he actually been boating in the dark? And if so, who had been with him? Was he taken by force or was he out fishing with someone he knew and trusted? For that matter, was he boating at all that night? Maybe he'd been murdered on land and then his body dumped into the harbor. To sleep with the fishes, as Mario Puzo might say. I was beginning to freak myself out, but for Lorenzo's sake, I forced myself to forge forward.

When I was finished with dinner, I studied the notes I'd taken so far on Lorenzo's troubles and the two deaths that had occurred this week. Lorenzo had dealt out several surprises, including the fact that he'd been abandoned as a child and then adopted and the fact that he'd known Cheryl Lynn a lot longer than he'd told me. But he was still the man I'd come to know and love and trust—I felt that in my heart. Didn't I? It was not that I didn't know Lorenzo; it was that I still didn't know Bart. Or Cheryl Lynn. Or why they'd been killed. Or who did it. I flipped through the photos I'd taken at the high school. Were the two deaths really connected? Did the answers lie in their past? If that was true, then the why and the who, I had a feeling, might be back in the pages of that yearbook.

I texted Officer Ryan and told him I had a question. *Fire away*, he texted right back.

Is there a teacher at the high school who's been there for twenty years plus, who might remember the kids from those days?

Try Debo Dingler. Nice lady. About the right time frame. Take care.

I texted the teacher at the number Officer Ryan gave me but got no answer. With an hour and a half to go before the seven thirty meeting at the Old City Hall, I decided to pay a visit to the man who designed and made the special forks for Bart Frontgate. I left a note for Miss Gloria about the leftover pesto pasta and begged her to hold off on the baklava for a couple of hours to let the honey soak the layers completely. Probably a lost cause, but who really cared? Any woman in her eighties deserved to eat whatever she wanted, whenever she wanted it. Then I buzzed over to Roosevelt Boulevard and hooked a right on White Street to the address that had come up when I Googled the Harrison Gallery, the home of fine art—and hand-hewn spear guns? It seemed an odd combination.

I wandered into the gallery, a small space showing modern artwork made of burnished wood, coral rock, and polished stones, displayed against white walls. I was admiring a stunning carved wooden bowl when a man in weathered jeans with a salt-and-pepper beard and a friendly face emerged from a door at the back.

"I'm looking for the fellow who makes the spear guns," I said, glancing around the room again. "I'm not sure I'm in the right place."

"That's my son," he said, his cheeks dimpling as he smiled. "He's not in right now, but I could take a stab at answering your questions." He grinned even wider. "*Take a stab*—get it? That's spear gun humor. Come on, we have some of his work on display in the back room."

I followed him across the gallery, down two steps, and through the office to a space that opened to a workshop on one side and an artist's studio on the other. On the workshop side, a handful of carved wooden spear guns hung on the wall.

"They are works of art," I said, and he grinned again.

"The smaller ones are made of Cuban mahogany, found right here in Key West," he said, pointing to the closest gun. "For the bigger ones, he uses teak, because it can be sanded down and oiled. And it's closed cell."

I nodded, though I was baffled. "Closed cell?"

"It doesn't absorb water. You've probably noticed

how often teak is used on decks and on boats. And it looks great, too, and it weathers better than any other wood."

"They're gorgeous," I said, "I can see why you'd include them in your gallery." The sharp metal tips at the ends of wooden cylinders gave me the shivers. I could imagine the flash of the steel piercing the silver sheen of a big fish. And then I couldn't stop the image of a teak-handled fork piercing Bart Frontgate's body from sliding into my brain.

He picked up one of the teak guns and handed it to me. Lighter than I'd expected. "Each one of these puppies is weight neutral," he added. "That's why it doesn't feel heavy or awkward."

I nodded my encouragement in order to hear more about the guns, though I had the idea if I got this man going, I'd be in for a long visit. I ran my hand along the length of the gun and fitted my fingers around the handle.

"Don't shoot the damn thing," he yelped, and I handed it back in a hurry. "Sorry, didn't mean to startle you. You can't shoot these things on land—they'll bite you back so hard." He settled the gun onto the wall rack, wiped his hands on his jeans. "What I mean by weight neutral is he puts the weights inside to make sure the thing is balanced correctly. And then when you shoot them underwater, they go right to the target and you barely feel the kickback."

"They're very handsome," I repeated, taking a step away.

"So you're a fisherwoman? Or shopping for a boyfriend? I'm Ben Harrison, by the way," the man added, reaching a hand out to me. I shook it, noticing the calluses on his fingertips. A musician, I suspected.

"Truth is, I'm not interested in the guns. I'm curious about the special forks your son made for Bart Frontgate."

"Uh-huh." He paused, no longer smiling, waiting for me to explain my curiosity.

"I'm a good friend of the man who's implicated in Bart's murder. I'm grasping at straws at this point. But I can't bear the idea of him going to jail, because I'm certain he didn't do it. And he wouldn't survive jail. He's an unusual fellow. Sensitive and sweet. That's it, really," I finished with a sniffle. "I thought if I came to talk with your son, he might have some insight into Bart's enemies or what he was up to, something. Anything, really. It sounds stupid now that I say it out loud."

"I'll help if I can. My son's not the kind of guy who usually manufactures barbecue forks," he said in his slow drawl.

"But he was willing to make an exception because?"

"Because Frontgate needed something perfectly balanced for his juggling act and he could see my son would produce the right instrument. They spent hours talking about how high he would throw them and testing the weights and so on. He could not afford to have them spraying out into the crowds, incinerating the tourists' polyester Hawaiian shirts."

"Were they friends?" I asked. "How did Bart even find your son? What was their relationship like?"

"Word of mouth, I guess. I don't believe they'd ever met. And if it was anything other than all business, I didn't hear about it. They did have one disagreement. My boy told Frontgate if he was going to put chunks of meat on these custom-made forks and set them on fire, he might as well just buy cheap Chinese-made junk from Kmart."

"Good point," I said, laughing.

"But Frontgate buttered him all up, said you do the best work around here, blah, blah, blah, and that's what I need. I met the guy once while he was in the shop—quite a smooth operator. And in the end, Frontgate paid him well enough that he couldn't afford to turn the work away."

"But after Bart was stabbed to death last week," I said, "I imagine that's the only set of three juggling forks your son will ever make."

"Probably so," said Ben, "though he made two sets of three."

"Two sets of three?" I asked dumbly. "Did someone else order them, or did Frontgate use both sets?"

"Frontgate wanted a backup. He originally wanted to order just one extra fork, just in case he lost one or it got bent or something. But my kid convinced him he'd be better off with an extra set, so the weights would be just right." He scratched his beard. "What difference does it make whether there are more than three forks out in the world?"

"Frontgate's body was found in the water. If—and this is a big if—he was killed in a boat, why would the murderer bring the murder weapon back to shore where the cops could find it? Why not throw it overboard? What if someone other than the murderer threw a fork in the Dumpster?"

"Good point there," said Ben.

"I need to call the police and let them know about the two sets of forks," I said. "It might make a difference."

"Of course, do what you need to do." Ben shook his

head sadly. "I'm only sorry my son's work had anything to do with Frontgate's death."

I thanked him for his time and returned to my scooter and punched Torrence's speed dial on my phone. When he answered, I said, "I'm wondering whether you actually found blood on the fork that was wrapped in Lorenzo's cloth. And if you did, are you certain it wasn't from the meat Frontgate used in his act? All this time I've been struggling with why in the world the murder implement ended up in that Dumpster if the man was murdered on the water."

"That's easy," said Torrence. "Lorenzo killed the man, panicked, and hid the evidence."

"But why?"

"The why is easy," Torrence said. "They'd been feuding for a year. Probably longer. They despised each other."

"That's lame," I said because I couldn't think of anything else. "Lorenzo doesn't own a boat, so how would he get him out to sea to kill him?"

Torrence sighed. "You may have noticed there is a plethora of boats on this island. Your stepbrother managed to purloin a personal watercraft within hours of arriving in the city. Remember?"

I remembered—it was a low, low point in our family history. "I thought you'd want to know that Frontgate had two sets of those special forks made by a man who works out of the Harrison art gallery. I'm not sure how it figures into the case, but I'm sure your crackerjack team of detectives will know what to do with the information."

"Honestly, Hayley, we are looking at everything and everyone. Unfortunately, the evidence still points to Lorenzo," said Torrence, his voice a little sweeter. "We all misjudge people sometimes. It's not only you, Hayley."

After hanging up with Torrence, I noticed that Debo Dingler had texted me back and said she'd be at home this evening and welcomed a phone call. I felt so confused and discouraged that it hardly seemed worth calling. But if Lorenzo ended up in the slammer, I wanted to be able to say I had done absolutely everything in my power to prevent that.

So I called Ms. Dingler, explained how Officer Ryan had suggested her, and told her I had a few questions about some former students.

"Oh gosh, I've been teaching for a million years, and a million kids have come through my classroom," she said. "But I'll try to help if I can."

"The man who was killed earlier this week, Bart Frontgate—it seems that he grew up in Key West and attended the high school—does that name sound familiar?"

"Oh yes," she said. "Poor Bart Gates. My niece graduated that same year, so I remember him well. His life had all kinds of possibilities, but he wasn't able to settle down and use his talents."

"Class clown," I said, and she laughed. "There was a photo at the back of the yearbook that showed Bart with his arms around two girls. It looked like they were very chummy. One of them was Cheryl Lynn Dickenson, who was also murdered this week. Do you remember her?"

"Cheryl Lynn," said Debo. "She came down from Miami during my niece's senior year and caused all kinds of chaos. By that I mean fights over girls, and drugs, and some petty thievery. Bart Gates was mixed up with her, too. She was not a good influence on a boy

who was having trouble maintaining boundaries anyway. They were thick as thieves until Victoria died."

"Victoria?" I asked.

A couple of dogs barked in the background, and
Debo excused herself to quiet the animals. "Sorry," she
said when she returned. "I adopted a new puppy and
the other three have not made the transition all that
gracefully. Kind of like when Cheryl Lynn came to
town." She laughed. "There's always something in my
house. You were saying?"

"I was wondering what happened to Victoria."

"Oh," she said slowly, "that was a tragic time. It
rocked the whole school for months and months. Young
people that age feel losses so deeply—it's like they haven't had experience with protecting themselves from
sorrow. Building up defenses, you know? My niece
cried every night for ages."

"What happened?" I asked again after a pause.

"Those kids went out boating and there was drinking
and probably drugs, too, and Victoria fell overboard. She
was too drunk to swim and the others weren't able to
rescue her in time. Tragic," she said quietly.

"Was there any question of foul play?" I asked.

She clucked her tongue. "Not that I'm aware of. Bart
left the island for a couple of years after he graduated,
but he bounced back like so many people do." She
laughed. "I never meant to spend my whole adult life
on this rock, either."

"It's like a drug, once you get it in your system," I
agreed. "So Bart left for college?"

"I don't recall that he even made it through the first
semester. Both of the guys in Victoria's clique were
stars of our Conch football team, but neither was good

enough—or maybe disciplined enough—to make it in college. And after Victoria died, they started using heavier drugs," Debo said. "Those four kids were tight as ticks, but the threesome didn't survive the transition. I think underneath the acting out, they were too sad about their loss. You know how hard teenagers take things—but I said that already. Now I can't believe three of them are gone, two of them murdered."

"What about the fourth, the other guy?" I asked. "He left the island, too?"

"Oh no, you see poor Louis everywhere around town. He makes those hideous hats." She snickered. "Don't tell him I said that. I gather he's rather proud of his work."

26

The light had faded to an industrial gray, and the breeze was as heavy as teakettle steam.
　　　　　　—Donna Tartt, *The Goldfinch*

After I'd hung up with Debo, I returned to the photos I'd taken in the high school and studied the one of the four students at the football game. Sure enough, the second player resembled a younger, unlined, undamaged version of Louis. My head was spinning with this latest revelation about Frontgate's past.

My first urge was to hunt for Louis and interrogate him about this history. I admitted to myself that it would be smarter to leave this to the police. Louis was a hothead to begin with, and probably drunk by this time in the evening. With a half hour left before the town meeting, I roared back over to the cemetery instead. Before I saw Torrence at the meeting and fed him more unwelcome suggestions and theories, I wanted to picture exactly how someone had killed Cheryl Lynn, then dragged her body over that tall spiked fence and stuffed it into the crypt. How was it physically possible? How would this not be noticed?

I parked outside the locked gate near the sexton's office and traced the sidewalk's path along Passover Lane toward Windsor. The homes along the Passover Lane side of the cemetery were set well back from the road, behind heavy vegetation and tall wooden fences. And some of them were rental homes that were unoccupied for periods of time. So it was quiet and dark. On the other hand, I imagined that police patrols would have been stepped up, given the cemetery burglaries that had plagued this neighborhood. And residents would be watching out for themselves and one another more carefully, too.

Twenty yards ahead, I noticed an empty grocery cart that had been pushed into the bushes against the cemetery fence. And suddenly I could imagine Cheryl Lynn's body being trundled across the road in the dark. But what then? It would practically take an acrobat to finish the job. Now I had some sense of how the body could have been taken as far as the fence, but not over it—and not why . . .

I trudged up the steep stairs to the meeting room at Old City Hall. The space was much more crowded than it had been when I attended the city commission meeting only days earlier. The odors of perfume and alcohol permeated the room. I found a seat on the far right-hand side, next to the nice older couple I had met earlier that day while looking for ideas for my cemetery story. We greeted each other warmly.

"I don't know how long I can sit here," said Brian to his wife. "My knee is killing me. I had a knee replacement earlier this year," he explained to me, "and it's still stiff and painful."

I nodded sympathetically but then zoned out and listened to the buzz of the waiting audience around us. The people on the island, especially those who lived around the cemetery, were not just worried about their stuff or their livelihoods. Now they were worried about their lives. I wondered what the chief of police could possibly say that would reduce the anxiety that gripped the town.

The chief approached the podium with the mayor, who was dressed in khaki slacks and a white Hawaiian shirt with pressed pin tucks down the front. "Good evening, folks," the mayor said in a genial voice. "We appreciate you coming out tonight. I promise this will be short. As you will have heard, the body of Miss Cheryl Lynn Dickenson was found in the cemetery yesterday afternoon. We express our deepest condolences to her family and friends." He nodded solemnly, adjusted his glasses squarely on his nose. "The chief and I and all of our commissioners understand that the recent events in our community raise concern."

A murmur of voices rose from the audience. "More than concern," he added, holding his hands up, as if to fend off a mob. "Fear for your families and yourselves. That's exactly why we wanted to bring you up to speed on the investigation. Chief?"

The chief stepped to the microphone, impeccably uniformed and taut with confidence. "Folks, it's been a difficult couple of weeks. We lost two islanders, first Bart Frontgate and now Cheryl Lynn Dickenson. These were not random events. They were the work of someone who felt a deep and personal rage."

This was supposed to be reassuring?

He cleared his throat and looked around the room, pausing to make eye contact with a handful of residents. "Now, what does that mean for you people? It means that you are not in danger when you walk your dogs in the morning. You are not in danger strolling home from dinner at night. You are not in danger."

The crowd began to shout out noisy comments, and a crop of hands waved furiously. The chief motioned for silence and pointed to a woman in the front row. "I'll take your questions one at a time."

"If you don't have the killer behind bars, I don't understand why we should feel safe." The volume of her voice rose until she was shrieking. "What you're saying makes no sense. We don't feel safe."

The mayor moved forward again and leaned into the mic. "Quiet, please. Let's show some respect. Let's all listen carefully to what our chief has to say."

"Did Bart Frontgate drown or did he die from the stab wound?" yelled out the same woman.

"Of course, the medical examiner will be the one to answer that question," said the chief. "There are many factors to consider, including the damage to his organs and the condition of his lungs. We will release those findings when they become available and when we determine the information will not hamper our investigation."

"Do you have any suspects?" shouted another man sitting behind us.

"We have a suspect in custody," said the chief, his voice raised so he could be heard over the din. "We believe that both victims were killed by the same person, someone strong and with a powerful vengeance." He explained about the department's excellent record in solving other cases and how this one was about to join those ranks.

I could count the ways he was wrong. First of all, they had Lorenzo in custody and I was certain he wasn't the killer. Honestly, I didn't think he was right about two victims, one killer, either. The methods were too different. One was sloppy. Stabbing someone to death with a fork in a rowboat seemed ridiculous. And then dropping the body into the water, where it washed up with construction flotsam and jetsam where any passersby could see. Seemed as though it hadn't been planned at all, but had suddenly occurred to the murderer in a fit of rage.

Cheryl Lynn's death, on the other hand, may not have taken more time to plan. But hiding her body took a lot of effort to execute. The murderer had to pry out the cover on the container and stuff the body inside, then close up the crypt and attempt to make it appear as though nothing had happened. Never mind killing her in the first place. And dragging the body over the fence that guarded the cemetery.

I leaned over to whisper to Brian. "I don't think they have it right about one killer. The scenarios are too different."

"Say what?" he said, cupping his hand to his ear. I repeated my observation, a little louder.

"Why don't you tell that to the police chief?" Brian asked. "It's time we started speaking up and not just accepting whatever the people with authority have to say. I, for one, would like to hear his answer."

Maureen nodded vigorously and leaned over to clasp my wrist. "I'll bring it up if you don't feel comfortable."

"That's fine; I don't mind." I raised my hand and wiggled my fingers at the chief of police. When the mayor indicated it was my turn to speak, I stood up, introduced myself, and explained what I'd been thinking.

The chief nodded briskly. "I appreciate that." He flashed a winning smile. "Lieutenant Torrence has kept me apprised about your ongoing interest in this case. And I'm sure you can appreciate, Ms. Snow, that there are details related to these crimes which we cannot disclose to the public, even to satisfy your well-meaning curiosity." Another tight smile. "Once the situation is resolved, then the details will become a matter of public record. But until the criminal is prosecuted and put away, we need to be very cautious about how much we can say."

As he was speaking, a man got up from his seat in the row ahead of me and stumbled across the laps of the people seated beside him. From the back, the man looked like Louis the palm-hat weaver—a man whom I now knew had a history with both of the murder victims.

And in a flash it came to me that he owned a grocery cart like the one I'd seen resting against the cemetery fence—that in fact he kept his palm-weaving supplies and his finished hats in this cart. Or perhaps he didn't own it, but he certainly made free use of it. And he could have used it to transport Cheryl Lynn's body to what he'd thought would be her final resting place. And if he wasn't an athlete now, he had been one in high school, when he played on the football team with Bart. According to my father, who knew these things and didn't hesitate to remind me of them when he was feeling oldish, a man who played sports as a youth never loses his athletic ability. Even if his joints get a little creaky and his waistline thicker.

Which meant that it wouldn't have been impossible for him to vault over that fence, even with Cheryl Lynn's body weighing him down.

I excused myself and slid past Brian and Maureen. I needed to visit the restroom anyway. Then I would take the opportunity to talk to Louis. If he confirmed that he had been involved in the murders, or even said anything slightly fishy, this room was crawling with cops.

All I had to do was shout.

27

It's not so much that we lack food, I re-
membered Simone Weil suggesting, as that
we won't acknowledge that we're hungry.
—Pico Iyer, "Healthy Body,
Unhealthy Mind,"
The New York Times

I hurried to the back corner of the room and exited the glass doors to the hallway that led to the back stairs and the bathrooms. But the area was empty, no sign of Louis. The door to the bathroom was closed. I certainly wasn't going to go in after him, but maybe . . . I rapped on the wooden door. "Louis, may I speak with you for a moment?"

I heard the lock click.

"Louis, I need to talk to you about your relationship with Bart Frontgate and Cheryl Lynn Dickenson."

"This is the men's room, for christ's sake. Leave me the F alone."

I knocked again. "You knew them both since high school—is that right?"

"Go away," he said. "Who do you think you are? The sheriff of Key West?"

I rattled the doorknob. If he would only say enough to point the finger, I could grab a cop from the meeting and turn the situation over to them. I knocked and rattled again.

"What part of 'men' don't you understand?" he shouted.

"Quite a bit, as it turns out," I muttered to myself. But then I felt something poking my back and heard a low voice hiss, "Don't make a move. Do not make a sound." The man grabbed my left arm and twisted it behind me. "Come with me down the stairs and no one gets hurt."

I craned my neck around: Edwin Mastin.

"What the hell?" I asked. Hard to take a fleshy restaurateur seriously.

"Do as I say," he said, "or I'll take you out right here."

"Help! Louis!" I started to yell.

"Shut up!" Edwin yelped, clapping a hand over my mouth and jerking me along with him. I stumbled down the stairs ahead of him, and he pushed me out the back door into the parking lot behind the building.

"Why are you doing this?" I asked, once I could speak again. "Where you taking me?"

"If you hadn't insisted on sticking your nose into things, this wouldn't be happening," he said as he looked wildly around. His gaze searched the few cars and bicycles in the lot and then the trellised-in overhang that separated the building's air-conditioning equipment from the parking lot. A door into the space was ajar; a padlock dangled from the latch.

"Seriously," I said. "What do you want?"

He paused to stare at me. "I wanted you to shut the hell up about these murders. Cheryl Lynn deserved to be avenged. And Victoria before her."

"Cheryl Lynn? Did you kill her?"

"Of course not," he said, shaking me and jabbing what I now saw was a small gun harder into my side ribs.

"Bart Frontgate, then?" I asked.

He did not answer, just pulled me along the west side of the building toward Greene Street, which I took as confirmation.

"I know that Bart and Cheryl Lynn were longtime friends," I said, scrambling to get the conversation going so we could stop and talk instead of running through Key West with a gun. He looked disheveled and distraught, and now I did not trust that he wouldn't hurt me, even if he didn't mean to.

"They were not friends," he said. "He killed her. And he had been killing her for years, anyway, with all the sickness he pulled her into."

I struggled a little harder and Edwin yanked my arms behind my back so hard I nearly fainted from the pain. Just then Brian and his wife, Maureen, limped down the access ramp and headed toward their little car, a blue Jaguar. Edwin quickly stepped me over as Brian opened the car door, and waved the gun so they could see it.

He pointed the gun at Brian but spoke to Maureen in a scary, low voice. "Ma'am, you get inside that trellis and you need to lie facedown, or I'll shoot your husband."

"Oh, come on," I said. "Don't get these people involved." He clicked off the safety on his gun and pointed it at Brian again.

Maureen squeaked, "Please don't hurt him." She took a few steps back into the shadows of the storage abutting the brick building, dropped to her knees, and then sprawled facedown in the gravel. Her shoulders shook with weeping as he locked the padlock.

"Pop the trunk," he said to Brian. The trunk of the little Jag flew open, revealing a small space lined with a blue plaid blanket. "Get in," he said to me. "Now."

"You know there's no way to get off this island unless you drive up the Keys," I said.

Of course he knew this, but I was stalling, hoping that a plan would pop into my mind. Or that Louis would come to his senses. Or that someone else might have noticed me leaving or had heard me yelling and alerted the cops.

"Once Maureen gets the police out here, they'll be crawling like flies on roadkill up and down the whole string of islands. You'll never get away with this," I said, cringing at my roadkill metaphor.

"Shut up and get in," he said. "Don't you imagine I have a boat?"

I didn't see another choice, so I climbed in.

"Now you get in the car," he said to Brian. "You're driving."

The metal of the trunk slammed shut over me. I closed my eyes against a flood of claustrophobia and tried to focus on breathing evenly and listening for clues about where we were headed.

Through the sheet metal of the trunk back, I could hear the rumble of Edwin's voice over the roar of the Jaguar engine. "Head toward Stock Island," he said. "I'll tell you where we're going when we get there. Don't try anything dramatic unless you want someone to die."

Within minutes, I heard the sounds of traffic and the eight-o'clock foghorn, which told me we were crossing over the Palm Avenue bridge, passing Houseboat Row, and then turning left on Route One toward Stock Island.

"Turn right here," said Edwin to Brian after several minutes. We bumped over a series of potholes and finally jerked to a halt.

"Pop the trunk and get the girl out, and then I want you in," Edwin said.

As I climbed out, gulping for air, Brian's face looked ashen; his jaw was clenched tightly against what I imagined to be his terror. We had parked near a boat ramp, where a collection of battered boats was tied to the docks. I couldn't stand the idea of Brian spending the night cramped in the trunk of his car.

"Please don't make him do this," I said. "He had his knee replaced recently. And he has a heart condition," I added, thinking that latter fabrication might call up more sympathy.

Edwin motioned to me to start walking toward the water. "Get in the trunk, old man," he shouted to Brian. Brian crawled in with some difficulty, and the door slammed.

We struggled down a trail through some overgrown bushes, finally reaching the rickety dock. We started up the finger, passing a line of well-worn dinghies and rowboats fastened to the dock with frayed ropes. The air felt heavy and smelled of gasoline, motor oil, and decomposing fish.

"Get in the last boat and sit in the bow," Edwin said shortly. "And don't try anything stupid. I mean it, Hayley. I don't want to hurt you, but I will if I have to."

Imagining that I'd seen a crack in his facade, I asked, "But what is the plan, Edwin? Where are we going?"

No answer. He untied the knots in the ropes holding the boat to the dock, threw them into the aft, and hopped in. Keeping his gun in his left hand, he inserted a key and started the motor. We shot away from shore, threading through a trail of mangroves and out into the open water. Edwin's phone rang. He extracted it from his back pocket, read the name on the screen, and cursed.

As we roared across the sound, my gaze searched the inside of the boat, looking for—what? There was no weapon that would stand up against his gun. Nor would I know how to drive the boat if he was not at the helm. But then I noticed rusty droplets toward the middle of the boat, only a foot away from where I was sitting; a splash of red gone gold stained the orange life vest pushed into the cubby. I stared at Edwin and he stared back.

"Yes," he said. "I did kill him. But he deserved it. I only regret that I didn't take care of him sooner."

"Tell me about it," I said, trying to sound empathetic, but fearing that I sounded like a wooden imitation of Eric. And besides, murder is murder in my book, whether deserved or not.

"He sucked Cheryl Lynn into so many terrible situations," said Edwin. "And she would no longer listen to any reason." The boat slowed down as he lost concentration, but then he roared faster again. Now he had to shout to be heard over the sound of the engine and the crashing waves.

"Start at the beginning," I suggested. "Cheryl Lynn was your goddaughter—is that right?"

"She wasn't legally anything to us. We just felt so

bad for her—she had no family to speak of—" He let go
of the tiller and dropped his head into his hands, and I
wondered if he was crying. Without his direction, the
boat sputtered and spun. "Cheryl Lynn moved to Key
West from northern Florida when Victoria was a junior.
She fell in with Bart and that hapless Louis, and my
daughter, of course."

I nodded, thinking of the football yearbook photo on
my phone. The second laughing girl must have been
Victoria Mastin.

"They were inseparable. And constantly in trouble, either at school or with the local police." Edwin turned the
boat motor off and we bobbed to a halt. "You would've
done the same thing," he said, a grim expression on his
face, "had it been your girl. They took my boat and they
went out drinking. Fishing, they told my wife. Four went
out, but only three came back. My daughter drowned and
it took two weeks to find her body."

"I'm so sorry," I said, feeling sick to my stomach to
hear his grief. "What happened?"

"Of course, it all depends on who you ask. Bart
Gates denied anything to do with her death. Cheryl
Lynn told me later that they'd been playing some kind
of card game. The loser drank a shot. Victoria got terribly sick and leaned over the boat to throw up. And fell
in. Cheryl couldn't help her; she couldn't swim. Forty-
five minutes later, Bart radioed for help, but my daughter was long gone when the Coast Guard arrived at the
scene. And later, when the police interviewed them, the
boys claimed they tried everything—life preservers,
oars, everything. But they were too drunk to rescue her.
And too stupid to call for help when it might have
made a difference."

The cords in his neck pulsed as he talked, and his face colored a frightening combination of white and splotchy red. "The police report confirmed that Louis and Cheryl Lynn had blood alcohol levels twice the legal limit that night. Bart's was over the limit, too, but not like that."

"You felt Bart was responsible for your daughter's drowning," I said softly. "You've been angry for many years. But why murder him now?"

His face darkened. I adjusted the words quickly. "I mean, why punish him now? Why wait twenty years?"

"I watched him destroying Cheryl Lynn bit by bit over the past few years. I offered to send her to a rehab facility—help her get clean, try to understand this latest absurdity, her need to steal other people's things. The last time we talked, I told her she had to get away from Bart, that I believed he was responsible for my daughter's death." He rubbed his upper arm, the place where Cheryl Lynn's tattoo had been inked.

"'I used to disregard regret, but there are some things that I can't forget,'" I said slowly.

"Cheryl laughed in my face and said, 'You're just figuring out now that he let her drown?' And I never saw her again. Until the cemetery . . ." His jaw worked furiously and his eyes glistened.

"Oh my gosh," I said. "I am so, so sorry. It's all almost too much to bear, isn't it? Both of them lost in terrible circumstances."

I gave him a moment to gather himself, while my own brain whirred with this new information.

"Wait, I'm confused," I said. "Who do you think murdered Cheryl Lynn?"

His face dropped to his hands and he smothered a

sob. He looked up, his cheeks tracked with wet. "He did. Bart. Honest to god, I didn't bring him out here with the intention of killing him. I wanted to warn him off Cheryl Lynn. Tell him we intended to do whatever it took to protect her."

"How did you get him to this dock?"

A pained expression on his face, he said, "We offered him money. Money always talked with Bart." He ran his hand along the length of his neck. "We stood on the dock." He pointed to shore. "He'd been drinking, of course. He started juggling those stupid forks, talking trash about Cheryl. Saying that she had threatened to go to the cops, have him prosecuted for letting Victoria drown."

"Why speak up after all those years of silence?" I asked.

"Bart said she was strung out all the time and crazy. So he had to take care of her. He said her death would be no loss to humanity. And then he described how he had often imagined choking her and disposing of her body in the cemetery. I became incensed, lost my cool, and grabbed a fork away from him." He swabbed his face with his sleeve, looked away over the glimmer of lights from Key West. "We struggled. It was him or me." He clutched his neck again. "I must have hit an artery."

"And then he fell overboard?" I frowned. "And you just let him drown?"

"No, no. We weren't on the boat. He died because of the stab wound. It was an accident. But he bled like crazy and I panicked, couldn't think what to do. So I dragged him aboard and then dropped him back in the sea once we got out into open water. Unfortunately, the body floated ashore faster than I ever imagined."

Edwin fell silent and I pictured the way he must have justified Bart's death as penance for his daughter's.

"Then I came ashore and went to Cheryl Lynn's house to tell her she had to get help. I didn't believe Bart would have killed her. I hoped he was jerking my chain. When I got inside I saw his things everywhere. He must have been staying with her. And I panicked, thinking that she would be blamed for his death." He choked back a sob, took a moment to collect himself.

"And then your goofy friend Lorenzo came up the path. I hid in the closet and saw him find the fork on the counter."

"Not the fork you'd used in the stabbing?"

He shook his head impatiently. "I threw that overboard, of course. But this was bloody, one of the implements from his ridiculous meat-juggling act. Lorenzo must have been worried about her, too; he washed the fork off and put it away in her drawer. When he went upstairs, I got the idea of diverting the cops toward him. So I wrapped the fork in the cloth from his tarot table and threw it in the Dumpster." He paused, his face and shoulders frozen. "I phoned in an anonymous tip. I'm sorry for the trouble to Lorenzo, but I was trying to protect Cheryl Lynn the way I couldn't protect my daughter. I simply didn't believe she'd already been murdered."

As Edwin talked, the boat had bobbed closer to the dock. Suddenly a big wave washed in from a yacht speeding by in the distance. Our little motorboat rocked precariously, and the rusty water on the floor sloshed from stem to stern. I bolted up, but as I prepared to dive overboard, he lunged for me. He knocked me off my feet and slammed my hip into the gunwale of the boat. I somersaulted backward into the cold water, hearing the sharp report of gunshots as I kicked away.

Moments later, he was in the water, too. He grabbed my legs and I scissored furiously, determined to fight to the bitter end. I broke through the surface to gasp for air. He knifed through the water beside me, and I slapped at his face, choking and sputtering.

"For god's sake, Hayley, it's me." Bransford. As the adrenaline drained from my body, I went limp, rubbery with exhaustion.

Bransford half carried, half dragged me through the weeds in the shallow water, and I reached for the arms of the cops who crouched on the dock. They pulled me up, and Bransford levered himself out of the water. Only yards away, Edwin Mastin was handcuffed, shoved in the back of a cruiser, and whisked off.

"There's a man locked in the trunk of a blue Jaguar," I said.

"We already found him. We've got it," Bransford said.

I clutched my hands together so he couldn't see them shaking. "Thank you. I don't know what would have happened—" My whole body began to shake, rivulets of water running from hair to T-shirt to sneakers. One of the cops grabbed a silver space blanket from his cruiser's trunk and draped it over my shoulders.

"I know what would've happened," Bransford said through clenched teeth. "You would've been killed, left somewhere like yesterday's carcass. Like Cheryl Lynn Dickenson or Bart Frontgate, only a smaller package."

"Yesterday's carcass?" A white-hot fury bubbled up. "Why do you have to be so mean?"

"You bring out the worst in me," he said. "I see you

lurch off into something so stupid with danger that it boggles my mind. I can't think how to get this across to you: It's not your job to catch criminals. It's my job. It's the police department's job. It kills me to see you in harm's way, but I don't seem to have any effect on you." He reached for me and reeled me in toward him, then kissed me with a fierceness that drove everything else out of my mind. Then he pushed me away.

"I'm not up for an on-again, off-again situation," I stammered, weak in the knees, mind whirling. "Been there, done that."

"This time I plan to date you until you beg for mercy."

"I need to take things really slow," I said. "I almost died here, remember?"

He grabbed me by the elbows and kissed me again until my legs felt like rubber erasers and my whole body hummed. Once I had pulled away, his eyes widened and I tried to focus on the cleft in his chin and ignore the wicked smirk.

"Meet me and Ziggy at the dog park at eight a.m. tomorrow?"

Eight a.m. was a lot earlier than I liked to get up and out. Especially after a night like this. "Make it eight thirty."

"Seven thirty, then," he said.

"Sure," I heard myself say.

28

*Nothing reveals itself so dramatically as
an egg gone bad.*

—Barbara Ross

By the time the cruiser dropped me off at Houseboat
Row, Lieutenant Torrence was delivering Lorenzo. "Oh
my gosh, am I glad to see you!" I threw my arms
around him.

"And likewise," he said, hugging me back.

We tromped up the finger to the houseboat. The little white kitty was out on the deck with Sparky and
Evinrude. She seemed to do a double take when she
saw Lorenzo. Then she darted over, scrambled up his
leg to his torso, scampered across his shoulders, and
bolted back down the other side.

Miss Gloria and I burst out laughing. "I think she's
glad to see you."

Miss Gloria herded us inside to the living room. "I'll
make some tea," she said. "And we've got Hayley's
amazing baklava. And your mother called. She wants
to hear everything when you get a minute. Sam's got

all kinds of research for you on copyright infringement, though I don't suppose you need that anymore. And Janet's booked her ticket back down in ten days because Sam insisted. As for you, mister," she said to Lorenzo, "we really hope you'll stay the night."

"I appreciate that invitation so much, I do," he said, stroking little Lola, who was now splayed across his lap like a limp dishrag. "I have so much to process. And after that jail bunk, I can't wait to sleep in my own bed."

I took a steaming-hot shower and then joined them at the kitchen table, with a glass of wine and a big hunk of honey-drenched pastry, to explain the night's events. "Detective Bransford"—I knew I was blushing as I said his name, but I couldn't help it—"said he saw me leave the meeting. When I didn't come back, he went out and ran into Louis, who told him what happened with Edwin. Then they found Maureen screaming bloody murder in the storage shed, and they were able to track her husband's car with his cell phone's GPS."

"That Edwin wasn't much of a criminal, was he?" asked Miss Gloria.

I shook my head sadly. "He was so desperate about the news of Cheryl Lynn. And his own daughter." I reached for Lorenzo's hand. "I'm sorry about your friend."

"At least there's some closure," he said sadly.

Miss Gloria piped up after a minute of heavy silence. "He has some good news, too. He got a phone call while you were in the shower."

"Sort of," said Lorenzo with a grimace. "A group of the performers called to ask me to stand in as president of the gang at Sunset. I can't say I want the job, but it's nice to be recognized."

* * *

The next morning I woke up as the dawn light crept in, fed the cats, and made coffee for Miss Gloria. We all felt a little lost without the adorable white kitten Lola underfoot in the kitchen. On the one hand, it was an utter relief to have Lorenzo out of jail and back at his New Town home. I planned to go down to the Sunset Celebration later this evening to make sure he was back in his usual place on the square.

For the cats, the loss of Lola was more visceral. They batted at each other, scurried around my ankles, and leaped onto the kitchen table, knocking silverware, the saltshaker, and a little bowl of sugar to the floor.

"Get out—go outside and play," I said, shooing them out with a broom. "Don't you know life is a series of adaptations?"

Miss Gloria came out of her bedroom, giggling. "Aren't we waxing philosophical this morning?" she asked. "How do you feel?"

"I feel fine," I said rubbing the side of my hip. "My leg's a little sore where I hit the side of the boat, but considering the shape I could've been in—"

"I don't even want to think about it," she said.

I didn't say that inside I felt numb. Frozen in time and space. Bransford's words and my reactions sat like a little frozen Tupperware of goodies in the back of my freezer mind, waiting to be unpacked. I ate a quick bowl of granola and headed off to *Key Zest*. When I hadn't been able to sleep the night before, I'd gotten back out of bed and written the piece on the cemetery that I'd promised to Wally and Palamina. I talked about how things circle about but eventually stay the same. How every thinking person should visit the graveyard from time to time to learn lessons from our ancestors—to remember that the things we sometimes judge to be critical to our hectic lives turn out not to be so important after all. And to remind ourselves that our time here is limited. And so very precious.

Wally was already in the office; I tried to sneak by him, but it didn't work. "How are you feeling?" he asked, poking his head out of his door.

"I'm fine," I said mustering a grin. "Everything is fine."

"Let me get you some coffee," he said, coming out of his office. He patted Danielle's desk chair. "Sit for a minute. I can't believe you even sent that article last night after all that happened. And it was excellent. Some of your best work. Palamina will think so, too. And I loved your lunch article, especially the opening." He read it aloud. "'Some folks treat lunch like a highway rest stop—keep their expectations low and visit quickly, so they won't be disappointed. But here at *Key Zest* we wonder why every meal shouldn't be the best it can be.'"

He paused, fidgeting with the collection of ceramic fowl on Danielle's desk. He moved the single white chicken out of the circle of colorful roosters and hopped her across the gigantic planner on her desktop, toward me.

"How about between us? Are we okay? I had the feeling that you were really disappointed the other day." He bit his lip, his expression all concerned.

"You know what?" I said. "I'm really fine. I would have called things off first, but I was afraid to hurt your feelings. Afraid to give you one more sorry bit of news in your life. With your mom so sick, I hated to break the news that you were a lousy boyfriend, too." The one zinger slipped out before I could bite it back, so I tried to make up for it by flashing a real smile. "But I'm looking forward to working with you. One thing I'm not letting go without a big fight, and that's my job at *Key Zest*. I love this magazine, and Palamina's not the only girl with great ideas and dreams for where we could go with it."

"Good," he said, a mixture of relief and sadness on his face. "Great. I want you on the team." He looked like he was going to either hug me or start to cry, and either one would feel unbearably sad. So I bolted.

As I arrived at the dog park on my scooter, across from the beach and Saluté, the restaurant where we'd held Connie's shower last year, Torrence pulled up in a squad car. He rolled the window down and pushed his sunglasses to his forehead. I got off the scooter and pocketed the key.

"What the H-E-double-L are you doing up so early? I thought you were supposed to be home taking it easy."

"Too antsy to stay home." I gave a sheepish shrug. "Besides, I'm meeting Bransford."

"Crap," he said. "Not him again. That guy is a sack of snakes, a nest of hornets, a—"

I cut him off. "I'm only going out with him once, see where it goes. Have coffee first, and then maybe lunch. Take it nice and slow. I know he acts like a jerk sometimes, but I don't believe that's the real him."

"You've told me a hundred times that he's the rudest person you've ever met."

I blushed. "I think he's rude and brusque because he's trying to cover up the fact that he really does care about me. Besides, he makes my synapses crackle," I said, feeling a silly grin spread over my face.

"You're beginning to sound like a pulp romance

novel," he said. "Don't you know that bad wiring equals burned girls?"

"But—"

"Have you ever tried electroconvulsive shock treatment, the kind that fries your brains?" Torrence asked. "Have you ever stuck your finger into a light socket while soaking in a tub? That's what dating Bransford would be like."

"But—"

"Have you ever tried to jump-start a car? But you touched the wrong terminal when you were connecting the cable to your battery and got blasted half to kingdom come? That's what dating Bransford would be like."

A little corner of me agreed. I had been singed by him before. And we still had to deal with the issue of his ex. Was she gone for good or simply waiting in the wings, ready to pounce if he drew closer to me?

"I could set you up with a nice man," Torrence continued. "Remember last winter, when Officer Ryan helped find your brother? He broke up with his girlfriend not too long ago. And he asks after you all the time."

The very same Officer Ryan who'd walked me into the school library a couple of days ago. He was adorable and sweet, but at this point, I practically had a master's degree in identifying sparks. In this case, there were none. Not one. Nothing but warm, brotherly feelings.

The wire gate separating the big dog pen from the little dog pen squeaked open; then the main gate opened. Ziggy darted across the grass and leaped into my arms, all shiny fur and squiggling angles. He lapped my chin with his pink tongue. The anti-cat. Evinrude would despise him. Bransford followed the dog out and stalked over to where I stood next to Torrence's car. He hadn't shaved and he wore a ratty sleeveless T-shirt, half-soaked with sweat. I felt an immediate charge.

Lieutenant Torrence glared at Bransford and then pulled his sunglasses down to cover his eyes. "It's possible—no, it's likely—that I'll kill you if you screw things up," he said to Bransford, tipping his chin at me. And then he rolled his window up and drove away.

Recipes

Raspberry Cake

Hayley imagines this cake could seal the deal with Wally on Valentine's Day. I think it would have, too—if only he'd tasted a bite before storming off the houseboat.

Serves 6–12, depending on the size of the slices

Cake
1¼ cups all-purpose flour
1¾ cups cake flour
1 tablespoon baking powder
2 cups sugar
¾ teaspoon salt
2 sticks unsalted butter, softened but still cool, cut into
    cubes
4 eggs, room temperature
1 cup milk
1 teaspoon vanilla extract
½ teaspoon almond extract

Frosting
1 (8-ounce) block cream cheese
1 stick unsalted butter
1 teaspoon vanilla
Confectioners' sugar

2 boxes fresh raspberries—about 30 for the frosting, and 40
   or so for decoration
3 to 4 tablespoons good-quality raspberry jam

Preheat the oven to 350°F. Prepare two 9-inch cake pans by buttering them well, lining with parchment, and then buttering the parchment, too.

To make the cake, combine the flours, baking powder, sugar, and salt in the bowl of an electric mixer and mix at low speed. Add the butter, a few cubes at a time, and continue beating on low for 1 to 2 minutes. Beat the eggs in one at a time, mixing well but minimally after each.

Mix the milk with the extracts.

Add ½ cup of the milk mixture to the flour mixture and beat until combined. Add the remaining ½ cup of the milk mixture and beat for about 1 minute.

Pour the batter evenly into the two prepared cake pans.

Bake until a toothpick inserted in the center comes out clean and the cake springs back when touched, in the neighborhood of 25 minutes. Watch this, because you don't want to overbake.

Cool the cakes in the pans for 10 minutes. Then remove the cakes, one to a plate and the other to waxed or parchment paper, and allow them to cool to room temperature.

Meanwhile, prepare the frosting by beating together the cream cheese and butter. Add the vanilla and confectioners' sugar to taste. (I used about 1 cup of sugar.)

Now gradually beat in about 30 raspberries until your desired pink color is achieved.

Spread one of the cooled cakes with a layer of frosting, then a layer of jam.

Layer on the other cake. Frost the top and sides and decorate with the remaining berries. Refrigerate until serving.

Once in a Blue Moon Blue Cornmeal Blueberry Pancakes with Cinnamon Butter

I first tasted pancakes like this at the Hell's Backbone Grill in Boulder, Utah. When I couldn't get them off my mind, I knew I had to try to recreate the recipe. They are wonderful with cinnamon butter and real maple syrup, but also good and filling with plain yogurt, some chopped almonds, and maple syrup. They make even a gloomy day a little better.

This recipe should serve four.

1⅓ cups blue cornmeal*
⅔ cup all-purpose flour
2 teaspoons baking powder
1 teaspoon baking soda
1 teaspoon kosher salt
2 teaspoons sugar
1½ cups buttermilk (or 1½ cups milk with 1 tablespoon
    vinegar added)
2 eggs, lightly beaten
1 teaspoon vanilla
4 tablespoons melted butter, plus more for greasing the
    griddle
2 cups blueberries

*If you'd prefer a little lighter batter, use 1 cup blue cornmeal instead of 1⅓ cups and 1 cup flour instead of ⅔ cup.

Cinnamon Butter
2 tablespoons butter
½ teaspoon cinnamon
½ teaspoon sugar

Stir together the blue cornmeal, flour, baking powder, baking soda, salt, and sugar in a large mixing bowl. In a separate bowl, whisk together the buttermilk, eggs, vanilla, and 4 tablespoons melted butter. Add the buttermilk mixture to the blue cornmeal mixture and stir until mostly combined. Heat the pan or griddle and melt some butter to cover the bottom of the skillet. Add the batter to the pan (about ¼ cup per pancake) and drop 5 or 6 blueberries into each pancake. Cook over medium heat until bubbles form and pop on the top, and then flip the pancakes over and cook the other side for 1 to 2 minutes. Keep the finished pancakes in a warm (200°F) oven until all the batter is cooked. To make the cinnamon butter, combine the butter, cinnamon, and sugar until the mixture is uniform. Serve with a small scoop of cinnamon butter plus real maple syrup.

Nocciolata Fudge

What can I say? I'm not even a fudge lover, but
I'm crazy for this recipe. Everyone else will be, too!

1 (14-ounce) can sweetened condensed milk
1½ teaspoons vanilla extract
1 cup bittersweet chocolate chips (make these good quality,
    as it will show)
1 cup Nocciolata (organic chocolate-hazelnut spread; I used
    the whole 9½-ounce jar)
3 tablespoons unsalted butter, room temperature, cut into
    ½-inch pieces
½ teaspoon sea salt or pink salt

Line an 8 x 8 inch pan with two layers of parchment
paper, overlapping the sides.

In a stainless steel bowl, stir together the sweetened
condensed milk, vanilla, chocolate chips, hazelnut
spread, and butter. Put an inch of water in a saucepan
and bring it to a simmer.

Place the bowl over the pot of simmering water. (The
bowl should not touch the water.)

Stir until the chocolate chips are melted and the mixture is smooth, 5 to 7 minutes.

Scrape the mixture into the papered pan, smooth the
top, and sprinkle with sea salt. (Use pink sea salt if you
have it on hand—so pretty!)

Refrigerate until the fudge is firm, at least 2 hours.

Lift the fudge out of the pan using the parchment paper. Cut the fudge into bite-sized pieces and arrange on a pretty plate. Store leftovers (if there are any) in an airtight container in the fridge. The fudge can also be made ahead and frozen.

Chicken Enchiladas in Tomatillo Sauce

Hayley's favorite thing to make with green tomatillos is an enchilada sauce. It isn't hard and it freezes just fine, so if you make extra, you can save half and freeze it for a winter supper. These yummy enchiladas don't take long, especially if you have access to half a roasted chicken.

The dish serves 4, or 2 with leftovers.

Green Sauce

15 or so medium tomatillos, paper husks removed and tomatillos washed (You can include a few green tomatoes if you're short on the tomatillos.)

1 onion, quartered

1 to 3 cloves garlic

2 cups organic chicken broth (or homemade, of course, if you have that lying around)

½ bunch cilantro, washed well, stems removed, coarsely chopped (This yields about ¾ cup. I know some folks don't like cilantro—and I'm sorry for you; I think you could substitute parsley.)

Place the tomatillos, onion, garlic, and chicken broth in a pan and simmer for about 10 minutes, until the veggies are soft.

Cool and then pulse the broth and veggies in a food processor, adding the cilantro at the end. The sauce should not be entirely smooth but rather a little chunky in texture. Set that aside. If you're cooking the enchiladas right away, oil a 9 x 13 inch pan and pour enough sauce in to generously cover the bottom of the pan. Preheat the oven to 350°F.

Enchiladas
1 onion, halved and sliced (white is fine but red is prettier)
2 to 3 green or red bell peppers, halved and sliced
Olive oil
½ roasted chicken, deboned, skinned, and shredded
4 to 5 ounces cheddar or Monterey Jack cheese, shredded,
    plus more for topping
½ cup sour cream or Greek yogurt, plus more for serving
1 package (about 8) tortillas (whole wheat tastes just as
    good as white and is better for you)

Sauté the onion and peppers in a teaspoon of olive oil until soft. Then combine them with the chicken, cheese, and sour cream. Spread a heaping spoonful down the center of each tortilla and roll tightly into little tubes. Nestle these into the sauce in the pan. Top with a little extra shredded cheese and a tablespoon or two of the green sauce. Bake for ½ hour or until bubbly. Serve with an extra dollop of sour cream if desired and a nice green salad.

Winter Walnut and Spinach Pesto

In wintertime, even in tropical Key West, vegetables are not at their best. Miss Gloria keeps a few pots of herbs and tomatoes on the deck of the houseboat so their food always has a touch of summer.

If you have the ingredients on hand, this is a super-fast meal that can be on the table in thirty minutes and looks as if you've been cooking all day. I serve it with a mixed green salad with winter radishes and some cherry tomatoes. We love this version of pesto—I think that the addition of the spinach tones down the sharpness of the basil just enough.

Serves 4

1 large garlic clove
3 ounces walnuts
3 to 4 ounces good-quality Parmesan
2 large sprigs basil, about 10 leaves
3 ounces fresh spinach
¼ to ½ cup olive oil
Salt and pepper

In a food processor, whir the garlic for 30 seconds, and then add the walnuts and Parmesan in succession. Add the basil and spinach and process until almost smooth. Pour in the olive oil, continuing to pulse until absorbed. Add salt and pepper to taste.

To serve, cook ¾ pound of good-quality Italian pasta until al dente (just soft) and drain. (I have gotten addicted to the pasta sold at Eataly in New York City. You can buy their products online. Yes, the pasta is three times as expensive as supermarket spaghetti, but it is honestly light-years better.) Add the pesto to the pasta in a large bowl and mix thoroughly. That's it!

Baklava

Quite a few years ago, I was asked to help our son's elementary school class make baklava, when they were studying food from various countries around the world. Though I've always been a fan of this pastry, I had never had the nerve to try making it myself. Believe me, if a group of schoolkids can make it, anyone can. The only problem we had was discovering occasional brush bristles in the finished pastry—this I blame on poor-quality pastry brushes and intense paint strokes. Hayley gets around this by using a silicone brush.

1 pound walnuts or mixture of pistachios and walnuts (I
     used $^1/_3$ salted pistachios and $^2/_3$ walnuts), plus roughly
     ground pistachios for garnish
½ cup sugar
1 teaspoon cinnamon
1-pound package phyllo dough, thawed overnight, then
     brought to room temperature
3 sticks unsalted butter, melted
12 ounces honey

Preheat the oven to 325°F. Butter a 13 x 9 inch baking dish.

Chop the nuts finely in a food processor and then add the sugar and cinnamon and pulse to combine. Set this aside.

Remove the phyllo dough from the package and unroll it on a clean counter. Into the baking dish layer eight of the phyllo sheets, one at a time, buttering each sheet with a pastry brush dipped in the melted butter.

While you work, cover the remaining sheets of phyllo with a damp towel so they don't dry out. (Don't sweat any little tears—they won't show up in the end.)

Pour 1 cup of the nut mixture over the eight layers of phyllo and spread it evenly to the edges. Continue to layer eight more sheets of dough, painting each with melted butter.

Spread another cup of the nut mixture over the top. Repeat the layers and the nut mixture until all the nuts are used, ending with eight layers of phyllo.

With a sharp knife, cut the baklava into diamond shapes. Bake for 45 minutes, or until golden.

Remove the dish from the oven and drizzle honey over the dough until it does not absorb any further. (I used a full 12-ounce jar of local honey.) Sprinkle with some ground-up pistachios if you like that look. (I did.)

Let it cool at room temperature for 6 hours or overnight, well wrapped. Then serve. Oh, the agony of waiting! But it's worth it. My guests told me this was the best baklava they had ever eaten. My hub and I had to agree. (There's no need to refrigerate the finished pastry unless you plan to keep it around more than a few days.)

Read on for a sneak peek at

KILLER TAKEOUT

the next in the national bestselling
Key West Food Critic Mysteries,
coming in April 2016 from Obsidian.

Resident islanders couldn't remember a hotter Key West summer. Not only hot enough to fry an egg on the sidewalk, they agreed, but hot enough to crisp bacon, too. So far, the advent of fall was bringing no relief. Today's temperature registered ninety-three degrees and climbing—fierce-hot for October, with the humidity as dense as steam from my grandmother's kettle. And the local news anchor promised it would get hotter as the week continued, along with the party on Duval Street.

Me? I'd rather eat canned sardines from China than march down Key West's Duval Street wearing not much more than body paint. But a hundred thousand out-of-town revelers didn't agree. They were arriving on the island this week to do just that—or watch it happen—during Fantasy Fest, the celebration taking place during the ten days leading up to Halloween, including a slew of adult-themed costume parties, culminating in a massive and rowdy parade.

Worst of all, the Weather Channel was tracking the path of a tropical storm in the eastern Caribbean. They had already begun to mutter semihysterical recommendations: Visitors should prepare to head up the Keys to the mainland and take refuge in a safer area. But based on the crowds I'd seen, no one was listening. These hordes weren't leaving until the event was over. Besides, with a four-hour drive to Miami on a good-traffic day, getting all those people out would be like trying to squeeze ketchup back into a bottle. Might as well party.

Since no right-minded local resident would attempt to get near a restaurant this week, I had fewer food critic duties at my workplace, the style magazine *Key Zest*. I was looking forward to covering some of the tamer Fantasy Fest events for the magazine, including the Zombie Bike Ride, the locals' parade, and a pet masquerade contest. And since restaurants were my beat, I'd promised my bosses an article on reliable takeout food, too. If that didn't keep me busy enough, my own mother, Janet Snow, and Sam, her fiancé, were arriving for the week to visit with my dear friend Connie's new baby, and then get themselves hitched on the beach.

In a weak moment, I'd allowed Miss Gloria, my geriatric houseboat-mate, to talk me into being trained as a Fantasy Fest parade ambassador. Our job would be to help patrol the sidewalks, which would be lined with costumed and tipsy revelers scrambling for the colored-glass-bead necklaces thrown off the floats.

"If we aren't going to go to the foam party or the Adam and Eve bash or the Tighty Whitey Party, we should at least attend the parade," Miss Gloria had said.

I closed my eyes to ward off the image of my elderly friend at any of those events.

"And if we're working as ambassadors, we'll be stationed inside the crowd-control barricades. We'll have the best seat in the house. Get it? *Seat*." She'd broken into helpless giggles.

At the time, the idea had seemed palatable. *Barely*.

I parked my scooter in front of the Custom House Museum, and Miss Gloria and I forded through the early-sunset crowds on the pier along the water. These were viewers seeking front-row positions for Sunset and for the zany Sunset performers, who were already warming up in their prescribed spots. As we passed by, we waved at the cat man arranging his cages of trained housecats and paused to watch Snorkel the potbellied pig practice his bowling. Ahead, a man dressed in a battered rice paddy coolie hat, a long-sleeved lavender shirt, and black pants was setting up a card table. Lorenzo, my tarot card–reading pal. His face glistened in the fierce rays of afternoon sun, and he had damp circles of a deeper purple under each arm.

"Did you come for a reading?" he asked after we'd greeted one another. "I would have brought the cards to your houseboat. Anything to get away from this madness." He fanned his face with his hand.

"No, actually, we're headed for the Fantasy Fest parade ambassador training," said Miss Gloria.

Lorenzo's mouth fell open as he first looked at me—on the small side, but plump like a baby leg of lamb, as my father used to say. And then his gaze swept over Miss Gloria—a true runt and scaring the far side of eighty years old besides. His dubious expression suggested that we were not the kind of volunteers that the organization had envisioned when they put out the call for people to help hold back the crazy crowds during the biggest parade on the island.

"Do you attend any of the Fantasy Fest events?" Miss Gloria asked him.

"No! I crawl as far away as I can. By Tuesday the brassieres are off, and by Friday these people are totally naked. It's horrifying," he said, clasping his arms to his chest. "What I ought to do is get out of town. The closest most of these folks come to understanding the tarot is Rocky and Bullwinkle asking the spirit rock to talk."

He began to chant and Miss Gloria joined him: "'Eenie meenie chili beanie, the spirits are about to speak.'"

"'Are they friendly?'" Miss Gloria asked, and they both cackled with laughter. "You're probably too young to have watched the show," she said to me.

"Stop it. I watched Rocky for hours on TV Land. We're going to be late," I said, smiling and tapping my watch. And to Lorenzo: "We'll see you soon, okay?"

By the time we located the Grand Cayman room in the Pier House resort, the room was almost full and the meeting had started. A tall young woman with long brown hair was stationed at the podium. The only two seats left open were in the first row, front and center. She waited while the two of us trooped up the aisle and sat down. She reintroduced herself—Stephanie—and then resumed talking.

"As I was saying," she said, waving for the chatter to die down in the crowd, "if you see unattended packages, alert an officer. Please don't announce that they are suspicious—we don't need a stampede on top of everything else. Public works employees will be emptying trash cans during the parade." She blew out a breath of air. "I don't need to tell you this, I'm sure, but full nudity is not permitted in public."

"Oh, drat," called a woman from the back, to a ripple of laughter. "Are bosoms okay?"

"Only if they are painted," said Stephanie, her face deadpan, but with a bit of impatience in her voice. She went on to discuss the finer issues of crowd control and safety, parade pacing, and closing gaps between the floats.

Managing this event sounded like an awful lot to expect from a bunch of greenhorn volunteers whose only props would be official yellow T-shirts.

"Talk to the float drivers," she said. "Have fun and show a pleasant attitude. Talk to the bystanders in your section and get to know them a bit. We know you wouldn't have volunteered if you weren't outgoing. Give your peeps beads. It makes them happy."

A woman behind us raised her hand. "Will we be issued rubber gloves?"

Stephanie made a face. "I don't understand why you'd possibly need them. You shouldn't be touching anything weird."

She pointed to someone at the back of the room, and Lieutenant Steve Torrence strode forward. I felt an instant wash of relief, seeing his familiar face. Over the course of the last two years, he'd become our trusted friend. The world felt manageable when he was nearby.

"I like the orange tie," Miss Gloria whispered. "Not so sure about the beard."

"Good morning, everyone! Or I should say afternoon," said Torrence. He laughed and twirled a finger around his ear. "That underscores my first point: As our ambassadors, we need you to be oriented to place and time, as many of our visitors will not be. Try to watch your beverage intake and remain in your right mind. You can join the party once the parade is over."

He went on to describe what we should do if we saw a fire (dial 911, duh) or caught fire ourselves (drop and roll—good gravy!). "We'll have police officers stationed all along the parade route, and undercover cops, too. Any questions about who they are, ask them to show a badge. If you feel unsafe at any time, please contact an officer for help. We thank you for your time and hope you have fun."

He gathered his phone and a pen that he'd set on the podium, then paused a moment. "One more thing, be aware that every year we have protesters come to Key West because they object to our parade. Key West wants this weekend to look like great fun—and to be fun. These people don't have the same thing in mind."

The radio clipped to his belt began to crackle, and then I heard the voice of my heartthrob, Detective Nathan Bransford, boom out: "Officer Torrence, report ASAP to the Bull and Whistle. Two of the Fantasy Fest Queen candidates have gotten into a mean hen fight."

OM0105

ALSO AVAILABLE
FROM NATIONAL BESTSELLING AUTHOR

Lucy Burdette

Topped Chef
A Key West Food Critic Mystery

Hayley Snow loves her job as the food critic for
Key Zest magazine, tasting the offerings from
Key West's most innovative restaurants. She would rate
her life four stars, until she's forced into the spotlight—
and another murder investigation.

When Hayley's boss signs her up to help judge the Key
West Topped Chef contest, she's both nervous and
excited. But when a fellow judge turns up dead, Hayley
has to find the killer before she's eliminated from
the show…permanently.

**"The victim may not be coming back for seconds,
but readers certainly will!"**
—*New York Times* bestselling author Julie Hyzy

Available wherever books are sold or at
penguin.com

facebook.com/TheCrimeSceneBooks

ALSO AVAILABLE
FROM NATIONAL BESTSELLING AUTHOR

Lucy Burdette

Murder with Ganache
A Key West Food Critic Mystery

For better or worse, Hayley has agreed to bake over 200 cupcakes for her friend Connie's wedding while still meeting her writing deadlines. The last thing she needs is family drama. But her parents come barreling down on the island like a category three hurricane and on their first night in town her stepbrother, Rory, disappears into the spring break party scene.

When Hayley hears that two teenagers have stolen a jet ski, she goes in search of Rory. She finds him, barely conscious, but his female companion isn't so lucky. Now Hayley has to assemble the sprinkles of clues to clear her stepbrother's name—before someone else gets iced.

"I can't wait for the next entry in this charming series!"
—*New York Times* bestselling author
Diane Mott Davidson

Available wherever books are sold or at
penguin.com

OM0143